W9-ARD-806

Acknowledgments

I am indebted to Nadine Laman of Cactus Rain Publishing
for her encouragement and patience with my poor book.

Susannah died, aged eleven years, in 1819.
All I wanted was to give her the life she never had.

Nadine helped me to do just that.

Diane Keziah Robertson

The Lacemaker's Daughter

Diane Keziah Robertson

CACTUS RAIN
PUBLISHING

Arizona USA

The Lacemaker's Daughter

Published by Cactus Rain Publishing, LLC
San Tan Valley, Arizona, USA
www.CactusRainPublishing.com

ISBN 978-0-9829181-2-8

Cover Design by Nadine Laman
Published June 1, 2012
Printed in the United States of America.

For
Pamela

ह&

in memory of

Susannah Brigginshaw
Lacemaker
1808-1819

The Lacemaker's Daughter

With Best Wishes,

Diane Keziah Robertson

Diane.

My Dearest Celia,

Your mother has asked me to write of my life, as legacy to you, my first grandchild. By the time you are old enough to read of it, I pray I will be on God's earth to answer any questions you may have.

I come from such humble roots, it is hard for me to understand why anyone would want to hear of them. Nevertheless, while it is hard for me to do, and to please your mother, I have agreed. Your life already promises to be so much more comfortable.

Known then as Susannah Brigginshaw, I was eleven years of age in the year of Our Lord 1770. I shall start my story there, for it just makes sense to me. When I think of it all now, it seems so long ago. Or only yesterday.

Your loving grandmother,
Susannah

Chapter 1 ❧
1770

I sat outside our cottage as I struggled to finish the piece of lace I had been working on for over a week. If I didn't finish tonight, it wouldn't be ready to take to the buyer when he came to the nearby Devon town of Honiton tomorrow. Once a month he made the journey to purchase lace for the ladies in London. Every piece we made had to be sold.

The wind blew all around the cottage, pushing the dried skeletal leaves in front of it, piling them up against the walls and the closed wooden door. The light through the trees that overhung the cottage grew dim, for darkness fell early in November. I sat on the three-legged stool, the large lace pillow stuffed with barley straw heavy on my knees. Low, grey clouds moved quickly above, hurried along by the same wind that blew the leaves around my feet. A woolen wrap helped to keep my arms warm, but without benefit of hose or shoes, my feet were bitterly cold. I had to stop my work often to cover them with my skirt, not that it helped much. My back and shoulders ached from the hours spent bent over the pillow, but my ma, your great-grandmother and me, all we could do was make the lace and sell it on, for without it our family would starve.

My hair was thin and curly, totally out of control. My arms and legs thin as twigs. I remember clearly the hunger, my constantly empty belly. My ragged hand-me-down dress was so big I had to tie it in the middle with my pa's old belt.

Most of the other women around made Honiton lace, which meant competition was fierce. Only the best lace was acceptable to the buyer; one small mistake, barely noticeable, and it was rejected. Ma also made lace, as I said, but the money we were paid between us didn't keep out the cold wind or rain as it blew through the holes in the roof and walls in winter. It certainly wasn't sufficient to feed us all for the month before the buyer returned; the last week was always a hungry one.

It wasn't too bad in the summer when Pa could poach meat in the surrounding woods. Wild vegetables and fruit were always to be found. But the winters, they were terrible. Even now, I dread the winters, when memories of Ma struggling to keep us alive all but overwhelm me.

Ma's given name was Emma. She was married at fourteen and had fallen pregnant within the year with me. From then she knew only hardship. Her face was so pretty, fine hazel eyes with laughter lines around them, or so I thought at the time. As I look back, I see now the lines were made by hard work and worry. There was no one else in the world I loved more. Her hair was long and thick, honey gold in colour, over a high brow. She would rub the end of her nose hard with the palm of her hand, and we would laugh. We would tell her it would fall off one of these fine days.

My pa's name was John Brigginshaw. He was a farm labourer, though for him work was rare. He was known as an unreliable drunk. He would say he would turn up, but more often than not, he failed to do so. Ma begged him not to drink, but he would shout at her, tell her he was the head of the house and he would do whatever he liked. Often during the day he was to be found asleep in what passed for their bed, his loud drunken snores heard throughout the cottage.

Peter had been born with a deformed leg and foot and, as a result, he had rarely been farther than the outside of the cottage door, round to the privy. But he could only get there in the summer; when the snow came, he had to use the pisspot. We didn't have a cart to take him to town, so he stayed at home.

The last born, also a son, we called William after our paternal grandpa. He had only lived for four days, sickly right from the start. Ma, fearing the worst, had sent Pa to the Rector in Upper Hambley, the nearest village to our cottage. She wanted the baby baptized immediately, but Pa hadn't returned until late into the evening.

The Rector had refused to come, saying it wasn't worth his bother. William died that night, though this time Ma sent me to the Rector to ask if William could be buried in the churchyard. I had to carry the message back that the Rector hadn't known of the birth, nor of William's sickly nature. He told me to tell Ma he would have come, if he'd been told. Pa had never spoken to him. I saw the light go from Ma's eyes that day, never to return.

Without benefit of a baptism, William could not be buried in the churchyard, though I did not understand why at the time. Ma sent me back again to beg the Rector for his mercy, but he remained steadfast. If we had money to pay him he might have agreed, though perhaps I do him an injustice.

Ma in her grief had insisted William's grave be dug in the plot of land to the back of the cottage beneath an oak tree. Pa had struggled hard to dig the grave, the roots hampering him at every attempt while he cursed loudly. But Ma wouldn't let him give up. She refused to bury her baby on the outside of the cemetery wall, as was usual for an un-baptized child.

'If they can't accept such an innocent, he shall be buried where we can easily tend the grave,' she had said. Work and food were our priorities, no time to keep trudging to the church. Except after the first while we didn't tend it, the tangle of weeds and nettles had soon re-claimed the tiny space where William lay. Three years after his death, we could hardly remember where the grave was. I am ashamed to say I thought of him hardly at all. Sometimes I would go out to his grave, move aside the undergrowth with my bare feet, impervious to the nettle stings, but the visits grew fewer. It was almost as if William had never been.

※※※

The lace pattern I worked was one of four pieces I had made this month. Ma had bought the patterns from the buyer on his previous visit. She always looked for new designs, so she could get more money for them. The more intricate the pattern, the more she would be paid. The buyer told the lacemakers what was required, sold the pattern and thread, and the lacemakers' job was to produce it.

I had learned how to work the lace when I was six years old, taught by Ma, and even though I say so myself, I was good. We couldn't afford any mistakes. The buyer, along with his helpers, would look over each piece carefully. If it wasn't perfect they would reject it, or lower the price if they thought they could get away selling it with a small mistake. I had only ever had one piece rejected, and that was because I had rushed to finish. It had been a costly lesson to learn.

With darkness almost here, it was time to go inside. I sat beside the candle at the end of the table, my fingers moving the lace bobbins smoothly like Ma had taught me. I loved how the bobbins clacked together as I worked them, the lace growing slowly before my eyes. I found the sound soothing.

My brother, Peter, had his small pallet bed by the kitchen hearth. When I came inside he was at work on a piece of wood with his knife. The knife had been a present from Ma and Pa one Christmas when they had spare money, but where the money came from, I've no idea.

Every night before bed, Ma would knead the dough for tomorrow's bread, then leave it to rise beside the fire overnight, where the smell of the yeast would set our bellies to rumbling.

I find it difficult to write of my pa. He was not an affectionate man to Ma, nor Peter and me. He always seemed angry, though why at us, mere children, we never knew. It wasn't our fault we were born, and none of us deserved the beatings. Peter thought it was because of his infirmity, but I didn't think so then, nor do I now. My belief is that he was just an angry man, never to change, not that it made living with him any easier.

Every evening he would go to the inn at Upper Hambley, returning late into the night, always the worse for drink. One particular night I remember with great clarity, though why this one, is hard to say, I suppose because of the events that followed.

Pa came heavily down the ladder as Ma was almost finished kneading the dough, and I was nearly at the end of a lace piece.

No one spoke. Ma cleaned the end of the table of flour, scraped it into her apron to easily tip it back into the flour bag, for none could be wasted.

She quickly looked up and just as quickly looked down as Pa put on his boots. Like me, she was worried Peter would ask him where he was going, for it would only make Pa angry. Please don't let him shout at Ma again, I prayed.

Thankfully, without a word he stepped out into the dark, pulling the door closed behind him. Ma and I looked at each other; we didn't speak, for what was the point? He was off to get a drink. He would spend the few pennies we had, and care not if we went hungry. Ma and me spent hours on the lace, sometimes ten hours to make but one inch. Then Pa spent the money we earned on drink.

I snipped the last threads and removed the finished lace from the pillow, handed it to Ma who held it to the candlelight for inspection, but I knew there weren't any mistakes. She smiled at me, carefully placing this piece with the others ready for sale as she hummed to herself. Ma did that a lot, and she told me she only did it when she thought of the goods she would buy with the proceeds of the sale, happy to know we would eat.

I leaned on the table and watched as she individually wrapped each piece of lace in muslin, then made them all into one long muslin roll tied with twine, leaving them near the door ready for tomorrow. With God's grace, we would get a good price.

The usual thin stew was heating over the fire, and none of us could wait any longer. Ma helped Peter to the table, while I filled the small bowls, set the spoons and this morning's bread ready. We bent our heads in prayer as Ma gave thanks for our meal. We all prayed for the same thing, I'm sure; better times to come. Rabbit again, eked out with vegetables scratched from the overgrown garden. The stew was full of bones, but we ate ravenously, not asking for more, though we were all so hungry, for we had to leave some for Pa.

We had two meals a day. The last had been breakfast, each given a slice of bread spread with wild honey. The time between was almost unbearable, our bellies were sore with hunger. The money that Pa would spend tonight, spent nearly every night, kept us in utter poverty.

Ma told me that Pa had been seven years old when he started work as an agricultural labourer. Like all children of our standing, he never learned to read and write. His parents in their turn had been dirt poor. With eight children, Pa being the second oldest, he was soon sent out to work. In summer he walked four miles to the local estate, worked hard for twelve hours, and then walked home. As a malnourished child, he was utterly exhausted on his return. He took a small noon meal with him, but that was quickly devoured, and he knew there would be little to eat when he returned home. He would fall onto his pallet, immediately asleep, until the dawn came too quickly, and his toil started again.

Ma said he dreaded the work. With so many other children having to earn their keep, those who came to the estate without their dinner often tried to steal his. Perhaps having to fight for his food, beating up the other boys, whether younger or older, made him believe that his fists could solve his problems.

In the summer it was hot, sticky work, plagued by flies and sharp, skin-cutting hay. In winter Pa would pick up any work that he could, he was always chilled through to the bone. Field work was not possible with the ground frozen hard. His clothing, passed down from his own pa, consisted of a thin pair of breeches and a shirt, an old leather jerkin, too-large wooden shoes that rubbed his feet raw, held on with strips of leather.

Life had been hard from the day he was born, so he had no sympathy for us, his own family. That was life, you either got on with it or you gave up. The bitterness in his heart was cultivated early.

'You'd best go to bed, it'll be full dark soon. We can't afford to keep the candle lit,' Ma said as she washed the few bowls with water I'd brought up from the nearby stream. I damped down the fire with turves for the night, then went out the door and round the back of the cottage to use the privy, rinsing my hands and face in the rain barrel on the way back. I returned to the kitchen, said goodnight to Peter and Ma. I had to gather my too-long skirt in one hand as I climbed the ladder to the small room where I slept. It was the one place I could call my own. Ma and Pa had the larger space next to mine.

My space was tiny, just enough room for a narrow straw pallet and a peg hammered into the beam to hold my clothes. With no window, in the summer the heat was oppressive. That's when I would creep downstairs to sleep outside. Used to the sounds of the night, they held no fear for me, and I relished the cool breeze on my skin. But now, in winter, the room was warmed from the fire below. The chimney breast climbed up the side of my room to the roof. I hung my dress on the peg, crept into bed and pulled the thin and bug-infested blanket over me as I eased my aching back into the straw pallet.

In the pitch-black room I stared up at the roof and wondered how much the lace we had made would fetch, if I could buy a ribbon for Ma's hair. She constantly brushed her hair back out of her eyes, sometimes pushing it under her cap, sometimes tying it back with a length of rag when she was at home. I dearly wanted to be able to buy a red ribbon for her, only wanting to see her smile.

Ma rarely smiled, only occasionally when she looked at me or Peter. But never when she looked at Pa; then her face was impassive, no love, no hate. Empty. My parents rarely spoke, as the most innocent word could set off his temper. Any complaint he took as an insult, and it always ended with one of us beaten. Peter would hold on to me at these times as we tried to close our ears to the sounds of the blows, Pa's anger and Ma's tears. Pa was always sorry after, and said it wouldn't happen again. Each time Ma would nod sadly and forgive him, yet knew full well that it would happen again. For the drink would come upon him, and the vicious cycle would begin again.

Chapter 2 ❧

I woke with a start to find Ma beside me.

'Wake up, child. Wake up!' she whispered urgently.

I raised myself on one elbow and rubbed my eyes against the candle's flame.

'I'm not well,' Ma said quietly. 'I can't go to town today; you have to go without me.'

'I don't know what to do, Ma. Why can't you go?'

'Of course you know what to do. You wait with the rest of the women and sell the lace. You've been with me before. I told you, I'm not well. You have to go.'

'But what if the buyer won't give me what it's worth?'

'You have to demand the full amount. Stay near Mistress Parnell. Ask for her help, if needs be.'

I opened my mouth, but Ma looked at me.

'Hurry now, you must be there early to get the best price,' she said. She left the candle so I could see to get dressed, then she disappeared down the ladder.

I was worried. I could see through the holes in the thatch; it was quite dark outside. It was a long walk to Honiton, mostly through the woods, but there was no other choice. With Ma ill, if I didn't sell our lace, we would have no money to buy food for a month. All I could think of was what was wrong with Ma?

Backwards down the ladder I went, the candlestick in one hand, making sure to miss the creaky rungs, so as not to wake Peter who slept below. I stopped to grab a crust of bread from the table, and to pick up Ma's woolen wrap. I crossed it over my

'Stay on the lane now, so you don't get lost,' Ma called after me from the doorway as I set off, to be quickly met by the first cold blast of wind. The cloudless sky was on the change from night to early day. A few faint stars were visible, but enough light came from the moon to find my way.

The town was about a three-mile walk, if I kept to the cart tracks. The wind soon blew through the wrap and the thin dress. Without boots, my feet were very cold. I hadn't walked far when I stopped and turned to look at the way I had come.

The cottage, well hidden in the trees, was already out of sight. I knew that if I stayed on the lane it would take a long time to get to Honiton, and I was already so cold. If I cut across the fields, then surely I would be in time to be at the front of the women, and have a better chance of a good price for all our effort. Out of sight of Ma, I made the decision to go over the fields, stepping quickly onto the dormant, tangled grass of the deer path that would lead me to Honiton.

The sun was peeking over the horizon, making the outline of the trees now visible. Disturbed rabbits scampered away to safety as I approached them. I glimpsed a deer through the trees, his antlers large and multi-branched.

A ten-minute walk brought me to the stream where I had seen otters before as they played, so I slowed, hoping to see them again. I stepped carefully on the stones that acted as a natural path. As if my feet weren't cold enough already, the water was icy as it frothed over my toes. I misstepped and caught my foot between the stones and felt my ankle wrench. I put out my hands to steady myself, letting the muslin roll slip from beneath my arm. I grabbed it before it had hardly touched the water, but it was soaking wet. Desperately, I reached for the far bank with my free hand and pushed the lace up out of harm's way. I pulled myself up beside it and sat down, holding my injured foot.

Ma would be angry, all that work gotten wet. If I had listened to her, this wouldn't have happened. I had no one to blame, but myself. I didn't dare open the roll, there was no need; I knew the lace was wet. All I could do was I put my head in my hands and weep.

'What's the matter?' a man's voice asked.

When I looked up, a large black horse stood nearby, though I hadn't heard its approach. The rider was informally dressed in a thick outer coat and a white stock showing at the neck. Long black leather boots reached above his knees, and a large-brimmed hat was pushed back on his head.

'What's the matter?' he repeated, louder this time, for without my answer he must have thought I hadn't heard him.

'I've hurt my ankle.'

'Well, crying about it won't help.' He slid from the saddle and led the horse closer. Letting go of the reins, he said, 'Let me have a look.' He knelt down before me and felt both my ankles. 'This one is a bit swollen. It must hurt?' he asked as he looked up at me.

I nodded as I wiped my tears and runny nose on the wrap.

'Come, girl, I'll give you a ride home.'

'I can't go home. Ma sent me to sell the lace to the buyer.' I pointed at the roll. 'Now, I won't be at the front of the women. Those at the front get the best price.' I didn't expect any of that to worry him, though, for this was my difficulty, not his. I struggled to stand, careful of my sore ankle.

He stood up. 'But you will be in time, if I give you a ride.'

I could hardly believe my ears. Before I could reply he bent down and put one arm under my knees, the other round my shoulders and lifted me onto the horse as easily as if I were a robin's feather, then he climbed up behind me.

'I suppose I should know the name of the young lady I'm riding with.'

'Susannah Brigginshaw, sir,' I replied.

'You're fortunate,' he said, as we started for Honiton. 'I'm not normally out this early. I needed to give my new hunter, Juno, a run.' He leaned forward to pat the horse's neck. 'You could have been here a long time waiting for someone to come.'

'I know it, sir. I'm grateful.'

'Is that the lace?' he asked after a while.

The side of his face was close to mine as he looked over my shoulder at the muslin roll.

'It is, but now it's wet, the buyer probably won't buy it.'

He made no reply while the horse plodded along. It wasn't long before I felt my eyes growing weary enough to close as I leaned back against him, feeling his warmth.

We were on the outskirts of town when I woke. Shortly after, the man asked where the lace buyer was to be found.

'In the High Street,' I replied. 'Ma had said to follow the women.'

It was early, though there was a small group of women who stood talking in the High Street. Those who were there carried pouches or rolls similar to mine.

The man kept quiet as he let the horse make its own way along the street. The women turned to watch as we approached, and I recognized one, who waved a welcome to me, but she wasn't Mistress Parnell.

'Have you sold lace before?' asked the man.

'Ma has always been with me before, but today she was unwell. She said to look for Mistress Parnell for help.'

'Do you see her here?'

'No, she's not here yet. Can I get down, please?'

He carefully lowered me to the ground.

'How will you get back?' he asked.

'I don't know. I hope there will be a cart headed that way and I can beg for a ride, for it is a long walk back on a sore ankle.' I gave him my thanks as I limped off to join the women, others hurriedly appearing from cottages and alleyways, some dragging sleepy children along. When I looked back, the stranger was watching me. I waved. Eventually, he turned his horse away.

As I took my place behind the other women, I prayed the warmth from my body would dry the lace before my turn came. The sun was now almost fully up, though no heat came with it. The wind was not quite so cold, sheltered as we were by the buildings, but standing on the cold ground my feet were frozen, and my ankle was more and more painful.

The lace buyer arrived later than expected. He was usually there by eight o'clock, but today the church bells at St. Michael's rang nine times before he appeared. Those in front of me moved excruciatingly slowly, while I tried to ease my ankle, moving carefully from foot to foot. There were many women behind me, making me grateful for the ride, which put me near the front. As I moved towards the buyer, I was frantic with worry, silently repeating, 'Please buy the lace. Please buy the lace.'

Soon, I found myself standing before the buyer who sat at a table. There were three chairs with two men who sat either side of him. On the table in front of the man on the left was a large tally ledger along with a money box. On the ground beside the man on the right stood a wicker basket that contained pieces of lace already purchased.

'Name?' the buyer asked loudly, though he didn't look at me.

'Susannah, I'm Emma Brigginshaw's daughter. She's not well today, so has sent me.'

'Your mother's health isn't my concern, girl. Did you bring lace?' he demanded. This time he did look at me, though with an angry scowl on his face.

I stepped forward as I held out the muslin roll in both hands.

The buyer motioned to the man by the basket to take it from me, and he spread it out on the table. All three looked at our work.

'It's wet,' the buyer said, as he fingered the lace. He frowned his displeasure as if he thought me a fool. Or worse yet, that I thought him one.

'I'm sorry, sir,' I replied, 'I fell in the stream on my way here.'

'Stand aside,' he said, waving me away. 'I'll look at the rest from the other women. I've no use for wet lace. If I decide to buy it, I'll call you back.'

I couldn't believe it and was now full of panic. 'It is just wet. It will soon dry. It's perfect with no mistakes; Ma bought the patterns from you last month.'

'There's plenty more to chose from. I told you to stand aside; I'll see what else is here before I decide on yours.' He roughly rolled it up as he spoke, shoving it back across the table.

To my shame I found myself begging as I told him we desperately needed the money, the lace would soon dry, I repeated.

But he motioned me again to stand away, the woman behind already pushing against my back as she moved forward to place her own lace for inspection.

With no choice, I limped to the side and slid down to the ground, my back to a wall, feet straight out in front of me. All I could do was pray the other women's lace wasn't good enough, though I didn't want to ill wish them, but that he would turn again to mine.

For the second time that day, I put my head down and wept.

Chapter 3 &

The anxious lacemakers dwindled down to the last few women, and I knew he would refuse me. The lace pieces already bought filled the basket. As each woman left, clutching her coins, they looked at me with pity in their eyes. Word of what had befallen me had passed rapidly amongst them. I knew Ma would hear of it. I felt only shame.

Two of the women came over to stand a little way from me, one asking if I was Mistress Brigginshaw's daughter. I replied I was, wiping my eyes on Ma's wrap as I looked up at them. The taller one asked if the buyer had taken any of the lace, and I had to reply he hadn't. That it was wet because I had fallen in the stream, but other than that it was perfect. I told them it would have soon dried, no one would have known.

Both nodded their agreement. They looked at one another, but I knew they couldn't help me. They must have sold their lace for a good price, but they needed every halfpenny themselves, with none to spare for our family.

She spoke again. 'I'm sorry, lass. Best get home to your ma.' They both turned away, clucking their tongues like hens as they shook their heads. I saw their fists clutched tightly, obviously their money held there, thinking how grateful they must be for it. Neither of them had come close, perhaps because they were afraid I would leap up to try to steal it.

I tried to take the weight off my ankle as I stood and looked around at the almost empty street. The lace buyer and his men had already packed up their table, along with the ledger and basket that held the precious lace. One of the men, the money box under his arm, came over to speak to me, but only to confirm the buyer would not take our lace.

'We have enough this month, no need of yours. Sorry, lass.'

It would take me at least three hours to get back to the cottage on my sore ankle. My feet and hands were blue, and my nose was running with the cold wind. As I started out, two wild dogs walked towards me, snarling and baring their teeth, the hair on the back of their necks standing upright. Unable to run, I had no choice but to stand my ground. I frantically waved the arm that didn't hold the muslin roll and shouted. I was making so much noise I didn't hear the horse as it approached.

'Get away, get away,' a voice bellowed from behind me. As the horse and rider drew nearer the dogs, the rider kicked the horse into a canter to frighten them both away. With one last howl they turned and ran between the houses out of the path of the huge, lunging beast.

I was shaken when he turned back to me.

'Did you sell your lace?'

I looked up at the man who had brought me into town.

'No, he wouldn't buy it because it was wet, now Ma will be angry with me. We need the money to buy food. He won't be back for a month. I don't know what we'll do.'

The tears started once more. I knew I looked dirty, my hair wild as it blew in the wind, skirt flapping against my legs, but it didn't seem to bother him, for when I looked at him, his eyes were on my face.

He dismounted and held out his hand. 'Let me see.'

I brought the roll from beneath the wrap and held it out.

The man unrolled it a little way. 'I can't look at it here. Did you eat today?'

I nodded, 'I had a crust of bread.'

'Follow me.' Holding the muslin roll in one hand, the reins of the horse in the other, he headed towards the nearby inn, leaving me with no choice but to follow.

I had never been inside the Cross Keys before. A few times, I've had to fetch Pa from the inn near the cottage, but that was a hovel compared to this. The man tied his horse to the ring outside, motioning me to follow as he stepped through the door.

He walked down a dark, wooden panelled hallway, and then turned to his right, me a few steps behind. Through another door we went, which brought us into a large room filled with tables and chairs, and a roaring fire burning in the hearth.

'Sit down,' he said, placing his hat on a long wooden table. I sat with my hands in my lap, so he couldn't see how dirty they were. He took a seat across from me and beckoned a serving girl, who came through a door at the back of the room. She looked to be a year or two older than me.

'Hanna, this young lady is in need of a good breakfast. I'll have the same, along with a small ale for both of us.' He didn't speak unkindly to her, all was said with a smile on his face.

The girl looked firstly at me then at the man, then raised her eyebrows as she looked again at me. Without a word to either of us, only a small curtsy, she turned on her heel to disappear out the back door.

'Let me have a closer look at what you have here.' He unrolled the muslin on the table, then began opening each individually wrapped piece, laying them out beside each other. The table was of oak, stained with years of wear, though it was very clean and dry, especially for an inn. The white lace stood out well against the tabletop. He said not one word as each piece was revealed. Pushing aside the muslin, he sat looking at the lace pieces.

'Did you make these?'

'My ma and me did.'

'Which ones did you make?' He leaned forward to look more closely at the lace.

I pointed. 'That one, that one, and the one by your elbow, the round one. That really pretty one over there, too.'

'Your ma made the rest?'

'Yes, but why do you ask, sir?'

'If I'm buying your breakfast, I'm entitled to ask.' Once more he smiled, taking away any hardness from his words.

The serving girl came back, left a pot of small ale before each of us, returning shortly after with the food. Looking at the plate, I know my mouth was open, for I couldn't believe my eyes.

'Who do I have to share this with?'

'Share? No one, it's for you. As this is mine,' he indicated his own full dish.

'What's the catch?'

He looked affronted. 'No catch. Eat while it's hot.'

So I did, shovelling in food at an unseemly rate, frightened someone would come to take it away before I'd finished, that I'd been given it by mistake. Eggs, pieces of bacon, a hunk of cheese, freshly baked bread and smoked trout. I was so hungry I couldn't stop eating. Between gulps of ale and the food, I had been far too busy filling my empty stomach to give thought to Ma and Peter.

'Susannah, what is to happen to this lace? All I can think is it has to be sold for a good price.'

'Well, he wouldn't buy it, the bastard,' I said, and the man raised his eyebrows at my words.

'No, he wouldn't, but I would. How much was your ma hoping for it?'

'At least five shillings,' I replied, stuffing bread in my mouth.

'For all this?' He looked down in amazement at all the pieces.

'Yes, that's a good price; it's worth more,' I said, defensively.

'Is it? I wouldn't know about that, but I do know a lady who would. I will give your ma a guinea for all of it and a shilling for something for yourself.'

That stopped me eating. 'A guinea? One guinea and a shilling? What do I have to do for it?' I asked, sure he must see the doubt on my face.

'I get the lace. Do we have an agreement?' He held out his hand.

I put down my knife. 'You're sure I don't have to do nothing?' I asked again, just to be sure.

'I'm sure,' he said with a laugh. 'To seal our bargain, I'll even give you a ride home.'

Without further thought I stretched out my hand to shake on the deal. I didn't spit in my hand first, like Pa would have. I returned to my food as I tried to work out why this man would be so kind to me. Why would he pay a whole guinea for the lace, well above the buyer's price? Wait until I tell Ma. She won't believe it. I'll be able to buy the red ribbon for her now.

As if he read my thoughts, he asked, 'What will your ma spend the guinea on, Mistress Brigginshaw? Food?'

'Yes, she will make sure we have enough for the month without having to fret.' I sat back on the bench, too full to eat more. 'I hope to buy a red ribbon for Ma's hair. I will keep the shilling aside, and not tell her of it. That it would be a lovely surprise.'

'It would indeed,' he said.

I looked past the man, out the window. I could already see Ma's face when I gave her the ribbon, and the very thought of it made me happy. 'Ma has beautiful hair, all curly, the ribbon will be perfect for her.'

ș ș

'I can walk from here,' I told him at the last corner before the cottage. 'I don't want Ma to know I came back on a horse. I don't know your name, either, though you know mine, so that's not right.'

'Thomas Stanton, at your service, mistress.'

'Do you live close by, Master Stanton?'

'My house is in Buckinghamshire, but I'm staying with my aunt, Lady FitzGerald, at Watermead, not far from here.' He waved off in the distance.

'I see,' I said, though I didn't really. 'Thank you, sir, for the ride home. Also for buying our lace.'

I slid down from behind him, then stood by the side of the horse looking up as I shaded my eyes from the sun.

'Thank you again, sir. We won't be hungry this month.'

I waved goodbye and limped down the lane towards the cottage, eager to tell Ma of our good fortune.

Chapter 4 ❧

'Ma, I'm back,' I called as I pushed open the door and stepped onto the dirt floor, but she wasn't downstairs.

'Peter, where's Ma?'

'She's abed with a fever. I had to get my food myself.' He spoke in a whining tone that irritated me, but I ignored him. I was too excited with my own news. Instead, I headed for the ladder.

'Ma, it's me. I'm back. I sold the lace like you told me,' I shouted as I climbed up.

Ma lay in her room on the narrow pallet, barely big enough for one, let alone two, her face red and shiny with sweat.

'Ma, what's wrong?' I asked as I knelt beside her, careful of my ankle.

'Just a small fever, I'll be better tomorrow. Did you sell the lace, Susannah?' She wiped her brow with a rag that already looked sodden.

I nodded, happy with my good news.

'I did, Ma, but not to the buyer. He refused it, said he had enough this month.' It wasn't a real lie, for he had said that, though I hated not being truthful to Ma, not telling her I had fallen in the stream. 'A gentleman bought it. Guess what he gave?' I didn't wait for her answer, for she could never guess.

'A guinea, Ma, one whole guinea.' I produced the coin from my dress, my other hand behind my back as I crossed my fingers to absolve me from the lie.

'One guinea? There must be a mistake, surely.' She tried to lift up to see, so I held my hand closer for her.

'No, Ma, he said he knew a lady who would like our lace.' Then I came to a halt, for Ma's eyebrows had pulled down in a frown, though I was the one that put our mutual worry into words. 'But what about Pa?'

'Hide the coin, Susannah, before he comes back. Hide it in a safe place, one where he won't find it. Quick now.' Ma waved me away, slumping back on the pallet.

For lack of anywhere better, I tied the coin into the hem of my chemise, then went outside to use the privy. As I walked to the front of the cottage, I heard Pa inside. I had barely been in time with the coin.

'Where's my dinner?' he shouted up to Ma.

'I'm not well. I've a fever and can't get out of bed,' came the weak reply.

'What am I supposed to eat? Didn't you sell the lace today?'

He must have heard me enter, for he turned to look at me.

'I sold the lace, Pa. I gave Ma the money for it.' I looked him boldly in the eye.

Up the ladder he went.

Peter and I could hear the demands for money.

Ma, too sick to argue or care, must have handed over a few coins she had kept hidden, but Pa was angry it was so little, demanding more. Ma was steadfast that there was no more to give.

Down the ladder once more, Pa said, 'I'm off.' He slammed the door behind him, on his way to the alehouse.

I crept up the ladder. 'Ma, did you give him all the coin?' I asked, worried.

She managed a small smile. 'No, lass. I have a little more hidden. I gave him only a few pennies, so never fear. We have enough for the month, more besides with the money you got today. You did well, Susannah.' Her face was shiny with sweat. She smiled, grateful for the money I had brought home. 'Quick. Go to Master Bentley's store, buy some food.'

I hadn't told Ma of my sore ankle, for that would lead to other questions. I stopped only to tell Peter where I was going, taking my own wrap this time. I also took the stick Pa sometimes used when he beat us, to help me walk.

I limped outside, down the path, and turned right along the cart track. The track lead past the field of cows and through the hedge, which led me up the lane to the hamlet. The stick took a lot of weight off my ankle, and I stopped only to pull the wrap over my head, protecting my ears from the wind. I knew I had to stay away from the alehouse, which thankfully was farther on from Master Bentley's store, as I didn't want Pa to catch me with another coin.

Upper Hambley boasted only one village store; everything imaginable and more was sold there. The owner, Giles Bentley, knew me well enough.

I stopped to untie the coin from my chemise before opening the door.

'Where's your ma?' he asked as he looked behind me, expecting to see her.

'She's abed with a fever, she sent me to get some food.'

'Did she now? How do you intend to pay?' He was suspicious, not that I could blame him. I was too well aware we were known for paupers, the tally with him growing longer each week.

'I have money, never you fear, Master Bentley. Ma and I sold our lace today for a goodly price.' I spoke forcefully to leave no doubt I could pay. I held out my hand, so he could see the coin.

'I'm pleased to hear it,' he said, reassured. 'Well, what is it you wanted?'

'We need flour and beans. Some potatoes, too,' but then I found my mind was empty. Ma hadn't told me what to buy; she'd only said food. 'I don't know what else we need,' I admitted, embarrassed. 'But I do want a red hair ribbon, for Ma.'

'Why don't you take that for now, come back later when you're sure. No point in taking goods your ma doesn't want and can't afford. I'll not add any more to the tally.'

That sounded right to me, so I agreed. I watched as he bustled around putting the order together, then realised I had no means to get it all back, for usually Ma came with me to help carry it. With my sore ankle and the stick, how would I manage?

'What's the matter now, lass?' Master Bentley asked gently, for he was a kindly man. Ma often spoke well of him. She knew he did what he could to help us.

'I don't know how to get it back to the cottage. I hurt my ankle this morning on the way to Honiton.'

I held up my injured leg for him to inspect. With all the walking, it was now very swollen, and even more painful. He bent over the table that served as a counter to look, his face screwed up in concern.

'That does look bad. Tell you what, I've to take a delivery to Watermead today, which means I will go past your cottage. What do you say, I bring your goods to you in the cart?'

'Would you? Would you really, Master Bentley? That would be very kindly of you, sir. But, can I take the ribbon with me now, please? I can't wait to see Ma's face. How much do we owe?'

'Three pence for today, but tell your ma and pa the tally is too long. I shall need payment soon, tell them I can't continue like this, that there are too many other families like yours.'

'I will be sure to tell her, sir. What will you want to bring our goods to us?'

'Nay, lass, you've a poor ankle, and with your ma ill, too, no payment for delivery is necessary. As I said, I'm going that way.'

'Thank you, Master Bentley, I'll be sure to tell Ma of your kindness.' I handed over the heavy coin, waiting patiently for the change. I wondered if I should pay some off the tally now, but didn't want to offer it without Ma's say-so. I decided to leave that for Ma to do next time she came.

He handed me the length of red ribbon, which I tucked safely away in the sleeve of my dress. I tied the change coins in the corner of my chemise and set off home.

A carriage pulled by two white horses passed me on the lane, making me stand aside. There was a lady in the carriage looking out the window at me. She smiled slightly. I gave a curtsy and looked down. It was only a second, but it struck me so that she had smiled at me. I looked a mess and knew it, but she smiled.

I walked down the lane, hurrying as best as I could. I was eager to tell Ma that the food would be coming in a cart, of all things, and for no cost! Why, she'd never believe it. But as I approached the path up to the cottage, my steps slowed, for I could already hear the shouts. Pa was home and not in a good temper by the sound of it.

Peter was in his bed, though he was crying, and Pa was upstairs. He must have cut across the fields to get home before me, for I had not seen him in the lanes. I was only grateful we hadn't met.

I hated him at that moment, for how could he berate Ma when she wasn't well? I went up the ladder as quickly as I could and saw Pa as he stood by the bed.

'Wake up, damn you. Wake up, I say.' He leaned over to shake Ma's shoulders harshly. 'Wake up, Emma. I'm hungry. I want my dinner.'

But Ma didn't wake up. Would never wake up again. I stood in the doorway, too scared to go closer.

'Pa, what's the matter?' I asked, though I knew already.

He turned to me, his eyes wide and fearful. 'She dead, that's what's the matter. Now what am I to do?' He slumped on the floor beside the bed, drunken tears on his face.

I forced myself to walk into the room to stand next to him. I looked down at Ma, who lay on her side with her eyes wide open. She was only twenty-seven, but the years had been hard; the lines on her face showed that too clearly. Now, in death, those lines were gone, her face smooth and pale. I reached out with a hand that trembled to touch Ma's already cooling cheek. 'Ma, can you hear me?' I asked loudly, but I knew she was already beyond hearing in this world.

I turned to Pa. 'Come, no good crying. She's gone, naught we can do about it.' Like an obedient child, he picked himself up, wiping his eyes and nose on his sleeve, following me down the ladder.

'What do I do now?' As usual, his only thought was of himself, not even a word of comfort for Peter who lay quietly now on his pallet, his eyes huge in his pale face.

I asked Pa if he would go for the Rector, or if I should go. We had to arrange for Ma's burial, but he just looked at me.

'Pa, what do you want me to do?' I asked again, my voice rising. I should have saved my breath.

He told me there was no point in walking all that way to Upper Hambley. The Rector hadn't come when William died; it would be no different for Ma.

'We'll have to pay for the grave, and he will want payment to come out this way,' he told me. 'I've no money.'

'In that case, we have to bury Ma here, so you'd best dig the grave next to William's,' for I had now become the parent.

He looked for a moment as if he would argue, but he knew full well Peter couldn't do it, and I knew I couldn't. He turned away, out through the door, round to the back of the cottage.

He cleared the weeds and nettles from beside William's grave, the thickened roots of the oak impossible to dig with the spade now, so he had to use the axe.

While Pa was digging, I carried a bucket of water upstairs to wash Ma's face and hands as I talked to her all the while.

'I'm sorry I haven't been a good daughter, Ma, but I did my best, you know I did. I have to keep your workaday dress for me, your linen, too.' I felt in the sleeve of my dress for a rag to wipe my dripping nose. Instead, I found the forgotten ribbon.

'I bought you a lovely red ribbon to set off your hair,' I told her as I smoothed her lank and knotted hair into order, laying the thick curls over one shoulder. I tied the ribbon into it, bright red against the golden hair, and the now so very white skin.

'You look right pretty, Ma,' I said, but I could no longer control the tears that came in a long, heavy sob.

Pa came back up, dirty and hot from the work.

'We need to wrap her in the sheet,' I told him.

Together we covered Ma up, but I couldn't bring myself to cover her face. Not yet. We struggled to carry her down the ladder, stopping but briefly for Peter to say his goodbyes.

Even though Ma was so thin, we were both breathing heavily by the time we came to the newly dug grave. Carefully we laid her in, then I made sure the red ribbon was still in place.

I looked at him squarely and said, 'Go get Peter.'

He stared at me with a confused look on his face, then did as I said. He came back carrying Peter without a thought of covering him for the cold.

'We should say a prayer, Pa.'

'You say it, I don't know any,' he shouted at me as he wrung his hands.

The only prayer I knew was parts of The Lord's Prayer, which wasn't much. All the time I spoke, I kept my eyes on Ma's face, knowing I would never see it again in this world. When I came to what I thought was the end, I bent down and placed a clean piece of rag over her face to keep the worms from her.

'All right, Pa.'

Peter clung to me while we watched Pa. He bent and shovelled, bent and shovelled until all the earth was back in the hole, and Ma was gone forever.

'Can we put a cross up?' I asked.

'What for, God didn't help her. What good is a cross going to do?' He turned away. 'I'm off.'

Without an embrace for me, and I daresay without even stopping to speak to Peter, he walked away, leaving me bereft.

I stood looking down at the untidy mound of earth. 'Whatever are we going to do without you, Ma?' Then I, too, turned away and helped Peter back inside.

Chapter 5 🍂

Peter and I lay together on his pallet before the hearth holding each other, both too numb to cry. It was only when I heard the sound of a horse coming along the lane that I stood up to look through the oiled parchment window.

Master Bentley had arrived with the food, and for a moment I forgot Ma was dead.

'You came, Master Bentley!' I shouted as I flung the door open and ran down the grass-trodden path.

'Of course I did, didn't I tell you I would? Can your ma come and help with these?' he asked as he reined in the old horse.

'She's dead, sir. She died of the fever while I was at the store. Pa and I have buried her already.' I stopped, for I didn't know what else to say.

'Oh no, child, I'm right sorry.' He got down off the cart, looked around. 'Where's your pa?'

'There's just me and Peter here, Pa will be back soon,' I said, for I knew Ma wouldn't have wanted him to know Pa had gone to the alehouse at such a time.

Master Bentley held out his arms, and without a moment's thought, I moved into them and felt the warmth of his body, his bristled chin on my head.

'I am sorry, lass. Let's go in to see your brother, make sure he's all right.' He took me by the hand, slowly leading me back inside.

Peter was raised up on one elbow.

'Hello, Peter, I'm sorry about your ma,' Master Bentley said, but Peter lay there without answering, eyes brimming with tears.

'Peter, where are your manners? Master Bentley's brought the food I couldn't carry. I have to help him fetch it off the cart.'

'Nay lass, you stay with Peter. I'll fetch it in.'

'Should we offer him a drink?' whispered Peter when he was gone. I thought we should, for that's what Ma would have done, though all we had was small ale, which was old.

Once all the food had been brought into the cottage, I asked him. 'Would you like a small ale, Master Bentley?'

'That's kind of you, but nay, I'd best be on my way. I've a long day ahead of me. Do you know when your pa will be back?' He could probably guess the answer as well as I could.

'No, we don't. Sometimes he's gone for a day or so. I expect he's off to find work, but he'll come back, never fear.'

Giles Bentley looked around the cottage. I too looked around, seeing what he saw, though as if for the first time.

To Peter and me, this was home, but to the likes of Master Bentley, used to a proper house, it must have looked very poor indeed. On his trips backwards and forwards to the cart he must have noticed the thin thatch, the gaps in the walls and around the door, for I'd watched as he stood outside, shaking his head at all the disrepair.

'I'll come by tomorrow to check on you like; make sure your pa's home.'

Peter added his thanks to mine, and Master Bentley moved to the door, his hand on the latch.

'Are you sure you'll be all right till he comes home?' he asked with concern in his voice.

'Yes, we are used to it.' I held my head up high, as I looked him full in the eye, daring him to argue.

'Right then, I'll be by tomorrow.' He walked down the path, then climbed back onto the cart. He clicked at the patient old horse to get it moving again.

Peter and I looked at the food spread out on the table. 'Well, we won't starve,' I said, with a smile in an attempt to cheer Peter. 'At least, not for a while.'

I slept downstairs that night, lying on the beaten earth floor next to Peter. Neither of us could really sleep. We lay in the dark, and occasionally we would talk.

'What will happen to us now, Susannah?' he asked, with worry clear in his thin voice.

'I don't know. I guess I'll have to keep making the lace. Ma had a bit put by that Pa doesn't know about, but it won't last long. We have to speak to Pa when he returns,' but neither of us were hopeful for any useful suggestions from him.

It was warm by the damped-down fire, and eventually both of us drifted into an uneasy sleep. Exhausted from the day before, the long walk, and Ma's death, we both slept past dawn.

❧❧❧

'Susannah, I'm hungry.'

I struggled to wake, looked around. Why am I down here? It didn't take long for me to remember. Ma's dead. We buried her with William. Why didn't I hear Pa come home?

'I'll get you some food in a while,' I told Peter as I stood up, stretching my stiff back.

Going quietly up the ladder, so as not to wake Pa, I looked in their room, but he wasn't there. Puzzled, and with no idea of the time except that it must be late for it was full light, I went back down the ladder.

'Peter, their room is empty.' We looked at each other, both relieved that he wouldn't be angry, or worse, beating us.

I cut a slice of bread from the loaf, the last one made by Ma. I spread honey on it and handed it to Peter. I needed the privy and opened the door to go out. It was raining again. Ma's wrap covered my head as I ran down the path, to return wet through.

'I'm still hungry, Susannah. Can I have more bread?' There was little enough left. If he had another slice, it would mean there wasn't enough for me, or for Pa, who would expect to eat when he came home. Then I thought of the breakfast I had been given yesterday and felt guilty. I cut him another slice to salve my conscience.

'I have to save the rest for Pa, so no more,' I told him. 'I'll make bread this morning, Peter, then you can have more.'

'All right,' he said, eagerly holding out his hands, then stuffing the bread into his mouth.

I sat at the table watching him, not daring to have bread myself. What was left must be saved for Pa.

He wiped his sticky hands on his jerkin, picked up his knife in one hand, a piece of wood in the other.

'What are you making?' I asked in an attempt to distract both of us from our hunger. I moved to the hearth and took the turves from the fire. Using the bellows to blow it back to life, I watched carefully for the flames to leap.

'A doll for you. It will be the most beautiful doll in the world, for it will look like you.' He bent his head as though embarrassed by his words, concentrating on his task.

I sat in what had been Ma's chair, the other side of the fire from Peter's pallet.

'Do you really think I'm beautiful, Peter?'

Without taking his eyes off the wood he said, 'I do. I think you're very beautiful.'

'Thank you, Peter.' I sat, my feet barely able to touch the floor as I listened to the scraping of the wood under Peter's knife, watching the thin curls of wood drop silently to the floor.

That evening, with dough set beside the fire for the next morning, we spent what was left of the day with Peter playing a hornpipe he had made a year or more ago. He was very good, all the tunes from his own mind, all lively, while I banged a spoon on a tin pot as accompaniment. We laughed until our bellies hurt so much that I had to beg Peter to stop.

&a&a&a

Master Bentley came again as promised, and saw that at least we were caring for ourselves. When suppertime came, there was no sign of Pa.

I made a stew of the beans and potatoes, with water fetched from the stream at the bottom of the garden, and picked some herbs as I passed through the overgrown patch.

'We don't have any meat to put in it, so this will have to do. If Pa doesn't come soon, I'll have to set the rabbit traps.' I tried hard to sound as if I wasn't concerned, but in truth I was very upset, for I hated to kill the rabbits. While we waited for our meal to cook, I made more bread dough with the yeast from the batch Ma had started. I had to kneel on the stool to get some weight behind me to work the dough on the table. At last satisfied, I set it back in the bowl beside the fire to rise.

'At least we'll have bread for tomorrow when Pa gets home.' But as we looked at each other, I knew Peter's thoughts, for I had no doubt they were the same as mine; if he gets home.

'If Pa's not back by tomorrow, I have to go and look for him,' I said, giving him warning.

'I know.'

'I may be gone awhile, but I'll leave the rest of the stew for you. The pisspot, too.' I could see the terror on his face and quickly tried to calm him. 'I'll come back, Peter, don't worry. I'll always come back.'

≈≈*≈*

When we woke the next day, there was still no sign of Pa. I put the dough to bake, and when it was done, I left it within Peter's reach, along with the pot of wild honey, two jugs of ale, and the pisspot.

'I'm off to find him. I'll be back as soon as I can.' With a last reassuring smile, I set off, leaving Peter alone.

It was another rainy day. Ma's wrap covered my head but, as usual, my feet and legs were soon cold and filthy dirty from the mud. I walked first into Upper Hambley and went straight to the alehouse. It had a branch above the door to denote its purpose.

An elderly widow, with the help of two small orphaned grandchildren, made a precarious living there. I had heard Pa talk of it often; indeed, Ma had sent me there on several occasions to summon him home. I walked through the door and looked around, but it was so dark and the roof so low, it was difficult to see. The smoke from the fire added to the gloom.

I decided not to waste time, calling aloud, 'Pa?' The few people inside stopped their talk, more to see if it was one of their own seeking them. When they found it wasn't, they lost interest. I called again, louder this time, but Pa didn't appear.

The old woman came up to me.

'Who are you looking for, girl?' She was sucking on her blackened teeth, her breath appalling.

'John Brigginshaw, if you please,' I replied, quickly taking a step backwards.

'Well, he ain't here. Haven't seen him for a week or more. Try the next village.' She returned to the ale pots, taking great care not to spill any, no wish to see her profits seeping into the earthen floor.

'Please, you, I don't know where the next village is.'

The old woman tutted, clearly reluctant to be drawn into another's business. 'Over yonder, about three mile or more.' She must have seen the worried look on my face and tutted again. 'Go down the lane outside and turn left by the last cottage. Follow the path, you can't miss it.'

'Does it have a name?'

'Don't be daft, girl, of course it has a name, every village has a name.' Now she was annoyed, and made it plain. 'It's called Lower Hambley, everyone knows that!'

'Thank you, mistress.' I was determined to keep a hold on my temper. I was by now very tired, and the thought of another three miles, then the return journey back to the cottage, all seemed too much.

Outside, the rain had stopped. Even the thin sunshine seemed bright after the darkness within, so it took a moment to get used to it. My ankle, though better, was again set to aching. With no other alternative but to find Pa, I had to go on. With the directions in my mind, I set off once more.

Within the first mile the rain started again, this time driven sideways by the strengthening wind. I walked on, looking out for the last cottage, seeing it at last with relief. The ground started a slow fall from there, down to Lower Hambley. All the while I tried not to think of Peter alone in the cottage. Nor of the return journey.

At last I came within sight of small cottages, hovels really, and I could have wept. I looked out for the branch above a door that showed a place that sold ale. I steeled myself as I entered, once more, into darkness.

Even though there were very few people inside, a silence fell as I appeared. Any strangers were reason for concern; even a small female child was worrisome to some.

'Pa?' I called. But again, there was no reply. Now weary beyond words, I groped for the stool behind me and sank down gratefully, close to crying childish tears. A man, the owner I supposed, approached me.

'Who do you seek, lass?'

'John Brigginshaw, if you please.'

'I know of him, but he hasn't been here for a long while.' A look of concern crossed his face. 'Are you all right? You look very weary. Are you hungry?'

'I am hungry, sir, cold and tired too, for I've walked a long way to find him.'

'Sit there,' he told me, pointing to a nearby table, the stool pushed beneath out of the way. He walked through a door set to the side of the ale barrels stacked from floor to roof. I closed my eyes, so very close to sleep. My clothes were so wet they clung uncomfortably to my thin body.

'Eat this.'

When I opened my eyes, a bowl piled high with meat and vegetables had been placed before me. A thick slab of bread spread with what looked like real butter lay on a dish, a tankard of small ale next to it.

'Thank you, sir, but I've no money so cannot pay.' I pushed the bowl away.

'There's no payment necessary. I'll come back when you're done.' He returned to his few customers, who all sat looking at me as they whispered behind their hands. He came back as I scraped the bowl clean.

'You'd best be off home, lass, the nights are drawing in earlier now.'

'Yes, thank you for the food, sir.' I slid down from the stool while all watched as I opened the door, stepping out into the rain. I stood outside for a moment, seeking the direction for my journey home.

The wattle and daub walls of the alehouse couldn't begin to contain the landlord's loud voice. It was easy enough to hear him say, 'Poor little maid. I hope she doesn't go through the woods, I heard the wolves were about again over Offwell way.'

Chapter 6 ❧

The journey home was even longer, or so it seemed to me.

I had no idea where to search for Pa. The only other place I knew of was Honiton, but I couldn't go there now, it was far too late in the day. Peter would be worried, wondering where I am. Through Upper Hambley I walked, on past Master Bentley's shop, now closed. It was almost dark and I was very tired. I took the shortcut through the fields. I could hear the cows, but couldn't see them. I wondered if they could see me, if they would knock me down, but I couldn't run in the darkness. I was relieved when I found myself walking in the lane, then down the path that led, at last, to our cottage door.

There was no light shining through the window. I opened the door to find it as dark inside as out. 'It's me, Peter, I'm back. Why didn't you light the candle?' I asked, annoyed that he hadn't gotten the candle for himself. I shuffled to the table, felt for the candle in its holder, and the strike to light it. I sheltered the flame with my hand so it didn't blow out until it had caught, then turned to face Peter. Still on his pallet, he smiled.

'I knew you'd come back. I knew you wouldn't be like Pa. I didn't light the candle, for I wanted to save it for when you came home.'

'I told you I would come back, there was no need to doubt me. Thank you for saving the candle, though.' I could smell the pisspot was full and quickly emptied it outside the door.

'Did you find him?' he asked eagerly. 'Is he on his way home?'

'No, he's not. I had to walk all the way to Lower Hambley, a long way past Master Bentley's store. I'm very tired. He wasn't there, and now I don't know where else to look.' I glanced at Peter's face. It had best be said, no point in not. 'We have to think that he won't be back. You know that, don't you?'

'Yes, I know it.'

We sat, each staring at the cold ashes of the fire, cold as the life we had once known, and for all its fragility, had felt safe in.

I re-lit the fire that Peter had let go out and heated the last of the stew for him. I had eaten, thanks to the landlord in the alehouse, so I would now wait until breakfast.

'If he isn't home by tomorrow, we have to think what to do, but let's not fret about it now. Tell me, have you finished the doll?'

Peter brightened instantly. 'I have, look.' He reached beneath the blanket that covered his legs.

The wooden doll stood about twelve inches high. It had a beautiful face, the nose tiny and perfectly formed. Legs and arms stuck out of the solid figure. To me, it was the most beautiful doll in the world.

'Can I have it?'

Peter passed it over, watching my face in the candlelight.

'She's beautiful. Thank you, Peter.' I sat in Ma's chair, cradling the doll while I thought of a name for her. 'I'll call her Emma, for she's beautiful, just like Ma.'

After Peter had eaten, I cleared away his bowl, then put out the candle, for it was precious. Besides, I was far too tired to make the lace tonight. Peter hauled himself up to sort out the blanket that covered the straw pallet. The only light came from the moonlight through the small window. Once again, I lay beside Peter to sleep, both of us needing the comfort.

⋅⋆⋅⋆⋅⋆⋅

In the morning, the sound of knocking on the door woke us.

'Who is it?' called Peter, frightened.

'Lady FitzGerald,' came back the reply.

We looked at each other, Peter silently asking me, 'Who?' I leapt up, smoothing my dress and my hair. I opened the door and curtsied, like Ma had taught me.

'Are you Susannah Brigginshaw?' In the lane stood the coach I had seen on my way back from Master Bentley's store.

'Yes, my lady. This is Peter,' I indicated my brother.

'Good morning, Peter. May I come in, Susannah?' I didn't answer, just held the door wide open.

Stepping inside, Lady FitzGerald looked around. I knew the cottage must look very poor, especially to this lady dressed so beautifully. She wore a cape in a mulberry colour, which covered her from head to toes. Peeking from beneath the thick cape, a cream silk dress was visible, embroidered with tiny flowers and birds. With the fire damped down, the cottage was cold, but she made no comment on it.

Instead, she said, 'I understand from Master Bentley that your mother has died?'

We both looked at her, Peter leaving it to me to answer.

'That is so.'

'I am sorry, Susannah. You too, Peter. Is your father to home? I need to speak with him.'

I shook my head. 'He left when Ma died, and he's yet to return.'

Lady FitzGerald stared at us each in turn, her eyes wide.

'You're on your own here? Who is caring for you?'

At this I pulled back my shoulders, lifted my chin. 'I am. I'm eleven; I can take care of us.'

'I don't doubt it, but you can't stay here alone forever.' She looked around openly, couldn't fail to see the utter poverty, the dirt floor, the holes in the walls.

'May I sit down?' We only had two decent chairs, one of which belonged to Pa. I didn't want this lady to sit there, he would be angry if he returned. The only other seat was Ma's rocker.

'Sit there, if you please,' I replied, pointing to the rocker, while I pulled a stool from the table.

We waited while she settled herself and was ready to speak.

'I understand you make lace, Susannah.'

'I do, very good lace, too.'

'Yes, that's what I've heard; indeed, it is the reason I've come. Do you have any I can purchase now?'

'No, I sold it all to a gentleman in Honiton. With Ma gone, well, I haven't made any more.'

'I understand, your grief is far too new.' She looked quickly around. 'Do you make it in here?' She could see how dark it was, but I couldn't light the candle during the day.

'Sometimes, but mostly outside where the light is better.' We looked at each other, sizing each other up.

'I would like to purchase the next lace you make. Don't take it to the buyer in Honiton in the future; instead, bring it to me at Watermead. You know where it is?'

I looked at her, my mouth open. 'I know of it, but I'm not sure.'

'Can you read, Susannah, or you, Peter?'

We both shook our heads.

'I thought not, so it's no use my writing it down. My carriage is outside, can you come with me and I'll show you? It's not far, the carriage will bring you straight back.' She looked at Peter and gave a smile to reassure him, while he in turn looked at me.

'I suppose I could. Though how do I know you would give me a good price for the lace? If I do come with you, I can't be gone long, I'm sure Pa will be home soon.'

'Of course you will want to be here when he returns. As to price, I'll pay double the price the buyer would give.'

'How do you know what he'd give?'

'Trust me, Susannah, I know. I won't cheat you, I promise. Indeed, I'll buy as much as you can make.'

Peter and I looked at each other, hardly able to believe what our ears were hearing.

'Yes, I'll come with you, so long as the coach returns me home again.'

'It will.'

I left the bread and jar of honey handy for Peter should he get hungry, picked up Ma's wrap, and looked at her, indicating I was ready.

Inside the coach, dark blue soft material covered the two long seats, and large fur rugs lay upon them. Lady FitzGerald used one to cover her legs against the day's chill while I sat looking around.

'Now pay attention, Susannah, for next time you come to Watermead you'll be on foot.'

I looked out of the window to get my bearings. The horses walked steadily, but it wasn't long before I realised we were on my usual way to Honiton, for I knew this lane well. The carriage turned off the lane, passing through a set of large iron gates, then onward down a long driveway.

'We turned in just past the large barn with the weathercock on top, Susannah. You'll remember it?'

'Yes, I will. I remember there's a pair of robins in a nest on the roof every year. I watch them when it's time for the babies to learn to fly. I walk into Honiton this way, so I've noticed the gates before, though never knew what was beyond them.'

Steadily up the long curving driveway we went. The trees, planted on each side, gradually thinned out, and the land turned instead into a large park filled with fallow deer rooting among the grass for food. They looked up inquisitively at the sound of the horses and carriage, but sensing no danger to themselves, returned to their foraging.

I leaned out of the open window to see better our progress, oblivious for once to the cold.

As we came round what would prove to be the last curve, there stood the house before us. The driveway was no longer bare earth; we now rode on small stones that made a loud noise when the carriage wheels passed over them.

I had never seen a house so big, not even in Honiton. With too many windows and chimneys to count, the roof wasn't made of thatch like our cottage, but tile. The walls were of stone, not wattle and daub. The carriage drew up outside the main doors.

'This is my home, Watermead. You'll have no trouble, Susannah?' asked Lady FitzGerald. When I confirmed it, she continued, 'Go round to the large door at the back of the house when you next come, and ask to speak to my maid, Mistress Dobbs. I will tell her to expect you and the reason for your visit.'

'Yes, my lady. I will. Thank you.'

'Don't forget, bring me all the lace you make, I'll make sure you get more than a fair price for it.'

She looked at me long and hard, as if she wanted to say more. 'The carriage will take you home now,' though I was almost certain that wasn't what she had really intended to say.

Helped by a footman who had ridden on a ledge at the back of the coach, she stepped down onto the gravel. The door of the house stood open to welcome her home, giving me a chance to catch a glimpse inside. A black and white tiled floor! A real floor, not beaten earth like we had at the cottage.

Before I could look any longer, the door closed behind her, then the coach was on the move once more as it turned around to go back down the drive. I leaned out of the window, looking back at Watermead. One day me and Peter will live in a house like that. The idea came so naturally that I didn't think about how unlikely that would be.

વ્ય.વ્ય.વ્ય.

Safely back at the cottage, I told Peter all about the ride, how the footman helped me up into the carriage, and Lady FitzGerald down from it.

Later that evening, with no sign of Pa, we sat for a long time talking about how we would cope. Peter was unable to walk, or at least walk far, so the main load would have to fall on my shoulders.

'We both have to do what we can, Peter. I can get water from the stream, collect wood for the fire, but you have to help do things here.' I indicated the cottage. He started to say he couldn't, but I quickly held up my hands to silence him.

'Don't say you can't, Peter. Unless you want us to go to Honiton and beg for food, you have to help. While I'm making the lace and also doing the other chores, you'll have to do more to help me.' I held up my hands yet again to stop him. 'Is that what you want, to live on the streets in the cold and wet? To beg for our food?'

'No,' he replied with a sullen voice.

'Then, that's the way it will be.' I sat in Ma's chair, moved Emma from behind me, and held her like a baby. 'So that's settled. From tomorrow on, you will help more. Ma has a good supply of threads for me to make lace.'

I looked at Emma. 'This is really good, Peter, which has given me thought.' I indicated Emma. 'You can make pieces in wood; I could sell them at market day in Honiton. I will collect the wood for you. Small things to start with, such as, I don't know, bowls and platters, some spoons. Easy pieces to start. Perhaps another doll. Then as you get better, you can make different things.' He looked at me, his face one large frown. 'Sell them? For coin?'

I tutted, irritated. 'Did you not listen to what I said? Of course, sell them. We need money, Peter; between us, we have to make money. So, as I said, from tomorrow I'll get back to making the lace to sell to Lady FitzGerald. You start with the wood, then I'll take it to market. The first pieces you must make are sticks, to help you walk around. I will bring some straight branches, ones you can work easily. That's settled then.' I sat back as I rocked Emma, humming to myself, just like Ma used to when she was happy.

That evening, Peter played the pipe again while I looked for a pattern for the next piece of lace I would make. With an idea now of how we would manage, I felt that everything would work out for me and Peter for the first time since Ma died and Pa left.

Chapter 7 ❧

The next morning, as soon as it was light, I went out to collect water from the stream, then prepared more bread dough.

'I'll need to go to the store today, there's hardly any candle left. I'll need it to make the lace again tonight. Ma had a pattern I've wanted to try, though she said it was too difficult for me. But I know I can do it. Perhaps Lady FitzGerald will pay even more, if it's really beautiful.'

I handed Peter a piece of bread spread with the honey. 'We are nearly out of ale. I don't know how to make it, so I'll have to buy some, then hope Master Bentley will deliver it. He'll charge for it, but it can't be helped. We have to drink more water from the stream to make the ale go farther.' As I spoke, I bustled about with the twig broom, sweeping the floor to push the dirt out, chasing the fallen leaves back outside that had blown their way in.

'On my way back I'll come through the woods to look for branches for you, so give some thought to what you'll make.'

'But you hate the woods, Susannah.'

'I know.' I shivered. 'But we need the wood. Besides, if it's daylight it won't be so bad.'

I took some of the money left over from the sale of lace to Master Stanton and tied it safely in the hem of my skirt.

'I'll be on my way, Peter. You have to make sticks to help you move around, so I'll look for wood for that. The pisspot's there, if you need it. Keep an eye on the bread. When it's grown a lot, beat it down like you watched Ma do, then set it back by the fire. Not too close, mind, for it mustn't get too hot or it will be ruined.'

I glanced out of the window. It didn't look like rain, but it was cold, even inside with the fire lit. With the wrap around my shoulders, I set off once again.

For the payment of one halfpenny, Master Bentley agreed to deliver two casks of ale to the cottage, along with the other items I bought. I took a deep breath, nervous now to ask about Peter's work.

'Thank you. I've to go home through the woods today to get Peter some branches. He is a right good woodworker; he'll be making some bowls and spoons, along with other pieces for sale. Would you be willing to take some for sale in your store?'

The shopkeeper looked aghast at my suggestion, and I didn't understand why. After a few minutes' thought, he did agree, though I felt he didn't think Peter's work would be much good, and he was only taking it through charity. He said he wouldn't make any promises, but he would look at Peter's work and give a decision after he had seen them.

I beamed with happiness, for all Peter and me needed was a chance, and hopefully he had given us one.

'Thank you, Master Bentley. You won't be disappointed, I promise. I'll show you a few things next time I come, for he hasn't started yet. That's why I've got to go home through the woods, to get some windfalls for him to use.'

I left waving happily. If Peter could sell pieces through the store, it would save me the walk to Honiton on market day, which meant I could make more lace with the time saved. Master Bentley would expect his share for any sales, but we should be able to make a bit as well. As Ma used to say, every little bit helped.

I hurried down the lane, waving to a group of women who had gathered outside a small cottage. Two of them, no doubt busy with the gossip, as Ma would have said, waved back.

When I drew nearer the woods, my steps slowed, I wasn't so happy or confident now; though I knew it was the best place to find fallen trees and branches, it frightened me. The wind blew through the treetops making strange noises, and the boles creaked and groaned while dry leaves clattered furiously against each other with each gust. Then there were the animals to fear, even wolves that the ale man in Lower Hambley had spoken of.

As I stepped off the lane, I said a quick prayer to ask the Lord to keep me safe, then lifted my head and walked on.

Shortly, I came upon some good branches, but they were too big to carry. Perhaps this wasn't such a good idea. For a moment I felt overwhelmed with worry, and could feel the tears starting to come. Don't you dare cry, Susannah Brigginshaw; it won't help you or Peter, for he can't find the wood. You just have to think of a way to get it all home.

I found smaller pieces that would do for spoons, even a candlestick if Peter was careful. I made a carrier of my skirt, placing the wood within. I found a few more branches, then hurried home.

At the cottage I called ahead to Peter as I walked down the path. 'Peter, I've found some wood, all good oak, too.' I struggled to open the door and looked to the hearth to see the look on Peter's face. His pallet was empty. 'Peter, Peter!' I cried in a panic.

'I'm here!' he cried.

I looked to the right to find him standing at the table.

'Peter! However did you manage?'

'Susannah, when Ma was here to do everything for me, I rather let her. But I can manage well enough, you'll see.'

I interrupted him, 'Wait, while I put the wood down.' I rushed to help him.

'No. I can walk a bit! It's not easy, but I can shuffle. Watch.' With the table as support, he moved his bad foot. In his own peculiar way, he was indeed walking.

'Oh, Peter, this is wonderful. It means when you make the sticks, you will be able to go anywhere! Even to the privy on your own!'

Peter's smile was from ear to ear. 'Yes, I'll be able to use the privy, not the pisspot!' He paused to steady himself. 'I had a thought while you were gone, Susannah. Ma and Pa's bed,' he jerked his head towards the ladder, 'I could use the wood from the sides to make the sticks. It's no good up there; I can put it to better use.'

It was then I realised that even the thought of using the wood meant we, Peter and me, had accepted that Pa wouldn't be back. But what would happen if he did return? I couldn't bear the thought of the beatings.

I stood beside him and gave him a hug. 'I'm right proud of you, Peter, that's a wonderful idea. I'll get the wood down, so you can get started. I'll also bring Pa's honing stone from outside. You will need to sharpen your knife with all this work.'

'We will be all right, won't we, Susannah?' He looked hard at me, eager for confirmation.

'Yes, Peter, we will. We will be all right; we'll make Ma proud, you'll see. When I went with Lady FitzGerald to Watermead in her coach, I caught a glimpse inside. It was beautiful. I wish you had been there to see it.' I stared off into the corner as I thought back. 'The floor was black and white, and there was a servant who opened the door for her. Just imagine! The house was very big, the small bit I saw very beautiful. One day we will go inside to see it, I promise, Peter,' I paused. 'One day maybe we will own a house like Watermead.'

He looked at me as if I had gone quite mad. No doubt thinking I was joking, he laughed. 'Will we have servants to open the door for us? A carriage and white horses like the lady who came here?'

'That we will, Peter. That we will.'

ê≈ê≈ê≈

Master Bentley brought the casks of ale the next day, rolling them down the path and into the cottage. When all was done, he said, 'Peter, I hear you're to be working some wood pieces. Do you have anything yet to show me?'

'Not now, but in a day or two Susannah will have a piece to show you. She brought some wood for me. All good oak, too. She did good for a girl. I can make nice candlesticks and spoons. You'll be surprised. I guarantee they will sell.'

Master Bentley looked at him indulgently. 'I'll look forward to them then.' He looked around. 'You'll be all right for ale for a while, I dare say. No sign of your pa yet?'

'No, no sign,' I replied quietly. I wiped my hand across my forehead, for suddenly I was bone tired.

'Ah well, he'll turn up when he's ready, I expect.'

I knew Master Bentley didn't really think so, and in truth, neither did I. He had already been gone too long.

'I have work to do; can't stand here all day. Show me what Peter makes when it's ready. No promises, mind.'

'We know, no promises,' we chimed together.

I remembered what I wanted to ask. 'Please, sir, how much is the wheelbarrow in your store?'

'Now, Susannah, why would you want a wheelbarrow, of all things?'

'I need it to gather wood for Peter. There are large pieces in the woods that he could use, but I couldn't carry them home.'

'It is more than you can afford, lass, it's one shilling.' I was disappointed, then quickly brightened.

'Could I pay you a bit every week until it's paid? Lady FitzGerald has promised to buy my lace for double the price of the buyer in Honiton, so I can afford the barrow.'

He looked from Peter to me, at our eager faces. 'I suppose we could come to an arrangement. Three pence a week till it's paid, then. I'll put two pence towards the barrow, one pence to pay off the tab still owed.' He held out his hand, firstly to Peter who spat in his palm like he'd seen Pa do, then to me, though I didn't spit in my hand.

'I'll deliver it next time I'm out this way, maybe in two days.'

We watched from the door as he climbed up into the cart. Peter said, 'He's a kindly man, isn't he, Susannah?'

'That he is, Peter, that he is. As is Lady FitzGerald.'

❧❧❧

On my way back from the privy, I stopped at Ma's grave to talk to her. I sat on my haunches as I brushed away some of the oak tree's fallen leaves.

'We don't know where Pa is, we've not seen him for days. I'm right scared, Ma. Peter depends on me, but I don't know what to do. We've got some food for now, and Master Bentley has been very kindly to us. Lady FitzGerald said she would buy any lace I make, so I don't have to line up in Honiton any more, for which I'm grateful. She'll give more than the buyer, so that's all to the good. But how I do miss you, Ma.'

Chapter 8 ❧

The next couple of days were spent in a hive of activity. Peter worked hard at the wood, totally absorbed as he smoothed and polished, the pungent smell of wood shavings filling the cottage.

He made six spoons for everyday use and two larger ladles. One large and one small candlestick were made. He had trouble carving out the holder for the candle, the knife digging into his hand a few times, bringing howls of pain.

'Take it slowly, Peter, it will be no use if you break it, or hurt yourself badly.'

While Peter worked at his tasks, I struggled with the new lace pattern, but at last, order was made from the chaos. The bobbins began their comfortable clacking sound once more as I fell into my usual rhythm. I dragged the table and stool over to beneath the window to take better advantage of the meager winter light.

'This will be nice when it's finished. It's a lot more difficult than I've made before, so I should be able to get more for it.'

❧❧❧

A few days earlier, I found two rabbit traps in the overgrown garden. I set them each night, but it wasn't until the fourth attempt that they both contained their catch.

The rabbits were alive and squealed loudly when I touched them, but it had to be done. I quickly broke their necks like I had seen Pa do. Then I sat on the stool outside the door to skin them. When they were ready, I put them, along with some wild onions and potatoes, in the pot. For the first time since Ma died, we had meat to eat. We sopped up the liquid with chunks of bread. Even if I do say so, it was a very fine dinner.

'Do you have enough wood made for me to take to Master Bentley tomorrow?' I asked Peter as I washed our two bowls.

'I believe I do. It would be best if he inspected my work before I make too much, so yes, take it tomorrow.'

'I will. I have to remind him about the wheelbarrow, also, but only if he thinks the work good enough to sell. We don't want to buy it, then not have a use for it.'

I knew I could use the barrow for collecting wood for the fire, but it was a cost we could do without.

୬ଈ୬ଈ୬ଈ

I was on my way early the next day, the pieces for sale cradled in my skirt. The sun shone, and compared to the last little while, the air was not too cold. I walked along the lane and watched a robin high in a tree above, his song loud in the early dawn.

'Please let Master Bentley like the wood,' I repeated, as if just saying it would make it come true.

Inside the store, he was busy with another customer, and I had to wait a long time. I tried to keep still, not hopping from foot-to-foot, but I could hardly stand the wait. Eventually the customer left, and Master Bentley to turn his attention to me.

'Well, lass, do you have some of Peter's wood for me?'

I placed the six spoons and two ladles, along with two candlesticks, on the wooden table that served as a counter. He picked them up, turned them round as he examined them from top to bottom, taking his time almost beyond endurance. He took one candlestick to where the candles were displayed and inserted one in the holder, then placed it on the table to make sure it stood straight, which thankfully it did.

He looked at me.

'These are good, Susannah. Peter has done a good job. Make sure to tell him so. Better than I expected, I have to say.' He looked again at the pieces, then turned back to me. 'Very well, I'll keep these here, though we have to come to an agreement on the price.'

I couldn't contain my relief. I rushed around the counter to wrap my arms round his waist, holding on for dear life.

'Thank you, sir. Peter will be so pleased. You'll see, people will buy them, they will buy every piece.'

'Well I hope so, or I'll have wasted valuable space on them,' he chuckled.

'How much do you think they could be sold for?' I asked impatiently, their price being my only interest. My hands were behind my back, fingers crossed for luck.

'Maybe a penny each for the spoons? The ladles, probably a penny and a half.' He stopped and looked again at the candlesticks. 'I would say four pennies for these.'

'Each?'

'Yes, each. I'll try them at that price and wait to see if they sell. Susannah, there's no promise they'll be sold. But if they are, I'll keep half, you keep half. Do you consider that fair?'

Added up, it all came to one shilling and nine pence. Peter's and my share would be ten and a half pence. Once Peter got used to the work, he could work faster, produce more pieces. I anticipated heavy demand for his work. With the sale of the lace as well, we would be able to survive. I shook hands with Master Bentley to seal our arrangement.

'Can I just rest awhile before I start back? I was up early and I'm very tired.'

He indicated a barrel in the corner. 'Sit there to rest.'

Thankfully, I hauled myself up, with my thin legs and grimy feet showing beneath my skirt. I watched him move to and fro as he lifted heavy sacks of flour recently arrived from the nearby mill, so he could sweep the wooden floor. I was terribly hungry, but dared not ask for anything to eat in case he changed his mind and told me to take the wood away. My stomach grumbled loudly. Master Bentley paused from his work to lean on his broom.

'Did you eat this morning?'

'No, sir, for I was in a hurry to get here. I'll eat when I get home.' I jumped down off the barrel. 'Thank you for letting me rest.' I was eyeing Peter's work on the table as I passed to leave when I heard the door open and turned around to look.

In the doorway stood the same two women I had waved at previously. I stood quietly, listening as they and Master Bentley greeted each other. They looked at Peter's work, which Master Bentley had quickly moved to display in a prominent position.

The taller of the two women spoke. 'These are nice candlesticks, Master Bentley. I haven't seen them here before?'

'No, mistress, they have just arrived.' He didn't look in my direction. The woman picked one up, like Master Bentley had, turning it upside down.

'How much are they?'

He told the price.

'That seems reasonable, for the work is very good.' She ran her fingers round the base to feel for rough spots, announcing, 'I'll take one, if you please.'

Before my very eyes, it was sold, instantly earning us two pence. Hardly able to contain my excitement, I clasped my hands together, holding them to my chin as I bit my lip in excitement, all hunger forgotten. Master Bentley didn't look at me, concentrating on his customers.

The other lady, a lot fatter than her friend, not wanting to be left out, also came to the table and picked up a ladle.

'I need a new ladle. What price for this?' He told her it was one and a half pence.

'I'll take one.' Examining each of the two in turn, she chose one, replacing the other on the counter.

I couldn't contain myself. 'My brother, Peter, made those.'

The ladies turned to me.

'Did he now? You're Susannah Brigginshaw, aren't you?'

'I am, mistress.'

'Has your pa come back yet?'

I shook my head, wondering how they knew he had gone. But then Ma had always said everyone knew everybody's business in a hamlet the size of Upper Hambley.

The two looked at each other. The taller lady asked, 'Are you still making the lace?'

'I am.'

'I hear you sell it to Lady FitzGerald now.' It was a statement, not a question.

'I do.'

They both glanced quickly at each other as if to say, 'I told you!'

'We'll let others know your brother is making pieces like these,' said the taller lady, who seemed to be the spokesperson. Each in turn handed over their money to Master Bentley for the wood, along with their other purchases, both nodding at me as they left the store.

'I told you people would buy it!' I cried once they had left. 'I told you Peter did good work!' I jumped up and down while Master Bentley chuckled.

'Yes, you did, and it seems you were right. But you have to remember, this is a small hamlet, and people here can use only so many spoons, ladles, and candlesticks, Susannah.'

'Yes, I know that I have to find other places to sell it all. I'll need that barrow now, Mr. Bentley! You said it was a shilling, but I'll pay you two pence now.'

He smiled. He must have thought me very forward to demand this and that.

He brought the barrow from behind the counter without comment, wheeling it to a stop in front of me.

'This should make life easier for you. Now, if we're to do business, I have to set up an account for you. Sit down while I do that.' He brought a large ledger up onto the counter, turned to a new page and wrote something at the top.

'I'll have to write down what you brought in, along with the price. Then mark that it was sold, and the price.'

I watched the quill skim over the paper, making the strange marks that I couldn't understand.

'Now I have to write down you bought a wheelbarrow and for what price, show how much you've paid now, how much you owe.' He looked at me. 'Can you read letters, add numbers?'

'I can add numbers in my head. Ma taught me. She said everyone should know how to add and take away, so no one could take advantage.'

'Well, if you're to become involved in trade, you need to be able to read and write numbers and words. Come here, let me show you.'

For the next hour, with only a few customers interrupting us, we sat side-by-side, he showing me how to form the numbers, me copying as best I could. My growling stomach kept intruding until eventually he disappeared, returning with a plate of bread spread with butter, and handed it to me without a word. While I ate, he returned to the page headed with larger marks, then went through everything he'd written, explaining how much had been sold, for what price, and how much we each received. Added to that was the cost of the wheelbarrow.

'Do you understand, Susannah?'

'I do. Thank you for showing me, Master Bentley.' I was anxious now to get on my way. 'I have to get back, though; Peter will be wondering where I am. Besides, I can't wait to tell him of the pieces that were sold. He will be so pleased.'

I waved goodbye, pushing the wheelbarrow towards home and Peter.

Chapter 9 ❧

When I told Peter that a candlestick, along with a ladle, had been sold while I was in the store, he couldn't believe it. He sat at the table with his mouth agape. 'I knew they'd sell, but not that quick,' he said, a huge smile on his face.

'Nor I, but we must not get too excited. Master Bentley rightly said it was a small village, and he'd soon run out of customers for your work. I have to find another place to sell the wood, Peter. I'll go to Honiton, but not to market day, goods are sold cheap there, and your work is too good to be sold cheap. The town must have a store like Master Bentley's, maybe more than one, so let me know when you have some pieces for me to take.'

Peter had been busy while I had been out, with several spoons and a new ladle waiting on the table. Candlesticks take longer, and larger pieces of wood were needed for those. I promised him I would go out later, but meantime I cut some bread and heated up a little of the stew from last night for him, as I had already eaten.

'Do you think Pa will ever come back?' He didn't look at me as he spoke; I knew he wouldn't want me to see the fear in his eyes.

'No, I don't. It's just the two of us from now on, but we'll manage. Never fear.'

While I was reluctant to voice my thoughts aloud, I couldn't help but feel it could only be for the good that Pa wasn't here. The little money we had at least stayed with us to buy food, not used for drink. Without the constant worry of trying not to anger him, I felt a lot easier, and I was almost sure Peter had to feel the same. Our only concern was what we would do if he did one day walk back through the door of what we now considered our cottage.

On one of our walks into Honiton with the lace, Ma had told me that the cottage had been built in the last century by the local lord as a bolt hole for himself and his mistress, by the name of Jane, who was my ma's great-great-grandmother. Upon his death, under suspicious circumstances, the cottage was left in his will to his mistress without encumbrance. Jane, the original owner, had borne two children as a result of the liaison; the eldest, Mary, and a son, Daniel.

Jane was well aware of the precariousness of her position. When her lover died, bequeathing the cottage and all its contents to her, she determined it would go to the female line upon her own death, and thus it passed to Mary. It was subsequently passed down to my grandmother. When she died, she in turn bequeathed it to Ma some twelve years ago.

I, Peter and William were born in the upstairs room. Pa had always referred to the cottage as his, though everybody in the area must have known the truth. Built of wattle and daub with a thatched roof, it had seen better days, even when Ma inherited it. Pa always said he would repair the walls, but it was only at the start of our life that Ma said he even attempted to do so, quickly giving up all pretence that he knew what he was doing. He made an attempt to mend the thatch, but as in most things, he did more harm than good. Now, the thatch is very thin, with it being green moss more than straw. When I laid on my pallet at night, I could see the stars through the holes made by rats, mice, and birds using them as entryways.

Ma and Pa had both been freeborn, so any children they conceived were beholden to no one. This would have been good for those fortunate enough to have land to work and a solid roof over their heads. For Peter and me, it meant that we didn't have a lord from whom we could seek protection or help. We were totally alone.

With Ma not leaving a will, or none that I knew of, the cottage would surely be mine. I should ask someone. Needing to know the answer, I decided to speak with Master Bentley the next time I went to the store. With that settled, I set the thought aside and turned my attention back to the lace.

❧❧❧

As I walked to Upper Hambley the next morning, small flakes of snow began to fall. Even with Ma's wrap around my shoulders, I was bitterly cold. My feet were blue, and the stones and pieces of wood I stepped on brought agony. By the time I reached the store, tears were flowing, unbidden, down my face.

'Whatever's the matter, lass?' asked Master Bentley, coming from behind the counter as I hauled myself up on a barrel. I wiped my nose with the back of my hand, just like Ma used to do. Rubbing my feet with hands just as cold, I tried to bring them back to life.

'The snow's started again, and my feet are so cold.'

'Haven't you some old rags you can wrap round them? That's what I used to do when I was a young'un to keep the cold out.'

'There may be some at the cottage I can use, I'll have to look. I didn't think it was cold enough for snow yet.'

Master Bentley took one of my feet in his hands, rubbing briskly. 'Well, just stay here until they're better. Keep rubbing them, they'll soon warm up.' With no fire lit, I thought that was debatable, for it was just as cold inside as out. When I looked at him he was dressed, surely, in nearly every piece of clothing he possessed, for he looked much fatter than when I had last seen him. He even wore his outer coat, though unlike me, he was lucky to have boots to wear.

After a few moments I asked him about the cottage; was I the rightful owner now that Ma was dead? However, he was unable to put my mind at rest. He advised me that a solicitor should be consulted, as Pa was, we presumed, still alive. He also told me there would be a cost for the advice. Unable to pay even the smallest amount, I decided to put it into a corner of my mind, closing and bolting the door to the thought. I would worry about that when, or if, the problem reared its head. For now, there were far more pressing things to think about.

Once back with Peter, our supper finished, I went upstairs to Ma and Pa's room. At the foot of the bed, set against the wall, was a small chest where Ma kept her treasures; a brooch from her mother, and the ring Pa had given her when they were wed. Right at the bottom, I found a dress of thick grey wool with some papers beneath it that must be the deed she had mentioned. I took the dress and held it up against me. It was far too big, but I knew I'd found the answer to the cold.

'Peter, guess what I've found!' I called out. I brought it down the ladder with me, holding it up to show him.

'Peter, look, it's Ma's dress; it was in the chest in their room. It's made of thick wool, and I can use it to make us something warm to wear!'

Peter wasn't as impressed as I had hoped. He looked quickly at the dress, but without interest. 'But you can't sew.'

'If I can make lace, then I can sew,' I replied, indignantly.

I laid the dress on the table, looking at it from every side. 'I can use the skirt to make at least two capes.' I held up the long sleeves. 'I don't know if we can use these, I'll have to think on it. There's lace round the cuffs and neck. I'll take it off carefully and see if Lady FitzGerald would buy it; it is very fine and beautifully worked. If I cut very carefully, make my cape shorter than yours, I may be able to get a skirt as well.' I sat down and pulled the dress onto my lap.

'I can't recall Ma ever wearing this, can you?'

'No.'

'It's beautiful wool, it's almost a shame to cut it up, but we need to keep warm with winter fully here. My feet were so cold yesterday, hopefully there will be some strips left over so I can bind my feet when I next go outside.'

My mind was busy with how else I could use the wool. Peter wasn't listening to me. He sat staring off into thin air, but I couldn't be bothered with finding out what was the matter. The brooch, in the chest upstairs, would do to hold the cape closed.

If Ma were alive she could show me how to cut the cloth, how to sew it, so it didn't come apart. Though if Ma were alive, I wouldn't need to, she would do it for me. Suddenly, sadness engulfed me.

'Peter, I'm going to the privy.' I made sure to keep my face turned away from my brother, not wanting to upset him with my tears. Though I doubt he even heard me, so lost was he in his own thought. I leant against the side of the cottage. Once I was calmer, I walked round the back and looked at the old oak, then down to where Ma and William were buried.

We don't even have a marker for them, no way to tell they are both here. Peter can make the markers. Perhaps Master Bentley would scribe their names for me, then I'll get Peter to copy them on the wood. I dried my eyes and turned to go back inside.

Those coming after us would know that here lay Emma Brigginshaw and her son, William, and that they were loved.

Chapter 10 ❧

To make matters worse, with the snow came ice, and the wood was impossible to find hidden beneath the drifts. It was needed not only to feed the fire for cooking and warmth, but also for Peter to work. Pa, when he wasn't drunk, had been the one to go scavenging, but like everything else, this now fell on my shoulders with even more urgency.

I remembered Ma talking about those lucky enough to live up on the moors; they at least could harvest the peat from the ground for their fires, but it was too far for me to walk, even if I knew where to go.

The blowing snow came in sideways. I was afraid I would get lost in the storm if I went outside again, so Peter and I lay huddled together using Ma's dress, still uncut, as a cover. Without a fire to cook the bread, we had the last of the hard crusts to eat. Unable to get out and check the traps for rabbits, there was no meat. This brought me back to the fact that without a fire, I could not cook anything, anyway.

The nearby stream, which flowed eventually into the Otter River, was covered in ice, making it difficult to get water. I looked around for a thick piece of wood to break the ice so I could reach the water flowing below, making me wonder if the fish could survive the icy weather. I had often been fishing with Pa. I knew how to do it, though I hated pulling the hooks out of their mouths, and always tried to leave that task to him.

'Don't be so feeble,' he would tell me angrily, 'they're just fish, they can't feel pain.'

I still couldn't do it.

For three days the storm raged. With every day that passed, we became more frantic with worry. Peter began crying in his sleep.

'Wake up, Peter. Wake up,' I said loudly, shaking him.

He leant on one elbow, rubbing his eyes.

'Why are you crying?' I asked, though I knew the reason.

'I'm hungry, Susannah. My stomach hurts.'

I knew the feeling all too well. My dress, already loosely hung, could now have taken two of me.

'I know, I'm hungry, too, Peter. Once it gets light I'll see if it's stopped snowing. If it has, I will try to get to the store.'

'But what if you get lost?' He was plainly terrified of being left alone, and rightly so. If I didn't come back, what would become of him? Would anyone come looking for him, or even know he was here? Only Master Bentley, but would he think to come to Peter's aid? Though, when I thought more of it, Lady FitzGerald also knew.

'I won't get lost. I know all the land around. I'll stick to the lanes. I'll not cut through the fields like I usually do, no need to worry about me.'

I was glad my voice sounded confident, for I was, like Peter, terrified. Terrified it would stop snowing. Terrified it would not.

'Try not to think about how hungry you are. Let's talk about what you will make next. Do you have any ideas?'

Peter settled himself, pulling his share of the dress back over his legs. 'I could make a small stool, if you find a good-sized log for the seat. Pa's saw is still sharp, though if I use it a lot I will need to get it sharpened or it will just rip the wood. I could make some bowls.'

I watched as the tension started to leave him, his mind on his hands working the wood, until eventually, just before dawn, we both drifted back into sleep.

⚜⚜⚜

The next morning even the birds didn't want to rise from their beds. With the light filtering through the oiled parchment window, I woke slowly. I had hauled my straw pallet downstairs the night before, the earth floor proving too cold and hard to sleep on for another night.

The snow and wind had blown too mightily through what was left of the thatch upstairs. Lying next to Peter, the dress over us both, we were relatively warm, but our cramping stomachs had woken us again.

The snow had stopped sometime during the night, the wind having almost blown itself out. I looked out of the window. It had to be warmer, as small drops of water were falling from the trees. Peter was lying abed, watching me.

'It's stopped snowing, and the wind has gone, so I have to go to the store. I will be back as soon as I can. I am afraid there is nothing left to eat, you will just have to wait. Can you get to the privy, or do you want the pisspot?'

'Don't worry about me, I'll manage. What will you get at the store?'

'I don't know, I have to see what Master Bentley has, what I can carry.' I picked up Ma's wrap and looked longingly at the woolen dress.

'But first, I have to cut some wool for my feet.' I sat at the table, the dress spread before me. I used Peter's small sharp knife to start, ripping the fabric as I had seen Ma do. With one long strip, which I cut in half, I bound one foot, tucking in the ends to secure them, and did the same with the other foot. I walked up and down the cottage.

'It feels strange when I walk, but it will help. I'll be back, Peter. Never fear.' Smiling at him with more confidence than I felt, I set off.

The wool strips certainly helped, and it didn't take long to get used to them. With my head down I walked steadily, but with little or no food for the past few days, I soon tired, having to stop frequently to rest. Keeping to the lanes as I had promised Peter took longer. The snowdrifts were deep, and I feared being lost in them. Off in the distance I could hear the howling of the wolves. They must be hungry, too. I tried to ignore them, hoping they wouldn't come looking this way for food.

By the time Upper Hambley came into view, I felt I could go no farther. It was the knowledge that Peter was all alone that gave me the strength to walk towards the store. Nobody was about, for it was early, though I had no idea of the exact time.

Twice I stumbled in the rutted cart tracks hidden beneath the snow. Hauling myself up on the step, I reached for the door handle, praying it would open. Before I could lift the snick, the door opened in front of me, Master Bentley standing there, amazement on his face.

'Susannah, you've walked all this way in this weather?' Before I could answer, I suddenly felt very odd, his voice seeming to come from a long way away. I fell at his feet in a dead faint, or so he told me after, for I've no memory of it at all.

I could hear a female voice, but again, as though from a great distance.

'She's just a little maid, walking all this way in the snow. Why, she must be exhausted. Just look at her poor feet! Wrapped in rags! She must have been so desperate.' The voice tut-tutted.

I tried to speak, indeed it seemed to me I was shouting. For some reason they couldn't hear me, for the conversation carried on around me.

'I hear her ma died. If that's not bad enough, her pa's taken off again with his fancy woman, though that's not what I'd call her. Whore, more like.'

Pa's gone off with a whore?

'Hush now, I think she's waking up.'

I opened my eyes to see not one, but three women standing over me as I lay on the floor. One, I recognized as Mistress Bentley.

'Now don't you move, Master Bentley will be back in a minute with some food,' she said. I closed my eyes again, only this time I must have fallen into a deep sleep.

I woke for the second time with a start and looked about. Master Bentley was talking in the other room to a customer. The door opened, Master Bentley's face slowly appearing in front of me. I realised I was lying in his private room at the back of the store.

'So you're awake, are you? You must have been exhausted, walking all that way in the snow. Hungry too, I don't doubt. Don't you move, I'll get you something to eat.' He disappeared again, with me not having said a word. He returned quickly, carrying a platter of bread and freshly made cheese, a steaming bowl of meat pottage, along with a bowl of ale, but the smells set my stomach to heaving.

'Now don't you move until you've finished all this, you will feel better after.' Leaving all beside me, he returned to the store, busy with customers clamouring for goods after the storm.

I ate like the wolves I feared, hardly tasting the food, which fell out of my mouth even as I pushed more in. It was only as I neared the end that I remembered Peter lying alone in the cottage, relying on me to bring him something to eat, too. I pushed the dishes away and carefully stood up. Thankfully my legs were no longer wobbly, the dizziness having passed. I peeked round the door.

Master Bentley must have seen the movement. He came towards me. 'Do you feel better, lass?'

'Yes, thank you, sir. I am sorry I fainted, but I was so hungry. Now I have to hurry home, for I need to buy food to take to Peter. Like me, he hasn't eaten for days. I told him I would be as quick as I could be.'

'Right, if you are sure you feel better. What is it you want?'

'We don't have any wood, so we can't light a fire, the snow has covered everything.' I looked around, confused.

'Sit there,' he said, indicating the barrel. Without a word, he began putting together some dried meat, three loaves of bread, along with some cheese from his personal supply. Then he added a large covered pitcher of milk, and when I peeked inside, it was fresh and creamy. He filled a large bowl with some of the meat pottage and covered it with a lid.

'How much do I owe?'

'Let's say one half-shilling, but only if I get the bowl and pitcher back.'

'But it must be more than that.' I lifted my chin, squaring my shoulders. 'I can pay you what it's worth, sir.'

'I know you can. Let's just say it is a small gift from me and my Goodwife, so not another word. Now wait here a moment.' He walked round the table then out through the door.

When he returned, he said, 'I have arranged for a carter who is going near your way to take you, along with all this,' he indicated the food with his hand, 'back to the cottage.' I couldn't believe it. I'd not have to walk all the way, and would be back in good time, though I had no idea how long I had been at the store.

'Thank you, I'll pay the carter for his trouble.'

'There's no need; he's going that way. He said he'd do it with pleasure when I told him your circumstances.'

I fairly leapt off the barrel. 'We're not looking for charity,' I said, my hands clenched by my sides. I felt my face grow hot with the shame of it.

'He's not offering any, lass. Just helping out, that's all, like the good church-going man that he is.'

Instantly I felt ashamed of my outburst. Sheepishly, I said, 'Well, that's all right then. I thank you again for your kindness.'

I sat waiting patiently for the carter, introduced as Joseph. After the supplies were loaded into the back of the cart, and with a wave to Master Bentley, we set off.

A very large, strong dray horse that made light work of the drifts of snow pulled us along. It was not until we had been going for a good while that I remembered the words I had heard the woman speak. 'Her pa has taken off with his fancy woman, though that's not what I'd call her. Whore, more like.'

Chapter 11 ❦

The journey home seemed endless. I knew Peter would be frantic with worry.

The old horse steaming with the effort, the carter used the whip to get it through the deepest drifts. Twice, I had been frightened we would overturn, but the carter knew his work, and brought me safely home.

Stopping at the cottage, the carter looked at it, then at me. 'You live here?'

'With my brother Peter, yes, I do.' Defiant again.

'Your ma's dead?'

'Yes.'

'So where's your pa?'

'We don't know.'

'But you can't stay here all on your own, surely. You must have kin who can take you in.'

'No, we don't. We don't need caring for. We can look out for ourselves.' Before he could say another word I jumped down from the cart.

'Thank you for the ride, Joseph, it was kindly of you. If you could pass down the goods, I'll be letting you get on.'

He didn't deserve the curt rebuke, though he did recognize a dismissal when he heard one, even if delivered by a small female child. Laying the reins down, he clambered over the bench seat, ready to hand down all the supplies one by one.

'Can I help carry them inside?'

'I can manage, thank you. Thank you kindly.'

He handed down first the bowl of pottage, which I placed by the side of the lane, then handed down everything else.

I made my way along the path, noticing the marks Peter's sticks had made on his frequent trips to see if I was returning.

'Peter, it's me. Open the door.'

'Susannah, thank God, you're back.'

I could hear him shuffling to the door as quickly as he could. He held the door wide, so I could bring the bowl in.

'There's more on the lane, I need to go back.'

The carter was still there, sitting back in his seat, watching.

'Who's that?'

'That's Joseph, a carter, Master Bentley asked him to give me a ride. The snow is awful deep, Peter; you have to thank him, for he's been very kind.'

'Thank you, sir, for helping my sister,' he called out, waving his arm.

Joseph nodded in return. Making 'giddy up' noises to the horse, he continued on his way.

Once safely inside, I said, 'I'm sorry I was so long, Peter, but the snow is terrible. Were you scared on your own?'

'Scared? No, of course I wasn't scared.' He turned his face away as he spoke, so I knew he had been.

With everything now on the table, I found the bread Master Bentley had wrapped in a cloth.

'Eat some of this quickly, you must be very hungry.'

He wasted no time answering. He tore off a chunk and stuffed it into his mouth while I sat in Ma's chair, watching him take his fill. He looked in the bowl containing the pottage, poured some milk into a beaker, and sliced off some meat, all the time making small grunting noises of pleasure. I watched him, knowing only too well the pain of hunger. At last, sated, he sat back on the stool.

'I lied, I was scared, Susannah. Scared you weren't coming back, for you were gone so long.'

'I know, Peter; I knew you would be frightened. I'm sorry. But the snow was so deep and I was so hungry, I was ill when I got to the store. It was such a long, cold walk that I fainted. That's why Master Bentley asked Joseph to bring me back.

'But let's not talk of it; the important thing is that I'm here, that we are together. This food will last for a few days, and by then the snow should be gone. I can find more wood, we can light the fire, and then I can make my own bread again.'

༈ ༈

He told me that evening how he had dragged himself to the door, struggling down the short path through the snow, to look along the lane at the way I'd gone. Praying I would return.

It was almost as if he had to talk, to lay the demons of the day to rest before he could sleep. He spoke of his thoughts and fears, making my heart ache even more for my poor brother.

'I sat in Ma's rocking chair, hugging myself for warmth, from fear, Ma's dress covering me.'

'Ma, I'm frightened, I'd cried aloud. Where's Susannah? Please let her come home. What will I do if she doesn't come back? No one knows I'm here.'

'I was too worried to think about being hungry. I told Ma that if it wasn't for my legs, I could have gone instead of you. I'm the man of the house now; I should be caring for Susannah. I am just a burden. She's better off without me.'

He turned to me and said, 'I cursed Pa for leaving us knowing we couldn't survive without him, especially with winter here. I curse you, I cried to the empty walls. I curse you.'

༈ ༈

Rocking in Ma's chair, with Peter already looking better for having eaten something of substance, I said a small, silent prayer for my safe deliverance.

I didn't know whether I believed in God or not. When Ma and Pa were here, we rarely went to church. At that time, all I could do was wonder that if there was a God, why had He let Ma die, leaving Peter and me alone? I tried to be confident that we would be all right, but in truth, I was very scared. Prayers couldn't hurt, to my way of thinking; perhaps they could even do some good. For good measure, I also added my thanks for keeping the wolves away, knowing I had no choice but to go back into the woods again. By the time darkness fell, both of us slept deeply, having been worn out from our day's worries.

༈ ༈

The next morning I brought down some wood from Ma and Pa's bed, telling Peter of my plan for the grave markers.

'Oh Peter! I forgot to ask Master Bentley to scribe it for me. I want you to make the same marks on the wood for markers for Ma and William. I can't bear to think they will lie here without anyone knowing who they are. The markers should be in stone, but we can't afford that. Yours will be just as nice.'

'But there's no one around to see them,' Peter stated rightly.

'Not now, no. But who knows, maybe one day this will be a proper village.'

Peter looked at me as though I'd gone quite mad.

'How could this ever be a village?' he said, derisively. 'There's no other cottage for miles and never will be, you mark my words, Susannah.'

We spoke a lot. Peter told me more of his thoughts during the long hours he had waited for my return.

'If we are to be alone, I have to be a man. Not a weak, angry man like Pa was, but a real man, responsible for us both. I must earn my own way, not rely on Susannah. It's what Ma would expect of me.'

⁂

Each day the snow melted a little more. I was able to return to the woods to look for wood for the fire and for Peter to work. Unfortunately, the ground was far too wet to use the barrow, with the wheel constantly sticking in the muddy earth. It took many trips to get sufficient firewood and small pieces, which had been buried beneath the bracken, but eventually it was done.

Washing my hands in the pail, I scrubbed at my face, weary beyond words, but there was no time for self-pity as I set water to boil over the fire. Once it was hot enough, I used the ladle to put some in the pail, leaving the remainder to bubble away merrily.

'We both need a good wash. You go first, strip off and use the rags to scrub with.'

While Peter bathed, I laid the dress on the table. 'I need your knife. I have to cut this. I can't put it off any longer.'

With Peter's small knife, I cut the cloth of the gathered skirt away from the waist. 'I wonder where Ma got this? It must have been costly, for the wool is very fine. We can easily each get two capes from this, and if I'm careful, a skirt for me, too.'

Yards of material were revealed when I laid it out flat. It proved to be almost twice as long as the table. Eyeing the length, I again used the knife, then ripped the material with my hands. It didn't take long to fashion the two capes.

I went up the ladder to Ma's room and returned with the brooch. The new cape reached almost to the floor. It would help to keep me warmer than Ma's wrap; I would save that for the warmer weather.

Even though he wouldn't be outside as much as me, Peter's cape was the same, though longer. Although he was a year younger, he was already taller, despite the lack of good food. For a fastener he sliced off a small sliver of wood, pushing it through the wool to hold it together, smiling at me with pure joy when he finished.

The skirt, however, proved to be a different problem. I didn't know how to sew the waist, so I ended up gathering it up, then tying it with a thin length of leather from Ma's trunk. There was a gap down the side where the two ends met, but I could cope with that. Ma had kept a bone needle in a small tin on the mantel over the hearth. I teased a length of the wool from the bottom of the cape and used it as thread to sew up the join in the skirt. Trying it on, I was so pleased, walking around the cottage while Peter stood clapping at my accomplishments.

Carefully picking the lace from the collar and cuffs of the bodice, I put them to one side, smoothing them straight. The sleeves of the dress had been very full and would make good leggings for Peter, which could also be held up with strips of leather. We looked at each other, both now laughing.

'You look very silly, Susannah.'

'I know, as do you, but there's no one to see. At least we're warmer.'

We fell silent.

'I miss Ma so much, Susannah. I wish she was here.'

For once, I had no reply, for I was beginning to despair. Even with Lady FitzGerald's offer, what would happen to us if I couldn't make enough lace, if no one else bought Peter's wood?

Peter had washed himself as best he could, and I used the water pail afterwards. My hair was knotted and dirty, but there wasn't enough hot water to wash it. It all seemed so much work, thinking of what to do, and what we'll need. How Ma used to cope, the Lord only knows.

My stomach felt odd. It wasn't a feeling of hunger, for I knew that well enough. It was a feeling of fear. What if something happens to me and Peter is really left alone? Who would care for him? I held Peter close until I felt his thin body start to relax and my own breathing calm.

'All will be well, Peter, all will be well.'

Telling him I had to use the privy, I went round back of the cottage to lean against the wall, taking in great gulps of cold air.

'Please, God, please help me and Peter.'

That evening I took up the lace pillow again, hurrying to finish the difficult piece. In the candlelight, shadows danced across the pillow. When I cut off the last of the bobbins I gave a huge sigh, sad that Ma wasn't here to see how well I'd done.

Once again I thought of the woman's comment at Master Bentley's store, 'Pa and his whore.' She had to be wrong; Pa would never have done that. Surely, he loved Ma? But if he did, then how could he have beaten her so? He'll come back when he's ready. Yet, do we even want him back?

❧❧❧

Within days, the weather was noticeably warmer. With more wood available, we were able to keep the fire alight to cook bread daily. Most of the snow had gone, though there were puddles and soggy patches on the ground. I could get back to the traps, but they were filled with only partial success, for it seemed that all the animals who had been cooped up inside their burrows, as we had been, were now too wily to be caught.

Peter had a good many pieces ready to take to Honiton, which was my next worry. I had only ever been to the lace buyer, never to visit the market with Ma. We hadn't been round the town, for we couldn't afford to buy anything, so what was the sense of looking? With no idea of what stores were there, all I could do was hope that someone would be willing to take the pieces Peter had worked hard on. Thankfully, this time instead of using my skirt as a basket, I could use the barrow. It would mean I couldn't cut across the stream, which probably was all to the good when I remembered the last time I'd done so.

'Market day in Honiton is on a Tuesday, which I think is tomorrow. I went to Master Bentley's on Thursday of last week, which was four days ago.' I planned to be off early in the morning. 'Put everything on the table you want me to take. Check it again first to make sure it's the best quality, so they can't deny us a chance.'

Lying beside Peter that night, I remembered to thank Ma for the dress. 'Peter thanks you too. If you could keep your hand on me tomorrow when I go into the town, that would be good, Ma. I'm worried what we'll do if no one takes the wood, for we can't live on the lace alone. I can't make enough on my own.'

Listening to the sound of Peter's slow breathing helped soothe me, and within a short time I, too, slept. The only noises outside were the fox yipping as it called to its mate and the owl hooting as it watched for a kill. So when the roof above gave way, it sounded as if all the Hounds of Hell had come calling.

Chapter 12 ❧

Woken loudly from our deep sleep, we both screamed. One of the large roof beams poked through over the table. I looked up at what remained of the ceiling, expecting it to collapse on us at any moment. Dust, pieces of old thatch, and birds' nests came down the ladder to choke the air, making it impossible to see.

Coughing, forcing myself to move, I shouted to Peter, 'Quick, get outside!' I ran for the lace, along with as many pieces of the finished wood as I could carry. Peter struggled upright, grabbed his sticks, then shuffled to the door and opened it. Both of us rushed outside. Taking a few steps down the path, we turned to look back in the moonlight.

The top floor had almost totally collapsed. The thatch that hadn't fallen inside had fallen to the ground. Two of the support timbers remained standing, but apart from that, the whole space seemed to have gone. We looked at each other, both pale-faced and shivering. It was dark, but the full moon harshly illuminated the destruction.

'What will we do now?' asked Peter, his voice quavering with fright.

'How do I know?' I wailed, instantly regretting it. 'I'm sorry, Peter. I shouldn't be angry at you, it's not your fault.'

'No, it's Pa's for not keeping the thatch up, the lazy sod.' He was openly crying.

I looked at him, amazed. 'That's the first time I've heard you curse him.'

'The first you've heard, but not the first time I've cursed him.'

❧❧❧

Luckily, we had our clothes, for we always slept in them, especially the new capes, though Ma's wrap was inside.

After a few minutes with no further collapse, I asked, 'Do you think it's safe to go inside?'

'We should wait a bit; if it's going to collapse, it will be soon.'

Shaking with fright, we sought a dry spot and settled ourselves, side by side on the path. Nothing to do, but wait.

ぇぇぇぇ

When the sun came over the horizon, nothing more had fallen, and we could see into the bottom floor of the house.

'I have to get Ma's chest down, there's a ring inside and I'm not losing it, and I must get the lace from Ma's dress. Don't worry, there's nothing left to fall, I'll be all right.'

Nervously, I headed back inside, the gathering daylight showing in stark detail the full extent of the damage. The ceiling sagged where the weight of the sodden mess rested above. It won't be long before it comes down. I thought, I should get Peter's woodworking tools first, then the lace pillow, and the bobbins. I wrapped the pillow in a large rag to keep it clean, though it was already covered in bits of thatch.

Taking all outside, I left them with Peter, and went back for the food and the large cooking pot and as many bowls as I could reach. The stools came next, then anything else I could either reach or carry. I put Ma's wrap round my shoulders.

Carefully, I climbed the ladder which had survived, but for a couple of missing rungs in the middle. The large roof beam had crushed the chest. Fortunately, I was able to reach inside to claw out the smaller things, trying to remember what else had been in there. But at least the important things, like Ma's ring, were saved. The deed to the cottage was also safe, if a little wet. I carefully rolled them up, adding them to the growing pile. I had stripped the pallet of all its covers long ago, and all the good wood was already used by Peter.

'Where shall we go? What's to become of us?' he asked once I was safely back outside.

'I don't know, Peter. Hush now, for I have to think.'

At least an hour went by while we sat on the path surrounded by our few remaining possessions.

'As far as I can see, first we have to sell the lace and wood. To do that, I have to go to Watermead and Master Bentley's. I've had a change of thought about something. I won't take the wood to Honiton, I know I can trust Master Bentley; I'll take it all there. They are in opposite directions, so I have to think which one to go to first.'

Peter sat quietly, watching me; I knew my face was creased with worry.

'We have to find a place to live, Peter. I think that place has to be Honiton, and as Watermead is on the way there, I'll go to Master Bentley's first. The barrow's not big enough, and once laden, it would be too heavy for me, anyways. Maybe I can get a cart to carry our belongings, not that there's many of them.'

We both looked round at our few retrieved possessions.

'You have to stay here, but I think it's safe to go inside, so long as you stay near the door; at least you'll be out of the wind. Leave everything out here.' I looked at the sky. 'It doesn't feel like rain, so it should be all right.' Putting the wood in the barrow that thankfully had been kept at the side of the house, I set off.

Keeping to the lanes made it longer, but there was nothing else for it. The store was open, and one customer was just leaving. I brought all the worked wood inside and Master Bentley checked each piece.

'The usual pricing for these, Susannah. I must tell you, Peter's work is already held in high regard. I've customers waiting for the spoons and ladles.' He spoke enthusiastically, but I was finding it difficult to concentrate, or to be happy at his words.

'Master Bentley, do you know of a carter going out our way today?'

'Why would you need a carter?'

'The top floor of the cottage has collapsed. I've moved everything out but Peter and me, and we've got to go to Honiton now to live.'

'I'm right sorry to hear that, lass. I don't know of anyone, but I'll tell you what. I'll get my Goodwife to care for the store, and bring my own cart. Do you know where you're going in Honiton?'

'That is very kind of you. No, I don't know where we will go, though first I have to stop at Watermead to sell the lace to Lady

FitzGerald, if it wouldn't be too much trouble. We'll need the money to find lodgings until we can decide what to do.'

Master Bentley called to his wife, explaining our problem. Willingly agreeing to take over the store, she cast sad glances at me as she made tutting noises, shaking her head.

'Husband, may I speak with you?'

'Not now, I have to get the horse and cart ready for Susannah. I'll be back before dark, there'll be time enough to talk then.' He left her looking after him.

It didn't take long to get back to the cottage. Peter was sitting outside, shivering, too frightened to find shelter inside. Looking at our belongings heaped on the path, I jumped down from the cart.

'I thought I told you to wait inside, Peter?'

'You did, but the ceiling started to come down again.'

We both looked at the ruins of our home, and suddenly it was all too much for me. I began to cry.

'Don't cry, Susannah. We will be all right. You'll see,' said Peter, trying to comfort me. 'Ma always said nothing would happen to us we couldn't cope with.'

But I couldn't be consoled, and continued to sob.

'Look, while you were gone I made two markers for the graves. They are very rough, but at least there will be some way of showing Ma and William are buried here.'

He held up two small wooden crosses, fashioned from the remains of the cottage. The crosspiece was held by twine wrapped round it, and the bottom of the main piece was sharpened to help get it into the ground.

'I know they aren't much, Susannah, and their names aren't on them, but it was the best I could do.' He looked worriedly at me with tears streaming down my face.

'It's not that, Peter, they are very good. I thank you for making them. It's just that all the way here I was thinking no one would know the graves were there; but now, thanks be to you, they will.'

Taking them from him, I turned to Master Bentley. 'Sir, may I ask you to wait a moment while we place these? We won't be but a few moments.'

'There's no need to ask, lass. I'll be here when you're ready. I'll start loading the cart,' replied Master Bentley gruffly, close to tears himself by the sounds of it.

Peter and I went round the back of the cottage, sweeping aside dead leaves. Kneeling down, I pushed the markers into the ground.

'Here you are, Ma, a marker at last. There's one for William, too. One day, I promise, there will be proper stones.'

Standing up, I joined Peter. We stood silently for a moment, then turned away, for what else was there for us to do?

With the cart ready laden, Master Bentley lifted Peter up onto the seat, while I clambered into the back.

'Tell me, Peter, how many times have you been to Honiton?' he asked as we set off.

'Never!'

'Well, you're in for a treat,' he said, trying to divert us both from the fact that we probably wouldn't see the cottage again.

'It's big and bustling, with shops, churches, fairs and markets. And the people! So many people it will make your head spin.'

'Is there a shop that would take Peter's wood, sir?'

'I think there's more than one, lass, at least two that I can readily think of. Your woodworking is selling well, Peter. Once you're in Honiton, you'll get more ideas, no doubt, and have access to more and better wood.' He paused. 'I know this seems a terrible thing to happen to you both, on top of what you've already suffered, but it's going to work out to be for the best, you mark my words.' He looked at Peter who, in turn, was looking around him, eyes wide at sights never seen before.

'We've to stop first at Watermead, so Susannah can sell the lace. You wait till you see that house, Peter, it's really grand!'

We plodded steadily along. Peter looked as if his heart had been lightened by Master Bentley's kind, thoughtful words. I, though, stayed consumed with worry about where we would spend the night. I felt saddest about leaving Ma and William. Ma always said, 'Never look back, for you can't change the past.' But I couldn't help myself. I turned to look over my shoulder at the ruins of our home.

❧❧❧❧

As was now the custom, I sold the lace to her ladyship's maid, Mistress Dobbs, at Watermead's kitchen door, then waited on the doorstep for payment. The large piece I had been working on was finished and was magnificent. I pointed it out specifically to the maid.

'This one is special, I think it could be used for a dressing table, or indeed any table in a lady's room. You can tell just by looking at it how well worked it is. I promise you'll not find any mistakes.' The maid looked it over carefully.

'Indeed it does look well worked. Wait here while I speak to her ladyship.' As she hurried off, I turned around to look at Master Bentley and Peter, waiting in the cart. Peter's mouth was hanging open as he looked at the building and over the grounds.

Coming back, the maid said, 'Her ladyship said she would give two guineas for this piece alone, so that means for all, I'm to give four guineas and four shillings.'

I couldn't believe I had heard right, and asked her to repeat it.

'Would you please thank her ladyship? Also tell her the cottage fell down last night, so we have to move to Honiton. I'll still be making the lace, though, be sure to tell her that. I'll come back with more as soon as I can.' I tied the coins into the corner of my skirt while I spoke, not wanting to risk their loss.

'I will. I wish you well in Honiton, child. Do you know where you'll be lodging?'

'No, I have to find somewhere for us, so this money is a godsend.'

Waving goodbye, I climbed back onto the cart. 'How much did you get, Susannah?' asked Peter as soon as I was settled.

'Four guineas and four shillings.' I was ecstatic.

'Four guineas?' repeated Master Bentley, utterly amazed, as he turned the horse around to head back down the drive.

'Yes, that means we can afford to stay somewhere tonight, not sleep outside. Do you know of a place, Master Bentley?'

'I only know of the Cross Keys near the square. I've never heard any bad talk of it. Better yet, you could ask for a safe place to lock your goods in, for there's a range of buildings out the back.'

'Then to the Cross Keys it is!'

With that, Master Bentley burst into singing the ballad of "Greensleeves." Peter quickly joined in, for it was one Ma used to sing to us. If it weren't for the fact that we were moving to Honiton as the result of such a tragedy, anyone looking on would have thought we were a happy family going on a much-anticipated journey.

I, however, couldn't shake the feeling that perhaps Honiton was where Peter and me were meant to be all along. Perhaps the roof had fallen to force us to go.

Chapter 13 ❧

During the journey to Honiton, I did a great deal of thinking while Peter was chattering to Master Bentley. With his talent for working the wood, why couldn't he be apprenticed to a joiner? He was ten years old, still very young, but anyone could see how talented he was. There had to be a joiner in town somewhere, or at least close by. I knew from listening to Pa that boys around Peter's age were apprenticed to a master to learn a trade. Why not Peter? When I mentioned it, he jumped at the chance.

'I think you'll find there's a fee required,' interjected Master Bentley.

'Really, how much do they pay?' Peter asked, excited at the prospect of a wage.

'No, lad, you have to pay the master, not the other way round,' he replied, laughing.

I couldn't believe it. 'We have to pay him? How much?'

'I don't know how much, depends on the master, I expect. Also the trade, come to think of it. It could also depend if he has any other apprentices, but you can inquire when you get to town.' With that, we had to be satisfied.

Master Bentley took us straight to the Cross Keys, the same inn Master Stanton had taken me to eat when he bought the lace.

He accompanied me inside, vouching for Peter's and my good standing. Poor we may look, he told the innkeeper, but we could afford the price of the lodging. The sum of two shillings a week, food included, was agreed upon.

Master Bentley explained our situation, telling of Peter's woodworking, of his customers' remarks on the quality of the work. He also asked where the best place was in town to try and place some of the pieces, then asked about an apprenticeship to the town joiner for Peter.

The innkeeper, Master Beaker, looked at me as if he had rarely seen anyone less able to afford his lodging, but at Master Bentley's urging, offered to approach the joiner on our behalf, an offer I readily accepted with thanks.

After the landlord showed us where we could store our belongings, Master Bentley and I unloaded the cart. I watched as the padlock was put on the door, accepted the key from Master Beaker, and clutched it tightly. We both thanked Master Bentley profusely.

Once Master Bentley had turned the horse and cart for home, we retreated to our shared room at the back of the inn. With wide eyes and a sigh of relief, we climbed onto the high bed with help from the small steps set there for that purpose. The mattress proved to be of feathers, not straw, nothing to prick our skin. The bolster pillow was large, the sheets clean and crisp linen. We both sat looking around at our new, albeit temporary, home.

My doll, Emma, lay between us. It was just after noon, and we hadn't eaten since last night, but even our growling stomachs couldn't keep us awake. Worn out with worry and care, we both slipped quickly into deep, dreamless sleep.

ༀ

We woke early the next morning to the sounds of the scullions as they toiled, preparing breakfast in the freestanding kitchen nearby. Neither of us could believe how long we had slept, but the smell of the bacon collops frying was too much to ignore.

Mingled with the smell of the freshly baked bread, we couldn't wait any longer to creep out of our room, making sure we locked the door behind us. We walked down the wet flagstone passageway, which had just been sluiced, in search of Master Beaker. The weather was wet, the accompanying wind causing the fire to smoke. We could smell it as soon as we left our room.

We came upon a large, wood-panelled room filled with trestle tables, benches and chairs, the same room I had eaten in before.

Master Beaker was already there, sitting at a table by the window as far away from the smoke as possible.

'Come in, join me,' he said, shuffling along to make room on the bench seat for Peter, who edged on to the seat, laying his sticks on the floor.

'Hanna, get in here, there are two hungry ones waiting for food,' he shouted.

Both Peter and I chuckled, for indeed we were very hungry. A short while later a girl swept through the door carrying a large platter laden with thick slabs of bacon, eggs, sausages, chicken, fish and kidneys, along with thick slices of fresh bread spread with butter. She placed it on the table before Peter and me. Quickly returning to the kitchen, she soon re-appeared with eating platters for each of us, pouring ale into beakers from the jug on the table.

'If you're to be lodging here,' she said, 'then you should know I am called Hanna.'

Peter and I smiled at her. 'I'm Susannah Brigginshaw, and this is my brother, Peter.' I looked at Peter, who sat silently, a silly smile on his face.

'Pleased to meet you both. Call, if you need more,' she told us, disappearing again.

Master Beaker watched as we piled our dishes with food, rightly deciding it would be a waste of his breath to talk again until we were finished eating. Indeed, it would have been hard for us to reply, our mouths so stuffed with food. At last, stomachs full, we sat back, Peter belching gently.

'Right, I'm off to see the joiner,' announced Master Beaker. 'Can you give me something to take with me?'

'This is very kind of you, sir. Peter chose a few pieces last night. I'll get them for you,' I replied, hurrying back to our room.

'I can't make any promises, lad. All I can do is ask, then it's up to him,' he warned Peter.

'I know, sir, but the work will prove I'm worthy of my hire. I don't doubt the joiner will take me on.'

When I returned with the four different pieces that had been selected, I heard Peter's reply. I felt so proud of him at that moment.

'Here you are, sir. As you can see, the work is of good quality. Be sure to tell the joiner that although Peter is lame, it doesn't stop him from producing good work.' I handed the pieces to Master Beaker.

He looked them over, smiled and said, 'I'll tell him.' He stood up. 'I hope to be back about dinnertime. I'll seek you out, hopefully with good news.'

Once alone, Peter and I looked at each other. In front of Master Beaker he had been sure of his acceptance by the joiner, but now I could see doubt creeping onto his face. Sometimes I forgot how young he was, still plagued with childish uncertainty.

'What if he doesn't take me, Susannah? What will we do?' He took a deep breath and looked to me for reassurance.

'Don't worry, Peter, how could he not take you? Your work is very good; everybody who has seen it says so. Don't sit here fretting—what are you going to do while you wait?'

'I thought I would go outside if it stops raining.'

Hanna appeared to clear the table, smiling at us both.

'If you're going out, you need to wrap up warm, the wind goes right through you,' she warned, looking down at our feet.

'Don't you have any boots?'

We shook our heads.

'You're going to need them here. You'll find the cobbles will hurt your feet.' She sat down beside Peter. 'Can you afford them?'

'We don't know the cost,' I replied, feeling embarrassed in front of this worldly girl.

'There's a bootmaker not far from here. When I'm finished my work, I'll take you round and show you, Susannah. We'll see what he can do for you. I know he sometimes has old boots people have no further use for. They would be less costly than new.'

Peter and I again looked at each other.

'Thank you, Hanna. We would be grateful, though you should know we don't have a lot of money.'

'Who does? Let's wait to see what he says. I'll be as quick as I can, then we'll go.' She hurried back to her work, humming loudly to herself.

Peter and I went back to our room. Sitting on the bed, he said, 'He won't have boots for me. My feet are all twisted and ugly.' He rarely complained about his infirmity, for what was the point with nothing to be done about it?

'As Hanna said, let's wait and see. It'll all depend on the cost. Now we are in Honiton, we can't look like country peasants!' We both fell back on the bed, giggling.

ঔঐঔঐ

Just before dinner, Master Beaker returned, knocking on our door.

'Peter, I spoke to the joiner as I promised. When I showed him your work, he wanted to know how old you were, then I realised I had neglected to ask.'

'I'm ten, sir,' he replied as he pulled himself up in an attempt to make himself look taller.

Master Beaker gave a huge sigh. 'Well, that's all right then, if you were younger he wouldn't have considered you. He has taken on lads as young as seven, but the work was too hard for them. He said you were just the right age. May I sit down? It's a fair walk and I'm not as young as I was. I'm sure that hill grows steeper with each passing year.'

Peter moved over to make room. Neither of us was interested in the steepness of the hill, only eager to hear what he had to say about the joiner.

'But you're not interested in the hill, are you?'

I immediately felt bad, not able to meet his eyes, for how could he have known what I was thinking?

'He was impressed with your work. He asked what tools you were using, but of course I couldn't answer. He is looking for an apprentice. I did tell him about your infirmity, and told him it seemed you could move around well, so he'll be prepared when he sees you. He has agreed to meet with you, but will want to know how you intend to pay for the apprenticeship.'

Peter and I looked at each other. So it was true after all. 'We hadn't known we had to pay, sir. We thought the master paid the apprentice for his work, not the other way round. We have very little money. Would he have mentioned what the cost would be?'

'No, he didn't. That would be one of the things to talk over with him.' He looked at Peter's worried face. 'Don't be disappointed, lad. Speak to him first. I said you would be there tomorrow morning at eight o'clock when his shop opens. It's about a twenty-minute walk for me, so it'll take you longer. Come and see me before you leave, I'll give you the directions. His name is Master Chapman.'

'Master Beaker's right, Peter, don't get downhearted. Wait until you speak to him, then we can discuss it. We'll find the money somehow.'

However, Peter continued to look worried.

Master Beaker hauled himself off our bed with difficulty. 'I've to get back to my work; I've done my best, lad, now it's up to you.'

Remembering my manners, I also stood up, curtsying. 'Thank you kindly, Master Beaker, Peter will let you know tomorrow if he's accepted.'

He looked at each of us in turn and, nodding, left us alone.

'We will need to leave in plenty of time to get there. I'll ask Hanna to give us food early, then we must leave straight away, for we cannot be late.'

I could see the look of concern on Peter's face. 'Rest easy, Peter, he liked your work that Master Beaker took to him. We know he's looking for an apprentice, so why shouldn't it be you? Try not to worry about the fee, we'll manage. Come on, we can't sit here wasting the day, let's go and see if Hanna is ready to take me to the bootmaker while you go exploring.'

Grabbing his hand, I started to pull him off the bed, while Peter howled once more with laughter, good humour at last restored.

Hanna was waiting for me. With Peter and me trailing behind, she led the way outside. 'It's not too far, Susannah. We will see what he can do for you.'

We both waved goodbye to Peter, leaving him standing at the inn door looking around, deciding which direction he would go.

The town looked so big, so busy. And the noise! When I came here with Ma to sell the lace it was always early in the day, hardly noisy at all. Now, I couldn't believe the difference.

Hanna chatted all the way, pointing out the different shops as we went. A candle maker, a bakery standing cheek by jowl next to it, with women already lining up to use their ovens. When I went to the High Street with Ma to see the lace buyer, I never had taken notice of what else was around.

Standing outside of the bootmaker's store, I looked at the boots on display in the bay-fronted window. Either black or brown, the boots were in two lengths, short or long. The sign above the door showed a boot, beneath the words, 'Jno. Bragg, Proprietor.'

'Come on,' said Hanna. 'Let's go in.' From the back room, which was out of view behind a curtain, came a young man bent over by a large hump on his back. A black felt cap on his head was pulled low, obviously to protect his ears from the cold. A leather apron hung from around his neck, tied at the waist. I would recognize him again anywhere, for there was a large hairy wart on his chin.

'What can I do for you, ladies?'

'My friend,' Hanna looked quickly at me, 'requires some boots. What do you have at a reasonable price, preferably ones that have already been worn?'

'Let's see your feet.'

I held up one foot.

'Hm, I should have something. Wait here.'

He disappeared into the back room. We could hear thumps and cursing, which set us both to giggling until eventually he returned, holding a pair of boots in each hand.

'Try these,' he said, putting down the first pair.

I looked around for a seat, and finding only a stool, I sat down and slipped on one of the boots.

'That's on the wrong foot, you daft thing. It goes on the other one.'

I giggled again, though this time from embarrassment. Feeling my face grow warm and changing feet, I tried again.

'How does that feel?' asked the bootmaker.

'It hurts.'

'Right, try these.' He handed over the second pair. I looked at the one I had taken off; it curved towards the front window, or so it seemed to me. Taking up the new one that also curved the same way, I tried it on.

'Well?'

'This one isn't tight.'

'Well try the other one, then,' he said, impatiently.

I did so.

'Walk around a bit; make sure they don't pinch you.'

They didn't.

'How much are they, sir?'

'How much you got?'

'I only have two pence.'

'That's what they cost, hand over the coin.' He held out a very grimy hand into which I placed the coins, instantly becoming the proud possessor of a pair of sturdy brown spiral-laced short boots.

'Could you please show me how to tie them, sir?'

He muttered, snapping his fingers in irritation, then bent down with great effort.

'Watch careful now, I'll only show you the once.' He quickly proceeded to do so, with me trying to follow along while looking upside down at his flying fingers.

'My brother also needs boots, sir, but he's lame. May I bring him, see if you can fit his feet?'

'I daresay,' he replied, which I took to be a 'yes.'

With the transaction over as far as he was concerned, he disappeared once more into the back without another word.

Hanna indicated we should leave, so I thanked the space where he had stood, but was now empty, and followed Hanna out of the store.

'How do they feel?' she asked.

'Very strange, but I'll get used to them, given time. Neither Peter nor I want to look as if we've just arrived from the countryside, even though we have. Hanna, I'm not sure I can remember how to tie them, he did it so quickly.'

'Don't worry about that, I can show you, it's not difficult.'

The church bells rang. 'I'd best be getting back to the Cross Keys, Susannah. They'll be busy soon.' Leading the way she strode off, me following along in my new boots.

As we walked up the High Street, I noticed Peter ahead of us, heading in the same direction.

'Peter, Peter,' I cried, waving my arm in greeting.

He turned and waited for us to catch up.

'I got the boots, and I'm to take you back. The bootmaker will see if he has something for you. Look!' I held up my skirt to give him a better view. 'They do feel funny, though my feet are a lot warmer, and it's much easier to walk on the cobbles.' I lifted my foot, turning it to and fro, admiring the boot. 'Did you enjoy your walk, Peter? What did you see?'

'Master Bentley was right, this is a big town, Susannah, I never realised. But all the walking has tired me; how far is it to the bootmaker's?' He spoke frettingly, and looked overwhelmed.

'Farther than I think you can manage. I'll see about hiring a cart for you tomorrow.'

Inside the Cross Keys, we stopped first at the room where we ate our meals, finding Master Beaker there, sitting at the same table as if he'd never left. The tables were starting to fill up with customers, so Hanna went straight through to the kitchen.

'Sit down, Susannah, Peter; I've some news for you.'

Peter slumped thankfully on the bench with a sigh of relief, while I sat on a chair. I pulled my skirt back, so everyone would be sure to see the new boots.

'I visited the church today and spoke to the Rector. Now, don't you get upset,' he held up his hands placatingly, 'but I mentioned your circumstances, how you were alone and trying to make your way in the world. I also spoke of the good work Peter has done.'

'Here in Honiton we are blessed with a comfortable living, what with the lace and the pottery, the market, not to mention the good agricultural land. Well, to make it short, Peter, the parish has access to funds made available by a late resident to be used specifically for boys to be apprenticed for a trade. That means that you, coming from Offwell, which is part of this diocese, can claim it!'

We looked at him, neither of us understanding.

'It means the parish will pay for you to be an apprentice. You won't have to worry about the fee!' he explained. 'I told the Rector about your work, and he's coming here shortly to speak with you.'

'Me?' Peter squeaked, 'Speak to the Rector?'

'Yes, lad, now don't get upset, he won't eat you. I've heard he only eats small boys on Thursdays.' He laughed at his own joke. 'His sermons are too long of a Sunday, but that is neither here nor there, where you're concerned. It's a rich parish, and we can well afford to help a young lad in need, especially one who shows such promise.'

Master Beaker had hardly finished speaking when we heard the inn door open, followed shortly by the appearance of the tall and darkly clothed Rector.

It didn't take long for him to make up his mind. He looked at the work Peter had done, and asked us both a few questions: where our parents; were we paupers?

I didn't know how much coin one had to have to be considered a pauper. Rightly or wrongly, I made the decision not to tell him about the money tied up in my skirt.

'Well, I think we can help you, young man. I'll go directly to speak to Master Chapman and make the arrangements.'

⁂

After a sleepless night for both of us, we set off early the next morning. Peter was riding in a small cart pulled by a bad-tempered donkey.

Hanna had fed us both well, maybe too well as far as Peter was concerned.

'I've butterflies, Susannah. I feel sick.'

'I know, but you'll do well, never fear.'

So much depended on his being accepted, the alternative not to be thought of, for our money would only last so long.

Master Chapman met Peter at the door of his shop.

'It's good to see you're on time, Peter. Come on in. Your sister, though, must wait outside.'

Peter gave one last look at me, while I tried to smile encouragingly.

The door closed behind them, my own unmentioned butterflies taking flight, threatening to lift me up to soar into the air.

Chapter 14 ❧

I paced up and down in front of the shop unable to stand still, oblivious to the chill in the wind. Uncertain of my bearings in Honiton, I daren't go far, for fear of getting lost. Not wanting to have to ask for help, I kept to the lane in which the joiner's shop was situated.

I passed a small shop with two steps leading up to a single door. A large window was on the left with one pair of gloves displayed on a small table. A lace curtain was discreetly drawn behind, giving privacy to those within. The large wooden sign, which showed a painting of a lady's glove, hung outside, creaking in the wind.

I watched two ladies enter together as another was coming out. All were well dressed, lace caps showing beneath their bonnets, long skirts held up out of the mud.

Master Bentley sold gloves in his store, though Ma could never afford the luxury. Some of the wealthier ladies in Upper Hambley wore them not only in winter, but also in summer to prevent the sun burning their skin. I just couldn't conceive of a whole shop filled with nothing but gloves.

I glanced back at Master Chapman's shop, but Peter hadn't been inside long, too early for sign of him. Rather than wait outside in the chilly air, I decided to look inside.

A small bell affixed to the frame above jangled noisily as I pushed the door open, alerting the lady behind the counter of new custom. Three sets of eyes turned in my direction, all taking me in with surprised glances, from the top of my head down to the toes of my new brown boots.

The lady behind the counter, obviously the owner, frowned at me as I entered. She didn't speak to me, continuing her conversation with the two customers as if I wasn't there.

There were tables to the left and right displaying gloves; long or short, in a variety of colours, some embroidered, some plain. Moving first to the left, I picked up a pair displayed alone. They were a beautiful shade of green that reminded me of the grass beside the stream at Offwell in the spring. Flowers were embroidered with great skill on the back, continuing up the long cuff. I liked the feel of the leather, butter soft when I stroked them with the back of my hand, and I gave a small sigh of pleasure.

'Don't you touch those!' shouted the lady. 'Get away from the table. We don't want the likes of you in here.'

I jumped and looked up, confused. 'But, mistress, I merely touched them. I've done them no harm.'

'Get away, I told you, or I'll call the Watch! Get out of my shop!'

I was now more confused. No one had ever spoken to me in such anger, not even Pa when the drink was on him. The woman came from behind the counter, shaking her fist, threatening.

The two customers, sensing trouble, quickly turned to flee from the store. Bumping into each other, they both tried to get through the door at the same time, their voluminous skirts pushing them together.

Realizing that nothing I could say would help, I followed them outside, turning in the lane to wait outside Master Chapman's shop. My knees were trembling, and my ears filled with her screeching.

I didn't understand what I had done wrong. I only touched them. I hadn't done any harm, though I knew she would blame me for the loss of the custom. Hugging the cape around me, I stood once more in the chilly air outside the joiner's, with no sign of Peter.

I leaned against the stone front trying to calm down, and looked in the direction of the glove shop. The two customers who had fled were hurrying down towards the High Street, waving their arms while talking so loudly I could hear them.

Hearing the shop door open, I looked back to find Peter beckoning me inside, while Master Chapman stood behind him, smiling.

'Susannah, I'm apprenticed! You have to come in to speak to Master Chapman!'

'Peter, I am so pleased for you. I never doubted you would do well.' I followed him inside, shutting the door behind me.

Master Chapman spent a few moments going over the terms of the indenture. Peter would live with him and his wife and would attend church with them on Sunday mornings. Sunday afternoon, from noon to five o'clock, he would have to himself. All his meals and clothes would be provided, though boots were our responsibility, due to his infirmity. The term would last for seven years, so he would be seventeen at the end of it.

The first year he would be paid a shilling a month, two shillings in the second and so forth until seven shillings monthly for the final year. I knew I had to concentrate, but my mind was taken up with my own unsettling events. I was also filled with so many other feelings. How Peter and me would be parted for seven years, leaving me, effectively, alone. However, all was tempered with how proud Ma would be of Peter.

'Are those terms acceptable to you?'

Peter and me looked at each other, silent agreement in our eyes. 'Yes, sir, they are,' replied Peter eagerly.

'Good. Come back at seven o'clock sharp tomorrow morning, Peter. I will have the legal papers drawn up; you must put your mark on them. I'm a fair master, so long as my apprentice pulls his weight. You won't have reason to complain about the training you get, and my wife will make sure you're well fed.

'The Rector, as well as Master Beaker, say you get around well, and from what I've seen, they spoke truthfully, not that I'd expect anything less from the Rector.' He stood up. 'I'll see you tomorrow, lad. Remember to bring your tools with you.'

'Yes, sir. Thank you,' Peter replied happily, stooping to pick up his sticks as we prepared to leave.

'You won't regret taking Peter, Master Chapman. He'll be the best apprentice you've ever had, you'll see.' I backed up towards the shop door, only to hear it open behind me.

'Here you are, you little thief. I've called the Watch; they'll be here any minute. Keep that girl here, Master Chapman, for she stole a pair of gloves from my store a few minutes ago.'

I looked at her in horror.

'I did no such thing, mistress, I only touched the gloves. I would never steal.'

'We'll see about that, the Watch will search you. If the gloves are found, it'll be the worse for you.' She guarded the door while I stood frozen in terror. Peter looked on in confusion, not knowing what had gone on before.

'What's this you say, mistress?' Master Chapman asked.

'This maid was in my shop and stole a pair of gloves. I had two customers eager to buy, though they fled when they saw her standing there in her rags, they were so feared.'

'No, mistress, they fled because you were shouting so loudly you frightened them,' I retorted, with no choice but to fight back.

The glover addressed Master Chapman directly. 'Well I never heard anything like it! Now she berates me! Me! What is this world coming to when a young slip-of-a-thing talks back to her betters! Where is that Watch?' She turned to peer anxiously out of the window. 'You'll be taken into charge, my girl. We know how to deal with thieves in Honiton.'

I was shaking, looking to Peter for help, but I knew there was little he could give, though he did try.

'Mistress, there must be a mistake, my sister would never steal. You have my word on it.'

'As if that means anything to me! Your word is as good as hers. Look at you; you're both in rags, obviously looking out for what you can steal.'

We all looked towards the door as it opened once more. It bumped into the lady's back, pushing her off balance.

'Now you're in for it, here's the Watch,' she said, smugly, crossing her arms beneath her ample bosom.

'What's this I hear, a report of a child stealing?' The Watch proved to be a large man, long grey whiskers hanging from the sides of his face. A battered old hat, which appeared too large for him, was placed lopsided on his head.

The lady from the glove shop began shouting once more, pointing at me, telling her story again. To my horror, with a few additions.

'She came pushing into the shop, demanding I give her gloves, said her hands were cold.'

'But that's not true, sir! I merely went in to see the shop while I waited for my brother. I've never been inside a glove shop before, I only wanted to look. I never spoke a word until she falsely accused me. That's the truth, sir.'

The glover took over again. 'I had paying customers in the shop. Then this rag-a-muffin came in and scared them. They fled immediately, not that I can blame them, but now I'm out their custom. Just the smell of her was enough. Look, she's wearing scraps! Look at those boots! I bet she stole those too!'

The Watchman looked from one to the other of us, taking in my boots, trying to decide which one of us to believe.

'Don't just stand there, you idiot, take her into charge!'

'Rest easy, mistress, I need to assure myself that she did take them first. What colour were they?'

'Red.'

'But, mistress, the ones I looked at were a beautiful shade of green, with embroidery on. I never even touched red ones. As for my boots, I purchased those honorably yesterday morning. The bootmaker will speak for me, as will Hanna from the Cross Keys, for she gave me the introduction and took me there herself.'

I turned to the Watchman, hands out, entreating. 'You must believe me, sir, I'm an honest maid, and I've never stolen.'

'Do you have someone who can speak for you?'

Peter and I looked at each other. We were strangers here, who would speak for me? For Peter? The only person is Master Bentley, but he was so far away.

'Not here, sir, but Master Bentley in Upper Hambley, he owns the store there. He would stand my friend.'

'That's not going to do you much good here, girl. No, I have to take you into charge until we decide who is telling the truth.' He reached out as if to take hold of my arm, but I backed away, bumping into Peter, causing him in turn to stumble.

'But, sir, if I had taken the gloves they would be with me, surely? Could you not have a lady come to search me to prove my innocence?'

The Watchman hesitated, betwixt and between.

A small crowd had gathered outside. They peered in through the glass of the window, hands shading their eyes. Children were pushing through the adults for a better view.

The two ladies who fled must have broadcast their fright abroad, others coming to see the alleged thief firsthand.

All was silent waiting as the Watchman tried to come to a decision.

Peter, standing next to Master Chapman, spoke again. 'Sir, Susannah is innocent, I would swear to it. The matter will soon be cleared up, but until it is, it won't affect my indenture, will it?'

Worry was etched on his face, his hands tightly clutching his sticks, afraid if he let go, he would fall. He was well aware of the importance of his position, not just for himself, for us both.

Master Chapman hesitated, looking between Peter and I. Luckily for us both, it seemed the joiner's philosophy was, 'Treat others as you would want to be treated.'

For certain, Peter had done nothing wrong.

'No, lad, it won't affect that. Be here at seven o'clock as I said before.'

Peter nearly sank to his knees in relief. 'Thank you, sir, you won't regret it. Susannah will be proven innocent, you'll see.'

The Watchman at last came to a decision, though not the one I wanted to hear.

'You'll have to come with me, girl. I'll find a lady to search you as you ask, but it has to be at the gaol.'

I started to shake badly, holding out my hands, pleading. 'But, sir, I'm wrongly accused. She's made a mistake, make her prove they are missing as she says.'

'How am I going to do that? No, there's nothing for it, you have to come with me. Don't make a fuss now; it will just be the worse for you.'

He took me firmly by the arm, leading me to a door.

'Stand away, stand away,' he called as he pushed his way through the growing crowd, hauling me behind him.

People were hissing and booing. I kept my head down, humiliated beyond bearing. What would Ma say, that I've come to this?

An unseen person pushed me, almost making me stumble, causing the Watchman to grasp my arm tight enough to hurt, while all the time shouting, 'Keep back, no pushing now.'

Down the lane and into the High Street we went, the wind blowing my cape behind me. I begged for release. Those we passed stopped to stare, some shaking their fists at me, though I doubt they knew of what I'd been accused.

All the way, I tried to plead my innocence. 'I've done nothing wrong, sir; there's been a mistake. Please let me be.'

However, the Watch was deaf to my pleas. We came to a halt outside a round stone tower. A wooden door showed on to the street, a small window, unglazed but covered with iron bars set to the side. He unhooked a large set of keys from his belt, and choosing one, unlocked the door, and thrust me inside. Before I could regain my balance, the door slammed behind me, the key turned raspingly in the lock.

'Let me out, please. Let me out, sir. I've done nothing wrong.'

There was no reply, only the echo of my own voice as it hit the damp, grey stonewalls.

Chapter 15 ❧

It was humiliating to be taken into charge and treated like a common felon. While I knew myself to be innocent, it didn't necessarily mean that I would be found innocent. Peter and I were new to Honiton, a town where everybody knew everybody else, along with their business. I was afeared that for convenience sake I would be found guilty. One of the penalties for theft was transportation to the colonies. Or worse.

After I had been taken into charge, Peter slowly made his way back to the inn. I had paid for a cart to carry him to the joiner's with me walking alongside, but with no alternative, he was now forced to walk back. Repeatedly stopping to ask for directions, he was wet when he arrived, for it had started to mizzle again.

Master Beaker met him at the door, word of my arrest having spread quickly.

'What's this I hear, Peter, Susannah taken into charge?'

'Please, sir, may I sit down, for I'm very tired?'

'Forgive me, lad. Of course, come away in.' Master Beaker led him to the eating room. 'Settle yourself, I'll get you something to drink.' He went through to the kitchen, calling for Hanna.

Peter laid his sticks on the flagstone floor, putting his head in his hands.

'Now, lad, don't despair. I'm sure it's all done in error,' said the landlord, coming back to rest his hand on Peter's shoulder.

'Master Beaker, whatever are we to do? Susannah's been taken away and has to be searched for the lost gloves. She will be so humiliated, and there's nothing I can do to help her.'

'No there isn't, it just has to be borne.'

Hanna came in carrying a jug of small ale, worry written clear on her face. 'Drink this, Peter, it'll make you feel better,' she said, pouring him a full beaker, but Peter couldn't think of anything other than the awful events of the morning, which had started so well.

'But to be accused of stealing, what would Ma say?' he said, his voice breaking into a sob.

'Tell me, from the beginning, what occurred,' said Master Beaker. Both he and Hanna took a seat at the table, giving him their full attention. Peter relayed the story such as he knew it, for he couldn't speak for events inside the glove shop.

'All I know is, this woman came into Master Chapman's accusing Susannah, though it seemed to me it was more of a problem that my sister wasn't well dressed.'

'That sounds like Mistress Tomkins, who's no better than she ought to be,' said Hanna with a loud sniff. 'But surely, Peter, once Susannah is searched and they don't find the missing gloves, that's proof that she didn't steal. Then they will release her.'

Peter looked pitiful, slumped on the bench, his face streaked with tears.

'Peter, did you get the post as apprentice to Master Chapman?' asked the innkeeper, thinking to try to divert Peter from his worry.

'Yes, I did. When the Watch came to take Susannah away, I asked Master Chapman if it would affect my position. Thankfully, I still have the post. I start tomorrow at seven o'clock, but now what of the room here? I will be going to live with my new master, but what of Susannah?' His voice trailed off, tears gathering.

'Don't you worry about that now. I think it will all soon be cleared up. You'll see,' said Master Beaker, with more confidence than he felt, for he knew Mistress Tomkins would make a fearsome enemy.

'So you have to be there for seven o'clock, do you? I'll arrange for a cart to take you, I know someone who owes me a favour, just be ready by six-thirty.'

He turned to Hanna. 'Make sure this young lad eats a good breakfast, for no doubt he'll have a long day ahead of him.'

'Now Peter, I need to get on, as does Hanna. Try not to worry about Susannah. I will speak to the Watch later today, find out what I can.'

With that, poor Peter had no choice but to be content.

Part of Hanna's duties was to collect food from various shops for the inn, which gave her good opportunity to hear the gossip in town. This morning all the talk, wherever she went, was of the recent events and me.

Later, Hanna told me that Mistress Tomkins had become the object of a great deal of attention, ladies just 'happening' to be passing by who came in to see if the new fashions from London were available. With each telling the story became more vivid, ending up with her, Mistress Tomkins, being actually pushed by the child!

The two ladies who had been present during the altercation didn't re-appear, the only ones who would have been able to set the record straight. When the Watch returned, asking for their names, they were given, somewhat reluctantly. He went off in search of them.

I, meanwhile, languished in what served as the gaol. I was peered at through the small window by the inhabitants of Honiton, as if I were a wild animal. I sat huddled on the dirt floor, arms wrapped around my drawn-up knees. I kept my head down, trying not to be seen. However, I could do nothing about blocking out the names that were called through the window and door at me.

The only way I knew it was dinnertime, besides the church bells, was when the Watch appeared. He looked through the window first to make sure I was away from the door. Following him came a woman, a grubby lace cap over her hair. She carried a tray on which a large hunk of bread and an equally large piece of cheese, along with a bowl of something greasy-looking, sat.

'This is my Goodwife; she's here to search you. I'll be right outside; so don't think of trying to escape. I'll make sure no one comes near the window, so don't be frightened.' Without any more ado, he left, firmly shutting the door behind him.

'Don't be frightened, maid, this won't take long,' said the woman as she bent down to put the tray on the ground.

I started to weep, unbelieving this was happening.

'Crying isn't going to help, so stop your sniveling. You must take off your clothes, I need to see you naked.'

Slowly I undid the cape, placing Ma's brooch on top of it, so it wouldn't get lost in the earth. Next came the skirt, untying the leather belt first, laying it all beside the cape. I now stood only in my chemise, my hands crossed in front of me. 'No more, mistress. I beg of you.'

'No, girl, I am required to see you naked, so naked you shall be. Willingly or otherwise.' She crossed her arms, waiting.

In utter humiliation, I pulled the chemise over my head, letting it fall to the earth. Head lowered, I sobbed.

'Turn around.'

I did so.

'All right, you can get dressed.'

I turned to face her again as she made to open the door to leave.

'Please, mistress! Don't open the door while I'm naked, I beg of you!'

'Hurry up then, I can't wait around all day. I've things to get done.'

I dressed quickly, nodding to the woman when I was ready.

Her voice softened, 'I'm sorry I had to do that, lass, but it's required of me in the case of female prisoners. You understand that, don't you? Eat the food while it's hot. Hopefully, you won't be here for much longer.'

The woman called through the window that she was coming out.

The Watch opened the door. 'Everything all right in there?'

'Yes, she ain't got 'em.'

'She ain't?'

'No.'

'Well, where are they?' he queried, but all she could do was raise her shoulders in a question mark.

I called through the window. 'Please, sir. Can I be released now?'

'Not yet, I have to speak to Mistress Tomkins.'

'But sir, it's been proven I don't have them.'

'True, but you might have passed them on to someone else, like your brother, for instance.'

'Peter? But Master Chapman can swear I did no such thing,' I said in desperation.

'Well, I need to hear him say that for himself. Have patience, girl, it shouldn't be too much longer.'

I leant my face against the bars and watched him leave, presumably heading back to the joiner's.

Thankfully, the few people outside had heard the Watchman's Goodwife's remark that I didn't have the gloves. Their disgust at my being taken into charge was turning from outrage to pity, a poor maid wrongly accused.

One woman approached the barred window. 'Don't despair, child. The Watch is a fair man, if he said it won't be long, then it won't. Eat the food his Goodwife brought. He'll be back soon.' Her face retreated, and I could hear her talking with others, passing on what she'd heard, and what she'd said to me.

With nothing left but to follow the woman's advice, I sat on the floor, taking up the bowl which contained the pottage, saving the bread and cheese for later.

ᘓᕒᕒᘐ

Peter, meanwhile, sat alone on our bed hugging the bolster pillow to his chest, rocking back and forth.

Master Chapman was busy at his work, half-listening to his wife talking to the chickens as she fed them. Hearing the door open, he walked to the front of the store to see who had arrived.

'Watchman, what of Peter's sister?'

'She ain't got the gloves. When she came back to your store from Mistress Tomkin's, did she have a chance to pass the gloves to the boy?'

The joiner set down his rasp on a nearby table, taking his time before answering, the consequences too important for misspeaking. 'No, I think not. He met her at the door, I was right by him, and nothing was passed between them then. Besides, he needed both hands for the sticks. We then went on to discuss the terms of his indenture, but he was sitting due to his infirmity, she standing. No, I can truthfully say nothing was given, nor received. Were the gloves not on the girl?'

'No, and she was stripped naked by my Goodwife. It looks like Mistress Tomkins has made a mistake in falsely accusing the maid.'

They looked at each other; this was indeed a serious offence, for I could level a charge of attainder, presuming I was even aware of it, against the glover.

'Does it now?' said Master Chapman musingly, stroking his chin. 'So if the girl doesn't have them, nor the lad, you must now look to the two women who were given as witnesses. And alternatively, the glover herself.'

'Yes, my thoughts exactly.' The Watch heaved a sigh. 'However, that's my problem, not yours. Firstly, I have to release the girl. Her brother will no doubt be frantic with worry. They are staying at the Cross Keys?'

The joiner nodded.

'Well, I thank you for your help, Master Chapman.' Walking back to the tower where I was held, his mind was racing. Indeed, he must now look to the witnesses, both supposedly pillars of the town.

I heard the key turn in the lock.

'Come on out, mistress. Master Chapman has spoken for you, said you had no opportunity to pass the gloves to your brother. As they are not on you, you're free to go.'

I continued to sit on the earth, my head buried in my arms.

'Didn't you hear me? You're free to go.'

I looked up. 'Thank you, sir, for I knew I wasn't guilty. Though what of the town, will there be a taint on me? Or on Peter?'

The Watchman came closer, his face questioning.

'Why would there be? No, the townsfolk are fair, in spite of the ones that pushed and shoved earlier. You'll find no trouble from folk here. If you do, let me know. I'll set them straight!'

I stood up, smoothing down my skirt and cape.

'Then thank you, sir, at least if only for that.' I picked up the bread and cheese, and walked past him into the cold damp air, which had never felt so good.

First walking, then breaking into a run, I went down the High Street on my way back to Peter. Running through the door of the inn, I called for Master Beaker and Hanna.

Hanna came through to the hallway, wiping her hands on her apron. 'Susannah! Oh, thank the Lord you're safe home! Peter is in your room; you'd best go straight there, for he's worried sick. The master is out, he had some errands to do, then was heading to speak to the Watch.' She stood clutching my hands, squeezing so hard it hurt.

'There's no need now, I've been proven innocent, Hanna! I'll go and speak to Peter, but I'll come back to find you later.'

Down the hallway, round corners I went, bursting at last through the bedroom door. 'Peter!'

'Susannah, is it really you?' he said, unbelieving.

I sat beside him on the bed. 'Yes, it is. I've been proven innocent, Peter. I was so worried I would be there all night, the last night we would be able to spend together for seven years! But the Watch let me go, and here I am!'

We hugged each other, both of us scared to let go.

'I was so frightened, Susannah,' Peter said, wiping his eyes with the cover of the bed.

'You must have been, as was I. But all is well now. Hush, Peter, let's just stay here together for a while.'

We lay back on the bed, clasping each other. Although it was early afternoon, we both slept, totally exhausted.

Chapter 16 &

Master Beaker, true to his word, had a donkey and small cart outside waiting for Peter just after six-thirty the next morning. Devoid of possessions, except for the clothes he stood in and his tools, it hadn't taken him long to get ready. Hanna had also been up early preparing a large breakfast for us, for which we were grateful. Master Beaker appeared somewhat sleepily just before it was time for Peter to leave.

'Are you coming with me, Susannah?' Peter asked nervously, pushing his empty plate away.

'Of course I will, I wouldn't miss it for anything. Ma would be so proud of you, Peter, she would never have dreamt that you would become apprenticed to learn a trade. Just remember to mind your manners with Master and Mistress Chapman.'

'I'll come and wait for you outside the shop next Sunday at dinnertime, and I'll expect to hear every single thing that has happened.'

I hugged his arm, trying to give him confidence.

'We'd best be off, you can't afford to be late on your first day!' I told him, but just at that moment Hanna came through from the kitchen to give him a big hug and kiss, which made Peter blush with embarrassment, while Master Beaker shook his hand, wishing him well.

'The seven years will pass before you know it, lad, then you'll be a joiner in your own right! Think on that if things get tough.'

'Thank you, Master Beaker. Thank you also for the cart.'

Peter followed me down the hallway, where once at the door we emerged into bright sunshine.

'See, Peter, that's a sign of good will! The sunshine means all will be well,' I said, trying to chase away his nervousness.

Master Beaker helped Peter up into the cart, loading his sticks in after him, while I clambered into the back.

'Giddy up, giddy up,' said the carter, urging the horse into a walk. With a final wave to Master Beaker and Hanna, we were off.

Master Chapman stood waiting for Peter at the shop door. As he helped Peter down, he looked at me.

'I was glad to hear you were released, mistress, but it leaves the Watch the job of trying to find out who did steal those gloves. Mistress Tomkins isn't happy; she thought she'd found the culprit! Anyway, that's all in the past. Come along in, Peter, have you eaten?' Peter confirmed he had. 'That's good, it means we can get straight on with the work.'

He turned and addressed me. 'Peter will be outside next Sunday at dinnertime, Susannah, so say goodbye to each other.'

We hugged again. 'You'll do fine, Peter, as will I, so try not to fret about me.' Releasing him, I stepped back to watch him go inside.

I turned, but was surprised to see the carter still there.

'Master Beaker instructed me to bring you back to the inn, mistress.'

'That's kindly of him, of you too, but I think I'll walk. The air smells so fresh this morning. Thank you, sir, for bringing Peter. As you could see, it would have been a long, tiresome walk for him. I'll be sure to tell Master Beaker of your kindness.'

I turned down the lane towards the High Street. To reach it I had to pass the glove shop. Holding my head high, I walked past. It was too early for Mistress Tomkins to be there, shops do not normally open until eight o'clock, so I wasn't afraid I would be accosted. Besides, what could she say? I had been proven innocent. Though when I thought about it some more, there was one thing she could have said. She could have given me her apologies, but I felt Mistress Tomkins wasn't the kind to easily admit a mistake.

Once in the High Street, I turned right to walk up the hill towards St. Michael's church. The five bells in the tower could be heard for miles, and I was interested in actually seeing them, if only from below. I had rarely been inside a real church. Pa hadn't believed in God, yet another reason why William hadn't been able to be buried in the churchyard.

All this made me think of Ma. Looking back, we had buried her in such a hurry; I had never given a thought to her lying in the churchyard. Pa hadn't mentioned it, had just dug the grave like I told him. She had been baptized, same as Peter and me, so why hadn't Pa gone to speak to the Rector?

He had said he didn't have the money to pay, but I doubted now if the Rector would have refused. How could I, a mere child, have known what to do? I was suddenly overwhelmed with grief, hurrying now to the church. I hoped the Rector would be there, and if he was, I would ask him if Ma would go to heaven even though she was buried beneath the oak.

St. Michael's, built over three hundred years ago, was beautiful from the outside, and easily seen as I walked up the hill. As I was about to pass through the lych-gate, I heard someone calling my name.

'Susannah Brigginshaw?' I turned, to find a lady just coming up the path behind me, the same one who had spoken to me through the window while I was in the gaol.

'Yes, I'm Susannah,' I replied with a smile, giving a small curtsy, remembering her kindness.

'I thought it was you when I saw you passing. I was glad to see the Watch had the wit to let you go, though it must have been an awful experience for you, and for your brother. I hear he's apprenticed to Master Chapman now?' She didn't wait for my answer. 'Do you have any thought as to what you'll do?'

'No. I make the lace like everyone else, but apart from that, I've no other thought.'

'Well, something will come up. Where are you lodging?'

'The Cross Keys.'

She nodded. 'You'll be safe enough there. Master Beaker is an honest landlord. Though I fear you'll find it difficult just relying on the lace for your living. If I hear of anything that I think will help, I shall come and advise you.' She gently touched my arm with her fingertips. 'Everything will work out, Susannah.

I find it usually does.' With a smile, she turned back the way she'd come.

I had now lost all interest in seeing the church. The woman telling me that I couldn't live on the lace alone had unsettled me, though I couldn't say if she was aware Lady FitzGerald was paying over the buyer's price. There was the room at the inn to be paid for. Peter had yet to go to the bootmaker to see about boots. No doubt they would cost a lot of money, indeed, and would probably have to be made especially for him.

Walking back down the hill, I passed Allhallows school. I could easily hear through the windows the boys inside reciting their lesson, and I stopped to listen. I felt envy of the children's parents, rich enough to allow them to attend school. Perhaps if I had been born a boy in Honiton, I, too, could have been inside learning a lesson. But I hadn't been, so no point in spending time in regrets.

I could understand figures, for hadn't I sat with Ma enough times, then with Master Bentley when he was explaining how much Peter would be paid for the wood. The wood! Of course! He had some of Peter's work in his store. Though it had only been a few days, surely it would have all sold by now. That would give us some much-needed money, hopefully enough to pay for the boots. I had most of the money from Lady FitzGerald, but I wanted to keep that safe, for who knew what other expenses would come our way. I have to return to Upper Hambley to collect any money owed us by Master Bentley. I would also have to speak to Master Beaker about getting a cheaper room.

As I walked down the High Street looking in shop windows, reluctant now to step inside in case I was wrongly accused again, I was well aware that people were looking at me. I presumed all had heard of my trouble yesterday, but I ignored them. I was warm, thanks be to Ma and her woolen dress; Peter had work; and I had somewhere, for now, to sleep with plenty of food provided. As far as I was concerned, I had everything I needed.

Once back at the inn, I stopped by Master Beaker's chancel room, the door standing wide open as usual. He sat at his desk, facing the door, a large ledger before him. I knocked gently. He looked up to greet me, a smile spreading across his kindly face.

'Ah, Susannah, you're back. Peter get settled all right?'

'Yes. Thank you, sir. Thank you also for the horse and cart, the man was very kind.' I fumbled for the next words. 'But I fear I can no longer afford the two shillings a week board. I will have to find cheaper lodgings.'

'That two shillings was for you and your brother, Susannah. With him no longer here, the cost is reduced. I was going to speak to you about that on your return. Can you manage one shilling?'

'I believe I can, sir.' I liked both him and Hanna, and had no wish to leave.

'Then a shilling a week from now on it is, all found.'

I laughed, reaching up to hug him. 'Thank you, sir, I shan't be a bother.'

Obviously embarrassed, he ushered me away, saying, 'You must be hungry. Find Hanna and tell her to give you something to eat. She'll be wondering where you are.'

With a lightened step, I went in search of Hanna. And food.

સ્ત્રઃસ્ત

A few days later, after washing in the barrel outside the kitchen, I noticed my dress was a little tight across the chest, and it definitely wasn't as long. Perhaps the boots make it appear shorter? It was a Sunday, which meant I could meet Peter at noon. I hoped we could go for a walk down by the river, the weather looked as if it would stay dry, even though it was a little chilly. However, without boots, Peter would find it difficult. The bootmaker wouldn't be open on Sunday; I would have to find out when he could see Peter's feet.

I waited anxiously outside the joiner's. At the stroke of twelve, the door opened and Peter came out with a welcoming smile on his face.

'Hello, Susannah, I knew you'd be here.' He looked up at the sky. 'Can we just walk for a little way, for I've missed the fresh air.'

We turned away from the High Street by silent consent, preferring to be alone.

'I have to speak to the bootmaker about boots for you.'

'There's no need, Master Chapman has already done so; indeed, he came to see me yesterday. He twisted my feet this way and that, had me walk for him, and said he could help! He's making a pair as a trial to see how I get on. Is that not good news?'

'Indeed it is! Did he also mention the cost?' Secretly I was worried, but tried not to let Peter become aware of it.

'No, but he said it would be reasonable. He also said we can pay it off a little at a time, if the full amount is beyond our means.'

'That's very generous of him, Peter. Did he say when they would be ready?'

'By next week, as they have to be made especially for me. I hope that next time I see you I will have boots!' The anticipation showed clearly on Peter's face.

'That is wonderful news, but tell me, how did your first week go? Tell me everything; leave nothing out, for I've done nothing but worry how you were getting on.'

We came upon a makeshift bench down a narrow side lane. We took a seat, bathed in the sun, huddled in our capes against the chill of the wind.

'It went well. Master Chapman seems fair. The work so far is not too taxing. Mistress Chapman keeps a very good table; we had roast chicken the other night. While it was cooking, my mouth was watering so much. I've my own room with a very comfortable bed, warm coverings, and a real pillow filled with feathers, not straw! The room is up a few stairs, which makes it a little difficult for me, but I'm getting better. Master Chapman said that before anything else, I have to make some proper sticks, not these old things.' He held up the ones he had made from Ma and Pa's bed. 'But they have served me well, so I'll not complain of them. Enough of me, what of you, Susannah? Are you still lodging with Master Beaker and Hanna?'

'Yes, Master Beaker changed the payment to one shilling, including all the food I can eat. Which reminds me, I think I'm growing, too! Look, I put my dress on today, I'm sure I'm getting taller!' I stood so he could see the difference.

'Indeed you are, the hem is well clear of the ground,' he said, which confirmed my own thought.

We sat for what was left of the day talking of Ma and Pa, wondering where he was, what he was doing. I had never mentioned to Peter about the woman's comment, 'Pa and his whore.' If it was true, why upset Peter? If it wasn't, well, he didn't need to know of it. I changed the subject.

'I want to find out if there's a stonemason in the town, Peter. I can't bear the thought of Ma or William's grave not being marked. When I get some money, I want him to make the markers for them.'

'I agree, Susannah, perhaps we can use some of my wages, depending on the cost of the stones.'

'No, for you'll have worked hard for it, I've no doubt. That money is yours to do with as you will. I'll think of something, though I'm afraid it won't be soon.'

We walked around for a while, eventually heading back towards the joiner's as St. Michael's bells tolled five o'clock.

'You'd best go inside; it will be time for you to eat soon. I'll be here again next Sunday.'

We hugged, parting slowly.

'Goodbye, Susannah,' he called, but I didn't turn around, it would have made the parting all the more painful. I was pleased enough to know that Peter appeared happy and that his master was taking good care of him. It was one less thing for me to worry on.

In the short time I had been at the Cross Keys, Hanna had become a good friend, sitting with me when I was in the eating room whenever her work allowed. Three years older than me at fourteen, she deemed herself to be wise beyond her years. Her sleeping quarters were in one of the outbuildings at the rear of the inn's stable yard, and she shared it with the cook and the other female kitchen workers. An orphan like Peter and me, she knew the feelings of sorrow that sometimes overwhelmed me, and did her best to cheer me at those times. She would often challenge me to a game of draughts, having to first teach me the rules, but I proved to be a fast learner, beating her more often than not.

With Christmas almost upon us, I knew my birthday was near, the last one celebrated with my family in Offwell. When I spoke to Hanna about it, she was determined to celebrate the day, but I was unsure of my actual birth date, always leaving that knowledge to Ma.

Hanna, never one to be defeated, 'bequeathed' me the day of December 20th, stating that from now on, that was my birthday.

༄༅༄

The morning of the 20th, the day I turned twelve years old, I went through to the eating room to find Hanna waiting for me, wearing a clean apron and cap in honour of the day. Master Beaker sat next to her wearing his Sunday best, and they gave me a resounding, 'Good Birthday Wish,' presenting me with a small gift wrapped in muslin.

'Master Beaker, Hanna, this is too much kindness.'

'Open it up, girl,' said the landlord gruffly, 'for how can you say that until you've seen what it is?'

Slowly I untied the parcel, to reveal a fine bone hair comb.

'It's beautiful, thank you both.' I kept my head down, hiding the tears. One of the young kitchen girls brought in large platters of food and jugs of ale, placing it all before us.

'The master said on this special day, I might eat with you!' Hanna plunked herself down next to me, giving me an embrace.

Overcome, I looked at both of them. How blessed I am to have these two people caring for me. I must remember them in my prayers, and remember to tell Ma she can stop worrying about me, for I'm going to be well.

I helped myself from the platter as Master Beaker, along with Hanna, raising their goblets in a toast.

After breakfast, I returned to my room to collect my cape, leaving the inn to walk up to the church. I found I was the only one inside, with no sign of the Rector. I knelt in the aisle, giving thanks for the day.

On my return to the inn Hanna met me at the front door. She tugged at my arm to bring me inside all the faster. 'Susannah, there's a man here for you; he's in the eating room. Hurry, he's been waiting awhile.'

I walked down the hallway, taking off my cape as I went. Whoever would come to see me? I stopped in the doorway, hardly believing my own eyes. The very last man I wanted to see on this, my given birthday.

'Susannah, you've kept me waiting awhile. Where's Peter?' He sat at one of the tables, a large tankard of ale in front of him, the long-remembered 'trouble brewing' look writ plain on his face.

'What's the matter, Susannah, you don't look pleased to see your old Pa.'

Chapter 17 &

'Pa! What are you doing here?' I stood in the doorway, hardly believing my eyes. I felt a rush of emotion that I couldn't put a name to. Hanna stood behind me, so close I could feel her breath on my neck.

'You'd best come to my room, Pa. We can talk there.'

I didn't want Hanna to think I was being rude, so I turned to her. 'Hanna, as you will have guessed, this is my pa. We have some talking to do, it's best if we do it alone.'

'Of course it is, Susannah. I'll make sure no one disturbs you. Can I bring something to eat? Or drink?' She looked pointedly at Pa, at the large, half empty tankard before him.

'No, thank you, Hanna.'

I turned once more to him. 'This way,' I said, more of a command than anything else. I walked out of the room and down the passageway. I heard the chair scrape on the floor as he pushed back from the table while I hurried to get my thoughts and feelings under control. I laid my cape on the bed, turning to face the door as I heard him enter.

Pa filled the doorway, his hands fussing with his hat, which he had removed, now held in front of him.

'What do you want, Pa?'

'Now is that any way to talk to your father, Susannah? Do you really want everyone to hear our private talk? Aren't you going to ask me in?'

He looked at me, his eyes narrowing. He could see already I didn't intend to fall all over him in gratitude at his return.

'You are in, Pa. I ask again, what do you want?'

'Can I sit down, Susannah? I'm very tired.' He looked at the chair in the corner of the room, my lace pillow beside it.

I nodded, but continued to stand as I waited for him to speak again.

'What do I want? Why, I came to see how you and Peter were getting on, lass. Can't a father do that?'

'A father can, but you have never been much of a father to either me or Peter. You abandoned us when Ma died.'

He made as if to rise in anger at my words, then thought the better of it, once more sitting down.

'I did my best, Susannah; no man can do more than that, surely. Besides, I was so distraught that I didn't know what I was doing. Haven't I come back now?'

'You may have done your best, but you didn't take care of your wife or children. A true father wouldn't have left Peter and me alone in the middle of winter. You never gave a thought as to how we would manage with Ma gone, did you? Surely you don't expect me to be pleased to see you? And you haven't told me what you really want.'

'Well now, Susannah, as you seem to be sour tempered, I see I've to be truthful to you. I've nowhere else to go. I went to the cottage, but it's fallen. Did you know?'

I didn't answer. Why else would me and Peter be here, if the cottage were standing?

'I see you do. Well, I had planned to come back to take care of you both, but when I saw the cottage, I didn't know where you had gone. I went to Upper Hambley where Master Bentley told me you'd both come to Honiton. It didn't take too long to find out where you were lodging. So where's Peter?'

I stood, deciding what to do. I didn't want to answer, for I knew Pa all too well. He would make a nuisance of himself, and we couldn't afford for Peter to lose his position. I could see no way around it; I have to admit I was flustered.

'He's apprenticed to the joiner for the next seven years.'

His eyes narrowed again while he thought this over. 'Is he now? How could you afford the fee? Apprenticeships don't come cheap, and Ma never had any money.'

I hadn't anticipated this, just stood silently looking at him.

'Not telling, eh? Well, it will be easy enough to find out.' He paused; I could almost see his mind turning as he looked around the room.

'Lodging here can't be cheap either, Susannah. How are you able to afford it?' He looked at the lace pillow. 'You and your ma never made enough money selling the lace to keep us before, I doubt if much has changed there. Selling anything else are you, Susannah?'

'What could I possibly sell, Pa? I don't know how to make anything else.' Suddenly the meaning of Pa's question hit me, leaving me too stunned to speak. There was a horrible, strained silence as I stared at him in disbelief.

He leaned forward, his arms resting on his knees. 'Come, girl, how many have there been?'

Suddenly the pent-up pain and anger raged. I screamed at Pa. 'Get out! Get out and never return! I'll call the landlord unless you go.'

He held up his hands, rising from the chair. 'I'm going.' He looked at the comfortable bed, a ceiling without leaks. His voice changed swiftly from its whining tone, becoming harsh and threatening.

'I'm still your father, Susannah. In my time of need, it's up to you to care for me as I cared all those years for you. My need is now. I'll ask the landlord if he has a spare room for me. I could do with a bit of coddling. Just like you seem to be getting, one way or another.' He gave a lewd wink. 'As I've no money, I'll tell him that you'll pay, I'm sure he'll understand.'

'Pa, go.'

'Now don't be upset, Susannah, think how nice it will be for us to be a family again, just the two of us, except this time you caring for me.' He opened the door, turning to look back.

I thought I saw a swish of a skirt behind him, and running footsteps. I continued to stand silently.

'I expect I'll be seeing a lot of you from now on, Susannah. Think what good times we can have.'

As he closed the door quietly behind him, I slumped back on the bed. I couldn't understand why Pa had appeared now, just when things were getting better for Peter and me. I wondered if I should hurry to the joiner's to warn Peter. Though what would we do if Master Chapman said he didn't want to get involved in family business and dismissed Peter? Could he do that? Hadn't Peter put his mark on the legal paper? Should I speak to Master Beaker? But surely, Pa would already be looking for him. The landlord could also feel the same as the joiner, not wanting to get in the middle of a family dispute. What a terrible mess we were in.

I lay on the bed trying to think, but my head was in a whirl, each thought not coming to a conclusion, just spinning round and round. I didn't even hear the knock on the bedroom door.

'Susannah? Are you well?' Hanna asked worriedly, peering round the door.

I looked at her through my tears. 'Hanna, Pa is going to ask Master Beaker for a room here. Worse, he expects me to pay for his lodging. Whatever am I to do?' I wailed.

She came and sat beside me, taking my hands in hers. 'Hush now, Susannah. I've already spoken to the master, he knows of the situation. He will tell your pa there are no rooms available, so don't fret.'

'So it was you I saw outside the door as he left?'

'Yes, I'm sorry I was listening, but I was worried about you, especially after what you told me of him. I'm glad I did, for it gave me a chance to speak to the master to warn him. I hope you'll forgive me?'

'Of course I forgive you; I only hope Pa doesn't cause a fuss and just leaves. It was such a good day before he came, Hanna. Peter is well and happy at the joiner's. I truly felt our lives were getting better. Why did he have to come and ruin everything?' I started to cry once more.

Hanna spoke in a firm voice. 'Enough of the tears, Susannah, they never solved a thing; all they do is make your face swollen and blotchy, so dry your eyes. I'll go and see what's happening with the master and your pa. Only when I've news will I return. Cheer up, Susannah, the day's not totally lost!' Rising from the bed, she moved to the doorway, her hand on the knob. 'All will be well,' she said, quietly closing the door behind her.

Will it, will all be well? Now that Pa knows where I am and where Peter is, will he stay in Honiton to make trouble for us both?

I remembered the day Ma died, when I had returned to the cottage to hear Pa berating her upstairs. I hated him at that time, and found myself hating him again now. Everything I had said to him was true. He had never been a real father to us, or a loving husband to Ma.

I would never forget his awful words of a few moments ago, accusing me of the unthinkable, for I was a good girl. I hugged myself as I tried to keep from shaking. Moreover, what else was it he said? 'You and your ma never made enough selling the lace to keep us before.' What had he ever made to keep us? Nothing. Our living, it had all been up to Ma and me.

I remembered Peter saying, when he had been alone in the cottage, he had cursed Pa aloud for abandoning us. I found myself now sobbing uncontrollably into the pillow, saying the same words as Peter. 'I curse you, Pa, I curse you.'

Chapter 18 ❧

I was afraid to go outside my room in case I bumped into Master Beaker. What would I do if Pa had caused a fuss, demanded a room? I knew I couldn't stay in my room forever, besides which I was hungry. Hanna had said she would return when she had news, but who knew how long that would take? Plucking up courage, I opened the door to find Master Beaker passing. He stopped to speak with me.

'Susannah, your father spoke to me about taking a room. Luckily Hanna warned me ahead of time, so I was able to answer that I had no empty rooms for hire.' A quizzical look came into his eyes. 'One day you must tell the reason for my having to lie for you, but for the moment, don't think of it. He won't be staying here, and there's no other inn in Honiton for him to ask. Don't fret about it, Susannah. We all have kin we prefer to keep hidden. You are no different.'

He took my arm, leading me down the hallway. 'Tell me, how is Peter? Did he enjoy his first week? Has he learned anything?'

I was grateful for the diversion of his chatter and answered readily enough. 'He is doing well, thank you. He seems happy. He enjoys the work. Master and Mistress Chapman are kind. He has plenty to eat and a comfortable bed with a real pillow.'

'Well then, what more could he want for?' stated Master Beaker, as we stood outside the eating room. 'You look hungry, girl. Get Hanna to feed you something.' With that, he walked off in the direction of his chancel room while I did as bidden, waiting for Hanna to appear from the kitchen. It seemed to me that Master Beaker's answer to life's troubles was to eat.

The first Sunday that I saw Peter after I had met with Pa, I told him what had occurred. While I talked, we walked along, though he didn't look at me, intent on watching his step.

'Did I do right?' I asked, worried he would be disappointed in me.

'Susannah, if what you told me is right, then yes, you did. It must have been hard for you to turn him away, but I don't believe either of us owes him anything, certainly not a lodging. Once he'd got his feet under the table, there would be no shifting him.'

We were heading for our usual piece of open ground on a small hillock overlooking the river. Peter sat gratefully, tucking his sticks alongside him. I remained standing, my stomach churning as I remembered Pa's words.

'Let's hope that's the last you see of him. What he said to you,' he couldn't bring himself to say the words, 'that was unforgivable, Susannah. He should know you'd never do any such thing. No, the more I think on it, the more I believe he will take off again. Try not to worry, we've both done enough of that, now is the time to think of happier things. Tell me, what's happening at the inn? How are Master Beaker and Hanna?'

I too wanted to think of other things, so took up the change of topic willingly. 'They are well and send their good wishes. I have plenty of time to make the lace; I have to take some to Lady FitzGerald next week. I'll also go from there to Upper Hambley, for we left some of your work at the store with Master Bentley. I must see if it has sold, and collect our money if it has.'

'I was thinking of that the other day. It's a long walk alone, Susannah; I wish I could go with you, but it's too far for me.'

'I know, Peter. I don't mind going alone, with the spring here the days are longer, the air warmer, it will be a pleasant walk.'

We spent the rest of our time together reminiscing about Ma, though I found now that some of the bad memories of Pa, of the beatings, were fading, replaced by happier thoughts.

I remembered the time when Ma fell into the stream because she overstretched to retrieve a dress she had been washing. Thankfully, it was summertime and we hadn't had a lot of rain, so the water was low.

I stood watching helplessly as she sat on the streambed, her skirt billowing out around her. How we laughed until our sides ached. Such a happy, carefree day.

'Well, it saves me washing this dress, too, Susannah.' She lay down in the water again, letting the small ripples wash over her. I reminded Peter of it now, the happiness of that time making us both smile. How I missed her.

When I left Peter at the store that evening, I made my way, reluctantly, back to the inn. I couldn't get Pa out of my mind, terrified he would be waiting for me, again demanding lodging. I kept telling myself that Master Beaker was right, that Pa would have left the town. That I had nothing to worry about. However, no matter how hard I tried, the fear wouldn't leave me.

It turned out that I worried for nothing. There was no sign of Pa, only Hanna sitting at one of the tables in the eating room, mending her hose.

'Hello, Susannah, how is Peter?'

'He is well, thank you.'

I sat next to her, tired from the afternoon. I watched the bone needle weaving through the woolen hose, then looked at Hanna's pleasant, innocent face as she concentrated on her task. I came to an immediate decision.

'Hanna, may I speak with you?' She stopped what she was doing, resting her hands on the table as she looked at me.

'Of course, Susannah. Would you prefer to go to your room?'

I jumped at the suggestion. 'Would you mind? I don't want to interrupt your work, but I do need to speak with someone.'

'Of course I don't mind. I'll bring this with me, it might be easier for you to talk if I'm sewing.'

She swiftly gathered up her various bits and pieces then followed me to my room. I closed the door behind us, climbing onto the bed.

Hanna followed, leaning back against the board. She set up her sewing again, patiently waiting for me to speak.

'Thank you for understanding about Pa.'

She stopped sewing, raising her head to look at me with gentle eyes. 'Nothing to understand; we all have family, I dare say your pa is no worse than mine.' She picked up her work again.

'I've never heard you speak of your family, do they live close by?'

'They used to. My mother died about three years ago, the fever took her. My father had always been a bit of a fly-by-night.'

The irony of this struck me. I paused, uncertain if I could ask the next question.

'Hanna, did your father ever beat you?'

'All the time, but I'm sure he didn't mean it, or at least, that's what my mother used to say.' She snorted, an opinion all of its own. She settled back, moving the bolster to a more comfortable position.

'We used to live in a small village by the sea; father was a fisherman, as was his brother. Between them, they owned a small boat. There was nothing else for them to do, but the fishing. They would put out to sea, no matter what the weather. One day there was a mighty wind, they were foolish, should never have left the harbour, but without fish to sell, there was no money. So, they went.'

Her hands stopped their work as she gazed off into the distance, re-living that day again. 'Mother and I, my aunt too, we all waited by the sea wall for the boat to come back. It was a rowboat, long past its best. It was called the *Katherine*.' She sighed. 'Funny the things you remember.'

'They should never have gone, but like I said, with no fish there was no money. Mother waited all night, as did my aunt, while I was sent home to sleep. As if I could sleep!'

'When the morning came there was no sign, but still they waited. Three days it took until the news reached us. Two men washed up farther down the coast, no sign of the boat. My aunt went to see the bodies, mother was too distraught. When she came back and told us it was Father and his brother, it was as if the world ended with that. The living he scratched from the sea was all that stood between starvation and us.'

'Ma did what she could afterwards, making ale and selling it, taking in washing. When she died of the fever, my aunt kindly offered me a home with her. Then, when the crops failed, we came here, hoping it would be easier living. My aunt died soon after, I believe from a broken heart. My aunt and uncle never had children of their own. That's when Master Beaker took me in.'

I sat in silence, for what could I say? I thought my life had been hard, but on hearing Hanna's story, well, it made me realise that we, Peter and me, hadn't been the only ones to suffer such a hardship and tragedy.

There had to be so many children left alone, scratching a living any which way they could. Hanna had been fortunate to have an aunt willing to take her in. Peter had been fortunate enough to be accepted as an apprentice to a joiner, thanks be to the parish. I had been lucky to be able to make the lace, and Lady FitzGerald to buy it from me.

Hanna interrupted my thoughts. 'What of you, Susannah? What of your family? I know of Peter, a little about your pa, but what of your ma?'

So I told her, holding nothing back. From as early as I could remember. It felt good to speak of it, as if I was laying the demons to rest. I told her about the beatings; the relentless, grinding poverty of our lives; baby William; and the cottage at Offwell, for all its humble state, it was home to us all. The terrible cold. The constant, constant hunger.

As I spoke, I also thought of Master Bentley and his many kindnesses. I thought of the innkeeper in Lower Hambley who had fed me when I was in search of Pa. Joseph the carter who brought goods to the cottage. Master Beaker and, indeed, Hanna herself.

I had lit the candle on the bed table long before. Hanna and me, in the flickering light, talked of our hopes and dreams for the future. As she was given Sunday evenings off work, time was not important, so it wasn't until late that she made her way back to her own bed. As I lay alone in the darkness, I added Hanna to my nightly prayers. I knew without a doubt that we had a lasting friendship.

The next day dawned bright, but more importantly, dry. I made the decision to walk to Upper Hambley to see if there was any money for us at Master Bentley's store. After eating, I returned to my room to pick up my cape, along with the finished lace wrapped in a cloth for Lady FitzGerald.

The church bells were just ringing eight o'clock, and the day was too good to waste. The sooner I was there, the sooner I would return. I thought of taking the short cut over the stream, then remembered I was carrying lace for Lady FitzGerald. I took the longer path, staying well away from water.

It felt so good to be away from the town and all its noise, the only assault to my ears the cawing of the rooks high up in the trees. The grass was growing well; with all the rain, it was already a vibrant shade of green, while most of the leaves were well out in bud.

As I walked, I looked down at my boots, now clearly visible beneath my skirt. The sleeves were shorter too, the bodice uncomfortably tight. I would need to look for a workaday dress, as Ma's was still too big for me.

I was so engrossed in thought I hadn't realised I was nearing the old cottage; the miles had flown by.

I turned the last corner to see one of the walls still showing. I found my steps slowing, almost as if something were holding me back, perhaps the fear that Pa would be there, ready to spring out at me. I stopped and talked aloud to myself.

'Don't be silly, Susannah; there's nothing here to harm you. Pa's not here. It's just a cottage, nothing to be feared of.' I forced one foot forward, then the other, drawing closer to the ruin.

The weeds and bushes had grown considerably, the short path down from the lane to the door now totally overgrown with new grass. The door hung drunkenly open, creaking in the breeze. How quickly nature covers up ugliness, softens hard corners. There were narrow paths leading this way and that; obviously, the rabbits were still around. Moreover, with rabbits usually came foxes.

I stepped onto the path and walked round the remaining wall to the back of the cottage, heading for the oak tree. The privy walls were still standing, though the roof had collapsed. I could barely make out the wooden crosses Peter had made for Ma and

William, grateful they, at least, were standing. There was a blackbird in the tree above, singing his joyous song.

During the walk, I had been wondering how I would feel, if I would weep. Finding myself at the graves, I felt only peace. A peace I had thought wouldn't be possible again, or if possible, not for a long time. I realised I was no longer afraid, I felt safe here. Loved. I walked on to Upper Hambley enjoying the day, taking in the beautiful countryside. The air smelled fresh, and even the cow dung made me smile.

The door of Master Bentley's store stood open, and I could hear voices inside. I was pleased beyond measure to be back. When I entered, the shop seemed very dark after the bright sunshine without, so it took me a moment to get my sight back.

'Susannah Brigginshaw! Well I never, what a sight for sore eyes, and right glad I am to see you,' said a familiar voice.

'Good day, Master Bentley. It's good to see you, too.'

He came from behind the table. I saw it had been replaced by a much longer and wider plank, which sat on a strong-looking base made of wood.

'I'm glad you are here, Susannah, for I've coin for you and Peter. All the pieces he made sold very quickly. I was going to bring the proceeds to you in Honiton, but my Goodwife has been unwell and not able to look after the store in my absence. I did have a lad from the village helping me; well, you saw him, he was useless. I wondered when you would return.'

As he spoke, he clasped my hands in his. 'But where are my manners, come into my room here,' he guided me to the back of the shop. 'You've walked all the way from Honiton?' He didn't wait for an answer, quickly adding, 'you must be hungry as well as thirsty. Come, let me get you something. I need to know how you are both faring, for I think of you often with great fondness.'

I followed, listening to his chatter, all the time bursting to know how much money he had for us. 'I'm sorry to hear of your Goodwife, Master Bentley, is she still ailing?'

'No, lass, she's a little better, though still weak. She keeps to her bed most days.' He paused, looking at me as if he wanted to say more. He obviously decided to speak out. 'The day you came here, when your cottage collapsed?'

He waited for me to acknowledge it.

'When I returned home after taking you and Peter to Honiton, my Goodwife wanted me to take you both in, but I knew it wouldn't be right for you. I hope you understand?'

'Of course I do, it was a hard decision for me to make to go there, but I knew it was the only one I could make.'

We looked at each other for a moment, no more words necessary between us.

'Tell me your news, are you still at the inn? What news do you have of Peter?' he asked, clearing his throat.

'I'm still there. Peter is doing well; he's apprenticed, thankfully, to the joiner. The parish paid the fee from a special fund. Master Beaker has reduced the room tariff to one shilling with Peter gone. I met with Peter yesterday, he's very happy. We both have boots, too!' I held out my feet for inspection, and he nodded in acknowledgement. I also told him how I felt sure I was growing with all the food I was eating, that I would soon have to look for a new dress.

While I was talking, he had been collecting food and drink, eventually putting a dish before me containing cheese, freshly baked bread and a tankard of small beer. However, before I could eat, I had to ask the one question that never left my mind.

'Sir, have you seen our pa?' Master Beaker looked away, taking his time before answering.

'Yes, Susannah. He came here asking after you. I couldn't tell a lie, I told him you and Peter had gone to Honiton. I'm sorry, lass.' His face took on an anxious look.

'No, don't be sorry. I wouldn't want, nor expect, you to lie. He did come to the inn, demanded lodging, but Master Beaker turned him away.'

We both sat quietly. I looked down at the dish of food for which, suddenly, I had no appetite. Master Bentley thankfully broke the silence. 'But the coin you are due, let me fetch it before I forget.' He disappeared into the shop leaving me alone for a moment, for which I was thankful.

'Now let's see, everything sold, quickly too, or did I already tell you that? I suppose now that Peter's apprenticed there will be no more?'

'I don't believe so, no. His days are long and it's important he does well.'

'Aye, that's what I thought. Well, I bought the ledger with me, the one you and I worked on that first day, you remember it?'

'Yes, I remember.'

'I'll let you check the entries for yourself, but I owe you two shillings.' He laid the two coins on the table. I looked at them, so small, but so very important to Peter and me.

'Thank you, Master Bentley. I'll not check the entries. If you say it's two shillings, then that's good enough for me.' I picked up the coins, tying them into the hem of my dress. We sat together while I ate. Master Bentley told me all the gossip in the village, though it didn't mean much to me, for I didn't know the people.

I was in Upper Hambley for about an hour, leaving with mixed feelings along with the promise to soon return. Back past the cottage I walked, though this time not stopping at the graves, on to sell the lace to Lady FitzGerald at Watermead.

Chapter 19 ❧

By the time I walked to Watermead, I was very tired. Lady FitzGerald's maid, busy with the dressmaker, couldn't come immediately to see the lace I brought, and I was kept waiting a half an hour. Not that I minded.

The little kitchen maid, Katherine, gave me entrance while I waited for Mistress Dobbs. She chattered away about nothing in particular, seemingly unfazed by my silence.

When eventually Mistress Dobbs appeared, I thanked her quickly for taking the lace, the coin in return.

I set off for home. It had been an emotional day, with so many feelings all now catching up with me. The thought of the extra three miles to Honiton seemed suddenly overwhelming. I sat at the end of the drive and leant back against one of the large stone pillars that supported the wrought iron gates.

No matter how much I tried, I couldn't clear my mind of Pa. What would I do if he came back to the inn again? I felt my eyes closing while listening to a bumble bee searching nearby for flowers. The gentle buzzing lulled me, unresisting, to much-needed sleep.

❧❧❧

The sound of horses approaching woke me, the riders' voices loud in the still air. I scrambled groggily round the side of the pillar, hopefully out of sight. Two men approached, one of whom was Thomas Stanton. The man beside him rode a smaller horse, and he was not well dressed. He seemed ill, quite plainly having difficulty keeping his seat. Thomas Stanton drew his horse to a halt just past where I lay hidden.

'Come, Hugh, pull yourself together, man. I don't want to be embarrassed in front of my aunt because you are drunk in charge of a horse!'

The other man mumbled something I couldn't hear, but Master Stanton urged his horse on, clearly annoyed. His companion followed at a slower pace.

I crept out of my cover to watch them as they disappeared down the drive towards the house. Once they were out of sight, I stood up and brushed down my dress to clean off the dried grasses left from winter. Checking that the coin from the sale hadn't slipped from my hem while I slept, I set off. I felt better for the rest and looked forward to reaching the inn.

※※※※

It was close to four o'clock by the time the Cross Keys came into sight. I hadn't been long in Honiton, but already it felt comfortable to me.

I went directly to the water pump at the inn to wash my face and hands, then made my way to the eating room. As I took the short cut through the kitchen, I stopped to talk to Hanna.

'How was your visit to Master Bentley?' she asked as she picked up a large, oval platter, heavy with food.

'It went well, thank you.' I held the door open for her and followed her along the open-air hallway until we came to the eating room. I ran in front of her, opening that door to ease her entry.

The room, much to my surprise, was full of men, the air thick with smoke from the fire. With difficulty, Hanna placed the platter on one of the tables, avoiding with practiced ease the roaming hands of two of the men.

'Are you hungry?' she asked. I looked around. I was indeed hungry, but didn't want to eat here with so many strangers, most of whom looked as if they had already drunk far too much.

'I am.' I looked around, and Hanna understood at once.

'Go to your room, Susannah, I'll bring you something.' She disappeared quickly back through to the kitchen. I walked between the tables, like Hanna avoiding the outstretched, groping hands, then ran down the passageway to the safety of my room, locking the door behind me.

I didn't have to wait long. There was a knock on the door, accompanied by a whispered, 'It's me, Hanna. Open the door.'

I pulled it open.

Hanna hurried in holding a platter of food in one hand, a jug of ale in the other. She placed the platter on the bed, the jug on the table beside the bed.

'I haven't time to talk now; indeed, I doubt I'll see you before morning, we are so busy. I'm glad your journey was good, but we will talk more on the morrow.'

Before I could thank her, she was gone, leaving me looking at the closing door, which I quickly locked again.

I settled onto the bed, the bolster pillow behind me easing my back against the hard wood. I ate the roast chicken along with the cooked vegetables, tearing off chunks of bread from the small loaf. Hanna had forgotten to bring a beaker, but I wasn't going out of my room again, so I drank straight from the jug, knowing I would have to rely on the pisspot kept under the bed for calls of nature.

Too tired to stay awake any longer, I moved the platter off the bed and slipped under the top cover, only to fall asleep within minutes.

⁂

The next morning I woke to the church bells ringing. Still dressed from last night, I unlocked the door, picked up the platter and jug, and walked down the passageway to the eating room.

There wasn't a sound anywhere; no kitchen girls, and no sounds of cooking pots being hurriedly banged around. Looking through the doorway, the room was completely empty. I left the platter and jug on one of the tables, then opened the door that led to the kitchens. There was not a sound.

I found my heart was beating quickly, my hands starting to shake. Should I go to the kitchen? What should I do? Where was everyone? I felt frightened. Should I get the Watch?

'Susannah, you're up early.' I jumped, my hands going to my mouth to stop myself screaming.

'I'm sorry, lass, did I frighten you?' asked Master Beaker, coming through the door.

I had to sit down because my knees were shaking so badly, while I felt close to weeping, unable to answer lest he realise how frightened I had been.

'Where is everyone? Where's Hanna? Why is it so quiet?' I asked after a moment when I could speak.

'Of course, you weren't with us last night, so won't know. I gave them all the morning off. We had such a lot of trade yesterday; all stayed so late that everyone was tired. Especially poor Hanna, running backwards and forwards like a scalded cat. I thought it wouldn't do any harm to let them sleep in, so I told them not to appear before it was time to get dinner ready.'

I stared at him, such a simple explanation with no need for me to be frightened. I began to laugh. 'I thought something terrible had happened to everyone. I heard the bells ring seven o'clock, and everyone is usually up and about long before this.' I wiped my eyes on my sleeve. 'I'm glad everyone is all right. However, may I find something to eat myself? I'm very hungry.'

'You can bring me something, too, if you would, Susannah. I'll be in my chancel room, come and talk with me there,' he said as he made his way out of the room.

I found some chicken, taking enough for both of us, then added some of yesterday's bread, a hunk of cheese, a large piece of poached fish which was kept under a muslin cloth, and a jug of ale along with two beakers.

The chancel door was open, and Master Beaker had cleared space on his desk for the food.

Once we both were settled and our first hunger satisfied, he asked how the visit to Upper Hambley had gone.

'Very well. All of Peter's wood had sold. It was good to see Master Bentley again. I stopped off at our cottage to visit the graves of Ma and baby William. On the way back I took the lace to Lady FitzGerald. I'm so grateful she continues to purchase it. I can't bear to think what would happen, if we had to rely on the buyer here.'

'So long as Peter is apprenticed, you shouldn't worry about him. As for you, well, we would come to some arrangement, don't worry about that. Besides, as long as Lady FitzGerald buys the lace, it's not something to worry about, is it?'

'No, it's not.' I remembered standing by Ma and William's graves, the sense of peace that had suddenly come on me. How I had felt that all would work out.

We talked until all the food had been eaten, after which I took the dishes to the kitchen and returned to my room to lay on my bed once more.

The next seven years stretched in front of me while I waited for Peter to add joiner to his name. It would be up to me how I spent those years. I had to decide if I would be content to continue to make lace for my living. Would my time be measured by the Sunday afternoons spent with Peter?

Chapter 20 ❧

I decided to spend the next few days giving serious thought to my future. Other girls of my station either worked on the local estate, or slaved in inns fifteen hours a day for their board. Some made lace, and some fell into a life of utter despair, selling their bodies for a pittance to anyone with the coin. Sometimes for much-needed food. If, as a result, they fell for a child, there was always the local wise woman to help them deal with it. A few days later they were back on the street, the circle going round again. Even in Honiton there were such girls, everyone knowing them for what they were.

It turned out that one was to figure briefly in Peter's life, not mine. Mistress Chapman had a sister, Sarah, the younger by four years, who married and moved away to live in the nearby town of Ottery St. Mary. Sarah and her husband had three children. The eldest, a boy, died shortly after his birth. Their sorrow was, however, tempered somewhat following the birth of two girls in quick succession.

The elder, Mary, quickly proved to be uncontrollable. Sarah and her husband wept many tears of despair at Mary's wanton behaviour, and in desperation, wrote to Mistress Chapman, asking if she would be accepting of Mary for a few months to try and 'make her right.'

Peter's master and mistress discussed it with him as they sat by the fire. He being part of their small family, and ultimately affected should the answer be yes, he was given a chance to speak. As usual, he spoke with confidence. As the apprentice, he rightly felt that his opinion would be given due consideration.

Peter told me what he had said to them, that, in his opinion, the whole venture was fraught with problems. How could Sarah expect Mistress Chapman to exert discipline into the girl when she had never had a child of her own? And Ottery St. Mary was nowhere as big as Honiton, that Peter felt it would be like sending the girl to a place, for however short a time, where even more temptation was to hand.

I had to agree with him, but as it wasn't my decision to make, I made no further comment.

After a great deal of soul searching, Mistress Chapman agreed to take the girl for three months, but made it clear in her letter of acceptance that she could make no promises that Mary would return to her family a changed person.

At fourteen years of age, Mary already showed a tendency to be too familiar with young men who gathered around her like moths to a flame. The family had hoped to have her married off by now, but her reputation had been sullied already, and any family of similar status refused to allow their sons to have anything to do with her.

Mary arrived on the coach, sullen faced and rebellious from the start. Greeted by her aunt, she barely acknowledged the welcome and walked to the shop with heavy, resentful steps.

Shown her chamber, she proclaimed it to be too small, too dark, too damp and definitely not what she was used to. On being told it was all that was available, she demanded to be shown Peter's room. Finding it more to her liking, she claimed it as her own. Peter, on hearing this, refused to move, saying he had been tenant there for the past four years, and that he had no intention of moving. Stalemate.

Mary sat on the top step of the stairs outside Peter's chamber drumming her feet on the board and screaming. Mistress Chapman flapped around her, telling her to quieten down or the neighbours would think murder was being committed.

Peter refused to move and went back downstairs to finish the dining chair he had been working on for the past four days. It was only when Mary realised that, for once, she was not to get her own way, she entered the small, dark, damp chamber and flung herself on the bed to continue the screaming.

Mistress Chapman, deciding to leave her to wear herself out, went downstairs to prepare dinner. Husband and wife looked at each other, both raised their eyes to the heavens, and both wondered what on earth had possessed them to accept this spoilt child. But accepted her they had, and now they had to get on with it.

Each Sunday when I met with Peter, he would give me the latest news of Mary. I had two reactions. Either one of utter amazement or one of laughter at the patently stupid things she did.

One evening when Master Chapman went out to feed the chickens before turning to bed himself, she was caught climbing out of her chamber window, balancing dangerously on the top of the window below. Rushing upstairs while shouting to his wife and Peter for help, he hauled her back in as she fought and scratched to be let alone. Peter stood to one side, laughing hard enough to burst at her folly, which only angered her all the more.

If one were generous, most of her adventures could be put down to childish enthusiasm, but eventually facts had to be faced. They couldn't control her any more than her own mother, and if truth be told, probably less. When she didn't appear for breakfast one morning, Peter offered to go upstairs to rouse her.

When there was no reply, he warned her he was entering, but upon opening the door, found the bed unwrinkled, the window ajar. She had gone.

Worried about giving such awful news to the Chapmans, he went slowly downstairs.

They had only had to take one look at his demeanour to know something was wrong, and when he did tell them, Mistress Chapman fell to the floor in a dead faint. Patting her hand to bring her round, her husband kept saying, 'There, there, it will be all right. We will find her.'

Peter was sent off to fetch the Watch who, he felt, came somewhat reluctantly. On the way to the shop, Peter found out why.

'She's got a right awful reputation, Peter. I can tell you for a fact this isn't the first time she has taken off, for I've seen her myself in the early hours, always with different people.' He looked sideways at Peter, his meaning clear.

'Why haven't you said anything?' asked Peter.

'She's of age, so I believe, nothing I can do. But I can tell you, she will come to a bad end, and sooner rather than later.' They passed the rest of the journey in silence.

Master and Mistress Chapman were waiting in the shop, both in turn poking their heads out of the door to look down the lane for the Watch and Peter.

'Do you want to see her chamber?' asked Mistress Chapman when the Watch at last appeared.

Peter could tell he didn't think it would serve any purpose, but thinking it would calm the woman, the Watch nodded.

'I'll take him,' Peter offered, leading the way. Opening the door to Mary's room, he was astounded to see her lying in bed, fast asleep, as innocent as any babe.

'Well I'll be damned,' said the Watch, looking to Peter as if he had brought him here on a fool's errand.

'I swear she wasn't here. She must have snuck in while the Chapmans were rushing around in panic.'

'No doubt. You'd best speak to them about her. Tell them what I told you. It's best they be aware of what she's up to.'

It was a task Peter didn't want to undertake, and decided to speak to me first.

We discussed how he would go about it. I couldn't see any other way but to tell them straight. Peter didn't want to hurt them, though how he thought he wouldn't do that, I haven't the least idea. I have always thought if the truth has to be faced, better to face it than wiggle around it.

❧❧❧

When we next met, I asked him how it had gone.

'They were very upset, demanded to speak to the Watch themselves to hear it from him rather than trust to me. He told them he had heard, without mentioning who from, that she was selling herself.'

'No!'

'Yes. And she's only been here a month, two more to go.'

'What are they going to do?'

'I don't know, I'm not asked to be part of those discussions. I think they should take her back to her family before she completely ruins their reputation.'

'You might well be right. It must be very hard for them, and neither are young any more.'

I, too, had heard rumours about Mary. I sat in the eating room one evening waiting for Hanna to finish work and overheard four men who were in conversation round the fire. The gist of the matter was they were discussing a young girl 'not from Honiton who is very worldly, if you get my drift.' They all laughed that dirty, throaty laugh men have when they think of the baser side of human nature. It had to be Mary they were talking about.

In the end, the most obvious solution was taken away from the Chapmans. Mary was found on her bed, sobbing her heart out early one morning.

Mistress Chapman, sitting beside her, stroked her hair, trying to soothe her. But no amount of soothing was going to help Mary. She had missed her monthly courses for the second month, she told her aunt. Only one explanation was possible.

Mistress Chapman, who had tried for a child for nigh on ten years, only to accept in the end she was not meant to be a mother, also sat and sobbed.

Facts, however distressing, had to be faced. Mary had to go home immediately. Seats were booked on the coach for the following day, and Mary packed her few belongings.

What her mother would say they both dreaded to think, but the girl must have fallen pregnant before she arrived in Honiton. Mistress Chapman comforted herself with that thought, that it hadn't happened while Mary was under her care.

Mistress Chapman told her husband and Peter that she would be staying a few days with her sister. Master Chapman and Peter once more quickly settled back into their comfortable routine, both glad to have the house back to its much-missed, much-lamented, tranquillity.

Chapter 21 ⨪

Peter's apprenticeship was progressing well, and he was happier than ever. Whenever we met, he talked of what he had worked on that week, how Master Chapman had shown him this and that, how much he loved working the wood.

Mistress Chapman taught him reading and writing, which in turn, he taught me on our Sundays.

I have to admit that I rarely thought of him during the week. Occasionally I would think, I must remember to tell Peter that, or ask him this, but most days went by when he never entered my head at all. When I told him of this, he laughed.

'Don't feel guilty, Susannah. I hardly think of you at all until Saturday comes around, then I begin thinking I will see you the next day. It means we are both busy and happy, and surely that's all anyone can ask.'

I suddenly felt very sad and lonely. 'I know you're right, Peter, but in some small part of me I feel that we are drifting apart.'

'No, we will never do that.'

I gave myself a shake, trying to rid myself of the sadness.

Peter said we were both busy, but secretly I couldn't agree.

I made lace. Hardly, after all the years I had worked it, something that kept my mind occupied.

Back at the inn later that evening, I lay on my bed thinking of the children who made the lace, how most would never be as lucky as I had been. They would never learn to read or write, figure numbers.

While on a walk, I stood outside Allhallows School and listened to the boys recite their lessons, wishing I could learn with them.

But I can read and write, thanks to Peter. Why couldn't I, in turn, teach the lacemaking children?

It would take them away from the lace and the badly needed income from its sale, but it would open up so many more opportunities.

Where could I teach them? What if the mothers said no? Where could I get some hornbooks?

The inn had at least two empty outbuildings. I knew they were dry and the floors solid, for I had been inside them recently looking for a cat who, about to sprout her litter, had taken to hiding in the oddest of places.

I could ask Master Beaker if we could have the use of one of the buildings in the morning. I sat up, fully excited with my plan. Yes, it would work!

As with most plans, the cold light of morning made me wonder what I had been thinking. I lay listening to the kitchen girls while I went through everything again. Each time I put up a barrier as to why I couldn't do it, I thought of a better reason why I could. Before I lost my nerve, I dressed and went in search of Master Beaker.

He listened without interruption while I told him my thoughts, then sat back, looking at me with raised eyebrows.

'You've given this a lot of thought, Susannah.'

I nodded.

'What makes you think the children will want to learn? Or that their mothers will let them?'

'I can't know for certain, I can only ask. It may be there are only one or two, perhaps the smallest ones who haven't yet learned the lace, or for some reason can't learn the lace. But what I do know is, that I have to try. There has to be more for these children than a life of drudgery for poor pay.'

'And you want the use of one of my buildings for this?'

'If you would allow it.'

'I will. You can have the use of it for a month, see how it goes. How do you intend to get the word out?'

'Mistress Parnell. She was Ma's friend, and if anyone can convince the women, she can.'

I got up, wrapping my arms round his neck. 'Thank you, Master Beaker. You won't regret it.'

I went directly in search of Mistress Parnell, finding her outside the baker's in the line of women waiting for the use of the ovens.

Asking the woman behind her to keep her place, I took her to one side, quickly telling her of my plan. She, like Master Beaker, never said a word as I spoke.

'Do you think you could help?' I asked when I had finished.

'Well, I could, but I wonder how the money lost from the sale of the lace could be made up.'

'I know, but I'm thinking that perhaps if the younger ones came, or those who struggle with the lace, I could teach them. I have to start somewhere, why not there?'

'All right, I will see what I can do.'

She returned to her spot in the line and I walked down the lane, turning between the first two houses to peek back. She already had a few of the women around her, the hand not holding the bread bowl gesticulating this way and that, pointing to the way I had gone.

On my way back to the inn, I suddenly had an overwhelming feeling of panic. What if children did turn up? I had told Mistress Parnell that the lessons would start the following Monday at eight o'clock in the morning, and that was six days away. I didn't have any hornbooks. Oh Lord, what have I done! I turned away from the inn, heading instead to the bookstore in the High Street.

The proprietor, Master Edward Catchpole, came through from the back room at the sound of the bell. We knew each other, though not on first name terms. I frequented the shop on occasion to see what new books were available, though only very rarely purchasing.

I explained what I wanted to do.

Listening patiently, he said at the end, 'I have two hornbooks you could purchase. Or why don't you use the Bible to teach them? Yes, the more I think of it, use the Bible for the youngest ones. And more people reading can only be good news for my humble shop!'

Of course, why hadn't I thought of it. We could work together.

'Thank you, I will take the two hornbooks for now, and later on, when they progress, use the Bible. That is a wonderful idea.'

We agreed on a price, and he hurried back to his room at the rear of the shop to get the hornbooks while I paced up and down between the shelves, my mind rushing here and there with all the things to be done.

꽃꽃꽃

In my absence, Master Beaker had spoken to Hanna about my idea, and upon my return to the inn, she was waiting for me.

'Can I come to your lesson, Susannah? I know I am probably too old, I'm eighteen, but I want to learn to read and write. Please may I?'

I laughed, filled with joy. 'Of course you may. You are my first pupil. But first I have to clean one of the outbuildings, there's so much to be done!'

'I can help with the cleaning, and I'll see if any of the other girls are willing to help. I expect they will want to come, too, so that will be five of us already. This is wonderful, Susannah.'

She ran off to speak to the girls while I returned to my room, wondering what on earth I had started, but knowing it could only be for the good of those who came. Who knew where it would all lead.

When Master Beaker heard that lessons were to start on the Monday at eight o'clock, he came knocking on my door.

'And what of the breakfasts?' he demanded. 'Who is going to clean that up? And prepare the dinners, if all the girls are learning their letters? I can't have my business brought down because of learning, Susannah.'

'No, of course not. I have been thinking how I could do that. If just a couple of the girls could come at a time, then they could teach the others what they had learned. The running of the inn wouldn't be affected that way.'

'Aye, well, that sounds better than them all being gone for the most important part of the day,' he said, beginning to calm.

137

I had very rarely seen him in a temper, and had no wish to make life harder for him than it already was after his many kindnesses to me.

I stayed up much of the night thinking of the opportunities about to open up for young children who never thought they would have the chance read or write.

Hanna and I had cleaned out the smaller of the buildings in the yard and used bales of hay for seats. When Sunday evening came around, I was very nervous.

'Do stop worrying,' said Hanna.

'I can't help it. What if no one comes?'

'I'll be there,' she replied indignantly.

'Yes, I know that, Hanna. But what if the mothers won't let the children come?'

'There's nothing you can do about that, Susannah. Why not go to bed and get a good night's rest.'

I knew she was right, but it didn't stop me tossing and turning, only falling asleep as it came close to dawn. When I awoke, the bells for seven o'clock were ringing.

❧❧❧

Rushing to wash and dress, I grabbed the two hornbooks and made my way to the building where the lessons would be held. Too nervous to eat, I sat on the straw and waited.

Hanna came just after eight o'clock, rushing through the door as if she was late.

'Am I the only one here yet?'

'Yes. I don't think anyone else is going to come, Hanna.'

'Stop it, Susannah, give them time.'

Together we sat and waited until nearly eight-thirty. Even Hanna had to admit it then, no one else was coming.

'Don't be disappointed. You can teach me, I'm eager to learn. And who knows, when the other girls see that I can read, they won't want to be left behind. Come on, cheer up, Susannah.'

'You're right. Thank you, Hanna.'

With an aching heart, I started to show Hanna the letters on the hornbook, and she repeated them after me.

The time went too quickly, and at nine o'clock Master Beaker poked his head through the door. 'No one turned up, eh? Ah well, it was worth a try, but I need Hanna back now, the inn is getting busy.'

Hanna and I looked at each other. 'Don't worry, Susannah. Perhaps I can come to your room tonight and we can continue with the lesson?' she asked, hopefully.

'Yes, of course. It was a good idea, but obviously making the lace comes first. Or perhaps the mothers don't see any need for the children to read and write. I will seek out Mistress Parnell tomorrow and ask her.'

Hanna went back to the kitchen, leaving me sitting alone.

It had been a good idea, and even if I only taught Hanna to read, that was one more that could read than before. And as Ma used to say, 'Small steps, Susannah, small steps.'

Chapter 22 🍂

Time passed quickly. Peter was nearing the end of his apprenticeship with Master Chapman, and it was just a short while before he could add 'Joiner' to his name. That sounded well, 'Peter Brigginshaw, Joiner.' He told me he spoke it out aloud every day, even more incentive to work hard. I couldn't believe how he had grown, both in height and girth, during the intervening years. Good, wholesome food had soon caused a growth spurt, and while nothing could be done about his legs and feet, at least he had boots to help him with the walking.

Over six feet tall, he had a handsome head of light brown curly hair. His face had filled out along with his body, blue eyes under well-shaped, tidy brows. His chin square and strong, skin clear. He turned more than a few heads when he went to church on Sunday mornings.

I was attending the regular Sunday morning service, though I didn't sit with Peter, for he attended with Master and Mistress Chapman.

Known in the town as a well-mannered lad with very gifted hands when it came to working the wood, I knew there were many of the town's females who had their eye on him. I watched as they poked each other in the ribs at the sight of him, whispering and giggling behind their hands. None seemed to note his infirmity, accepting him for what he was, a gifted and handsome man.

Under the terms of his apprenticeship, he wasn't allowed to step out with anyone, all his time and energy to be used for the wood. However, shortly his apprenticeship would be completed, and then he would be free to do as he pleased. I knew he couldn't wait.

After the first year, Master Chapman had allowed me to enter the shop to meet Peter, instead of waiting outside, then again when we returned. Both he and Mistress Chapman were obviously fond of him, especially since they were themselves childless. He told me he had never had a moment's regret about taking Peter on, knowing from the first that a lad like this came along rarely, and for some masters not at all.

Peter's drawings made before the work started were detailed and explicit, nothing left to chance. His work was always done with meticulous attention to detail, while he was rapidly gaining an excellent reputation in his own name.

Mistress Chapman and I became good friends. She would greet me as I waited outside the shop for Peter. When I was eventually allowed to enter, we would often sit and talk. If I have to be honest, she was more of a mother figure to me, not that anyone could ever replace Ma. I found I could talk to her of my hopes and dreams without censure.

Mistress Chapman's only regret, well, the first of two, she said, was that Peter would soon be leaving them. The second, that they didn't have a daughter for him to wed.

Her husband wasn't getting any younger, indeed, neither was she. The slowing down of his steps, the arthritis claiming his hands and knees was all too apparent. The time would come when he could no longer lift the heavy pieces of wood. Peter had been a godsend during the last while. Even with his infirmity, he did better than some without.

Mistress Chapman had grown well used to having Peter in the house. She spent her evenings teaching Peter to read. He had proven to be a quick study, absorbing the letters like a sponge. He was quickly able to read short sentences, and from there progressed in leaps and bounds. Reading was fundamental to his trade; contracts had to be composed and signed, tradesmen's invoices scrutinized and paid. Without the reading, he had no hope of progressing.

Master Chapman had been happy to sit beside the hearth of an evening, his clay pipe in hand, watching and listening to his wife give instruction by candlelight in winter, and outside in the garden during the milder months. Mistress Chapman would see him watching them, knowing he regretted the lack of their own family, but it had been God's wish they should be childless. It was far too late for anything to be done about it now.

Peter read everything he could get his hands on. Having read all the books the Chapmans had, which admittedly weren't many, he borrowed from friends of his master. He lay in his bed of an evening, for he only felt comfortable reading lying down where he could rest his legs and feet. He always read late into the night, the candle flickering beside him.

Once he had mastered reading, he spent Sunday afternoons teaching me. He patiently explained the different letters and sounds, just as Mistress Chapman had done for him.

Master Chapman left Peter to speak to customers when they called, he now taking a more passive role. Peter would ask their requirements; was it intended the piece be used, or put on display? What wood was to be used, or would they leave the choice to his discretion? Using paper and pen to quickly sketch his thoughts, he would show the customers, certain of their approval.

'A quotation will be ready in two days,' Peter would say. When asked why it couldn't be available earlier, his answer was always ready, 'We are very busy at the moment, it will be ready in two days.' He already had the exact figure in mind, had worked it out while sketching, but he didn't want to appear too eager for the business. 'Let them think they are fortunate to get our services,' he would tell his master when they had the shop to themselves.

With increasing work coming in, the days flew by for Peter, with Sundays coming around at a rapid rate. Mornings were spent in St. Michael's church on the top of the hill, along with most of the town. The small Allhallows chapel was halfway up, ideally situated for those who couldn't, or pretended they couldn't, go the extra distance. Ever since the fire of 1765, in which a large part of the town had been burned to the ground, some of the remaining buildings had to be used for more than one purpose. During the week Allhallows served as the school room, and Sunday it became the chapel.

The Rector, a man who liked nothing better than the sound of his own voice, usually managed to make his sermons last for up to an hour. This was fine for those with nothing better to do on a Sunday, but it meant Peter had to hurry back to the shop in time for us to meet, undeniably the most important part of the day for both of us.

During the week I made the lace, which Lady FitzGerald continued buying. I often wondered what she did with it all, a prodigious amount made and sold over the years. All of it was, of course, perfect and beautiful. Perhaps she sold it on, though once sold, it was immaterial to me. All that mattered was the money I received.

I was by this time eighteen years of age, a woman fully grown. Most maids were married by now. Like Peter, my hair was thick and curly, but its colour had become a beautiful honey gold. Though not as tall as my brother, I was slim. My eyes were the colour of a blue sky, framed with long dark lashes. Even though I do say so myself, I turned many heads.

I often thought about leaving the Cross Keys and finding a room elsewhere, but each time I decided to stay, feeling safe there. I was comfortable with Master Beaker and Hanna; indeed, I even thought of them as family. The room was more than adequate, food so plentiful that I was amazed I hadn't grown fatter. And where would I go, anyway? There were no other inns in Honiton offering lodging.

I was teaching reading to the local children in a building at the back of the inn. Sometimes two children came, sometimes none. If I moved, Master Beaker might tell me I couldn't use the space any more, and I didn't want that.

Mistress Parnell, Ma's friend, was in contact with me. She still made lace, though now, she told me, her eyes were failing fast. She attributed that to too many long hours in poor light weaving delicate threads, but truth be told, she wasn't young anymore. Uncertain as to the actual year she had been born, she thought herself to be in her fortieth year. If that were true, eyesight could never be what it was when a person was of twenty years.

Through her, I heard news of the other lacemakers in Honiton and the outlying areas, and it bothered me greatly to hear of the hardships they endured. Those who were alone, either with or without children, led a pitiful existence. The trouble was that the lace, depending on the pattern required, took many hours of work. Some laceworkers, including young boys and girls, took weeks to finish one piece, and the reward for all their work was very small.

But what choice had they? They couldn't work on the land, and only so many servants were needed at Watermead. It was too far to the coast to fish, and besides, who ever heard of a woman fishing for gain? The lace was all they had. I set aside a shilling a month, then when I heard of a particularly sad situation, I would share the money, hoping to ease a little of their hunger. I was all too well aware I had been so very fortunate to have Lady FitzGerald purchase my lace and felt it my duty to help others in need.

❧❧❧

One morning, through Hanna, I heard that Mistress Edgemore, the milliner in the High Street, was in need of assistance. I discussed the possibility of taking the position with both her and Peter. It wasn't for the money, although it would always be useful, but sitting making the lace all day was a solitary occupation.

The other lacemakers worked from home with hearth and children to care for, though they did occasionally meet, in the summer months. Each brought their lace pillow and stool to sit outside one of the houses, gossiping the time away while their hands were busy. I never joined them, feeling awkward, knowing they were aware I wasn't in such great need as they. The money paid for the lace I made was usually a guinea a month, sometimes more, sometimes less. I didn't have a husband or children to care for. I didn't have to cook, wash and clean. My room at the Cross Keys cost one shilling a week, all found. Apart from the expense of a few clothes, my boots, boots for Peter (which were my biggest expense), and by being very frugal, there was always money left over. I kept this in the chest Peter had made for me.

As I said, it wasn't for the money; I felt it would be good to meet more people. Therefore, I presented myself accordingly at the milliner's. I had been in the shop twice before in all the time I had lived in Honiton. I had never bought anything, for our money didn't stretch to fripperies, but there was no cost for looking. The milliner and I knew each other, if only by sight, for Honiton wasn't a large town.

After spending time telling me of the duties, should I be so fortunate as to obtain the position, she told me she would let me know within two days if she would hire me and to return to the shop on the Wednesday for her answer. She must have used the intervening time speaking to various friends as to my honesty and reliance, though oddly enough she never spoke to Master Beaker, for I asked him.

Wednesday came slowly, but at ten o'clock, I returned. Mistress Edgemore informed me the position was mine, that she would pay two shillings a week. She also mentioned that there was a room above the shop, should I wish to take it for sixpence a week, though I would have to find my meals elsewhere. I was taken aback about the room, for perhaps this was the answer to my quandary.

'May I think about it, mistress? I lodge at the Cross Keys and am quite comfortable. But thank you for the position, when shall I start?'

'I have no need of you until Monday, my other girl is leaving Friday. Be here at seven o'clock sharp. If you decide to take the room let me know before, so I have time to prepare it.'

'Yes, mistress. I will have made up my mind by tomorrow about the room.' Curtsying, I left.

If I took the room for sixpence, I would have to find my food. At the inn, my room was only one shilling, with all the food I could eat. I would have to think carefully, perhaps discuss it with Hanna later.

That evening the two of us sat on my bed. 'The way I see it,' said Hanna, as she inspected her chapped, worn hands, 'is that you live over the milliner's but have to go elsewhere for your food. I can't think of anywhere nearby where you could do that. It would mean either coming back here every day or going the other way, up past the church to the King's Head, and I wouldn't eat there, no matter how hungry I was. Whatever you decide, it would be a long walk twice a day, especially in the winter. Who knows what else she'd get you doing, you being so convenient upstairs. I'd say that's fraught with no end of problems, Susannah.'

'I never thought of that. I also have to think of Peter. His apprenticeship ends in a few months, and what's he going to do then? What if he wants to move away from Honiton? Set himself up in business elsewhere? He would probably want me to go with him. No, Hanna, the more I think on it, I'm best to stay here until I know what Peter's intentions are, and make a decision then. I'll ask him on Sunday, and tell Mistress Edgemore I won't be taking the room.' I felt glad I had come to a decision.

The two shillings a week would definitely help. Peter's boots had to be specially made, and he continually scuffed them, wearing out the toes. He also outgrew them quickly, not that he could help it, it was just the way it was. The bootmaker had always taken a bit off the price, but they were still expensive. Hopefully, though, his feet were fully grown, with just general wear and tear to be considered.

The bookshop in the High Street had been a place of frequent visits ever since Peter had taught me to read. I was slow, my finger moving along the line as I worked out each word, while my tongue stuck outside my mouth in concentration. I loved the books, and thought that perhaps with some of the money from the milliner's I could afford to buy one of my own. If only Ma could see Peter and me now, she'd never believe it. She'd be that proud of us.

It had been nearly a year since I had returned to the ruins of our home in Offwell. It was too far for Peter to walk, even with boots. With only Sunday afternoon off, it just wasn't possible for him to come with me. So we hadn't gone back to Offwell.

I had walked to Watermead to deliver lace, the day fine and clear. With money in my workaday dress pocket, I stood at the end of the drive, homeward bound. To the left was Honiton, to the right, Offwell. It was only three miles; besides, I had nothing else to do that day.

As I walked along, my head was filled with memories of the family we used to be. I wondered what our lives would have been like if Ma and Pa were here. I couldn't see it would have ever changed, Pa wouldn't stop the drinking, Ma and I would be always be making the lace. We would always be living from hand-to-mouth. At least now, Peter and I had enough to eat, and boots. When I thought of Ma, it was only with regret that she couldn't see how we had both grown. When I thought of Pa, it was with anger that he could have neglected us all so.

I was all the more determined that when I wed, it would be to a man who would care for me, love me. But I was young, with no husband in sight. There were certainly enough young men in Honiton who would be only too happy to woo me, but I made it plain I wasn't interested. Making sure Peter had everything he needed, the accumulation of money was my only concern. There was time enough when Peter's apprenticeship was over for all of that.

The cottage had fallen completely. It was summer, the garden overgrown. In another couple of years, every indication that we had lived there would be gone, anyone passing hardly aware it had ever been. Around the back, the oak was still there, even taller, the bole now large around. Ma and William's graves were totally lost in the undergrowth. I wondered if Pa had told the Rector Ma had died.

It was a fine day, no sign of rain, and the air warm. I decided to go on even farther to Upper Hambley to see if Master and Mistress Bentley were home.

I couldn't get over how much the village had grown, more houses, some even made of stone with tiled roofs replacing the thatch. Strangers weren't plentiful here; they were an object of speculation, sometimes of fear. I was aware of being watched as I walked towards the store. Opening the door, I heard Master Bentley talking to someone in the back room while I stood waiting for him to finish.

Shortly he appeared.

'Yes, mistress?'

'Good morning, Master Bentley,' I replied, smiling. He looked at me, mouth agape.

'Susannah? Little Susannah Brigginshaw? Well, I never! Come on in, girl, don't just stand there.'

He called to his assistant to care for the store while he ushered me towards his private parlour.

'My, but you've grown into a pretty young thing,' he said at different times, wanting to know all that had happened, asking after Peter, how we were coping, what news I had.

He was constantly interrupted by customers, the assistant seemingly unable to be of much use. Our story took awhile to tell, with Master Bentley bobbing up and down to run into the store every so often, but at the end, he was delighted with all our news.

'I'm so glad Peter has landed on his feet,' he said, pleasure clear on his face. 'And only another while to go when he's a joiner in his own right. Your ma would be right proud of you both.'

'And what of you, sir?'

'Well, you won't have heard, but my Goodwife was killed some three years ago. She'd been ailing for a while, but I think I told you that when you were last here. One day she decided to go outside, get some fresh air. A runaway horse knocked her down, killing her instantly, just outside here in the street. We never even had a chance to say goodbye.' He stopped to clear his throat. 'It's been hard without her, for we'd known each other since we were babes, but I'm slowly getting used to being on my own. If one ever does.' He sighed. 'But, tell me more about you.'

'There's not a lot more to tell. Peter gets a good wage; I'm still making the lace, and I will soon start work with Mistress Edgemore, the milliner, which will bring in more coin. We manage well. Have you seen or heard any more of our pa?' I was suddenly aware that this question had been at the back of my mind all along, perhaps the only reason for my journey here. Master Bentley looked uncomfortable.

'Tell me, sir. Even if it's bad news, it's surely better than none.'

'Well, yes, you're right, of course you are. He did come here, it must be a good year ago now. Appeared out of the thin air as if he'd never been away. He had a woman with him, not the same one he had before. I don't know where he found this one.' He looked uncomfortable, but I needed to know the answer, and would press him for it if necessary.

'She was carrying a child, a boy about two, I'd say, another one coming soon by the looks of her. He didn't ask after Peter or you. He did say he had seen you once, that he needed lodging, but you had refused him.' He looked at me, unspoken questions in his eyes.

'I did refuse him, for right or wrong.'

'There's no need to defend yourself to me, lass. I know you would have followed your heart. I don't like to speak ill of your pa, but he's a bad lot, he would never have changed.'

'I know. Peter and I are doing well. Everyone has been very kind to us,' though I never told him of the stolen gloves. 'We have enough to eat, people who care for us. We can both read and write. Peter has an excellent trade, which will keep him in work for the rest of his life. Don't be sorry for us, sir, there are many far worse off. But I'm sorry for you, for the loss of your Goodwife.'

I stayed for another half-hour, telling Master Bentley of all the gossip in Honiton. He rarely came to the town, but promised upon my leaving that next time he would stop by the Cross Keys and visit me.

'You said everyone is kindly to you there?'

'They are. I have a friend called Hanna who works at the inn. She's older than me, but we get on well with each other. Master Beaker is very good to me; the inn is well kept and clean. I couldn't have made a better decision, for both of us.'

Shortly after, I took my leave, walking back past the cottage. I hoped that with the wages from the milliner's I could afford to have proper markers made for the graves. With a lightened step, I set off for home, for Honiton.

Chapter 23 ❧

The Sunday before I began my new position, Peter and I spent a long time discussing what it would mean for us. I told him of my hope that the extra money would at last enable us to buy markers for the graves.

'But, Susannah,' he protested, 'I told you I would willingly help pay for those a long time ago.'

'I know you did, Peter, and I thank you for it, but it's more important that you save your wages as much as possible. With your apprenticeship ending, you will soon need to set yourself up in business. You will need to find premises, buy tools and wood. It's far better that your money is spent in that way. You will have other expenses, too, some no doubt we haven't even thought of. Up to now Master Chapman has been clothing and feeding you, but you will have to find somewhere else to live, be responsible for yourself soon.'

'Besides,' I continued, 'I have been saving my money, too, but find myself reluctant to spend it on the markers.' I laughed as I looked at Peter's confused face. 'I know, it doesn't make sense. I have spent all these years saying I wanted markers made; and now, when I am able to afford them, I can't spend the coin. I will buy them, I promise, it will just be when I feel more comfortable.'

Peter had made a strongbox as part of his training, which he kept in his room. With two hefty locks of black iron, it was made of solid English oak, intricately carved with his initials on the domed lid. It sat, two feet long and one foot wide, at the foot of his bed. The town blacksmith had made the locks and the one key, in themselves a work of great beauty. Rightly proud of his work, Peter polished it weekly with beeswax. Inside he kept his spare linens. His rapidly accumulating wages were also kept there in a felt bag sewn for him by Mistress Chapman.

'Have you given any thought to what you're going to do when your time here is over?'

'I have, but I need to get it all clear in my mind before I speak of it. Perhaps we can talk of it next Sunday?'

'Of course, there's no rush, still plenty of time.' I knew that the time would fly by, but I couldn't hurry him. It would be his decision; I hoped he would choose to stay in Honiton.

The morning I started work, Hanna inspected my appearance before I left the inn, and pronounced me 'very suitable.' So it was that I was waiting at the steps of the milliner's at seven o'clock in the morning, as instructed.

Wearing my best workaday dress along with a clean lace cap, I knew I was well turned out. That knowledge, however, did little to stop the butterflies fluttering in my stomach. The door opened, Mistress Edgemore standing there.

'I'm glad to see you're timely at least, come along in.' She didn't address me by name as politeness dictated, leaving me to wonder if she was upset I had not taken the room. I followed her inside, which smelt very dusty after the clear morning air.

'The first thing you must do on your arrival is to dust, especially so after market day. The sheep and cattle walking up the High Street stir it all up, and most of it seems to land in here! There's a rag under the counter there,' she indicated a shelf. 'When you have finished that, the floor must be mopped, you will find a bucket and some rags in the back; water you get from the pump outside. Under no circumstances are you to be involved with money; I will handle every sale, Susannah. Not that I don't trust you.' Now she had made me fully aware I wasn't trusted, for why else tell me. She gave a small smile.

'While you are dusting, take note of where everything is so you may quickly lay your hands to it should a customer ask. I don't take kindly to constant interruptions, I have my own work to do and can't keep running in here to do yours, too. You may have a half-hour to eat your dinner when the bells strike twelve.

I presume you brought something with you, for I'll not provide it.' I nodded.

'We open the door at eight o'clock, so best get on. I'll be in the back finishing a bonnet for Lady FitzGerald. Her maid will be in later to collect it, but you are not to deal with her. I'll come out the moment I hear her voice.' She bustled off, full of self-importance.

I wondered if she knew I sold the lace to Lady FitzGerald and was well used to dealing with not only her maid, but the housekeeper, too. Smiling to myself, I picked up the dusting cloth, starting my new work.

The shelves were full of ribbons, different colours and widths, and lengths of lace for edging. Even more ribbons and lace hung from racks on the ceiling. The lace wasn't the Honiton that I made; these lengths must come from somewhere else, used to edge the bonnets and caps. Different widths hung in order, some very intricate and would obviously be more costly; simpler pieces less so. I touched one, noting that whoever had made it was very good at their craft.

'Don't just stand there daydreaming, girl, and don't touch the lace! You're supposed to be dusting! We've a lot to do before we open!'

I hadn't heard Mistress Edgemore come behind me, so intent was I on looking at everything.

'But, mistress, you told me to note where everything was, so that's what I'm doing.'

She immediately bristled. 'Don't answer back, for I won't stand for it. If you want to keep this position, learn your place.' Once again, she bustled off.

Oh dear, what have I let myself in for?

At eight o'clock, as the church bells rang across the town, the milliner called through to me, 'Turn the sign to show we are open, Susannah. Don't forget, when Lady FitzGerald's maid comes, I'm to deal with her.' She spoke as if I were a simpleton, unable to remember being told this before.

'Yes, mistress.' Using the stop to keep the door ajar, I turned the sign that leant against the window. I stood for a moment in the doorway looking out. The shop was located on the shaded side of the lane in the morning, though once the sun moved, hopefully the inside would be warmer, for it was definitely chilly now.

Before dinner, there was a constant flow of ladies either to collect finished bonnets or to consult with the milliner on new requirements.

All this seemed strange to me, for didn't you choose a shape, a colour, the ribbons and the lace, then had the bonnet made? It was amazing how some ladies could not make such a simple decision.

Upon entering, on the right-hand side of the shop was a large oblong table, on top of which was placed a freestanding mirror. Also available on the table was a hand-held mirror, so customers could see themselves from all angles. An armless chair was placed in front of it, while to the side a more comfortable chair was available should the customer bring a friend with her. This was encouraged by Mistress Edgemore as, more often than not, if one lady bought a new bonnet or cap, invariably her friend also had to purchase something new, not wanting to be left out. Various hat frames were available for inspection, these formed with buckram stiffened with starch, fabric and ribbons, then draped over them to allow the customer to see how the finished bonnet would look.

When the bells at St. Michael's rang at noon, my feet and legs were hurting badly, for I wasn't used to standing all day. Pleased though I was to have boots, I longed to take them off.

'Mistress, where may I eat?'

Mistress Edgemore looked around as if she'd never seen me before, bemused.

'I don't know, not in here certainly, I don't want customers seeing you eating. You'll have to go into the garden, but you're only to take half an hour, there's much work to be done.'

I wasn't sure what work needed to be done. I had dusted and tidied already, what more was there to do? I also didn't understand why I couldn't eat dinner inside. The shop closed at noon for one hour, indeed, all the shops in town did. Everyone knew it, all at their own homes eating their dinner. I gave a small shake of my head, deciding to eat in the garden listening to the sparrows arguing with each other in the trees, rather than question her rule.

I was thankful I hadn't moved into the room above the store. Hanna had been right, who knew what else Mistress Edgemore would have me doing. At least when I left the shop, I was going back to the Cross Keys where there were people who would welcome me. I had to admit, the milliner seemed particularly sour tempered.

While I ate, I thought again I had made a mistake taking the employment. Then I told myself it was just my first day, not to make a hasty decision; I would wait to see how it went. It would get better, surely.

Lady FitzGerald's maid came in just before three o'clock, expressing surprise when she saw me behind the counter.

'Susannah, whatever are you doing here?' Before I could answer, Mistress Edgemore came through from the back room, a smile, for once, on her face.

'Mistress Dobbs, you've come for the new bonnet for her ladyship? It's just ready and looks beautiful; I'll fetch it for you.' While she returned to the back room, I tried to take advantage of her absence, turning to answer the maid, but I didn't get the chance, the milliner quickly returning.

'I placed it in a large box to protect it, I'm sure it will be to her ladyship's liking,' she glared at me to keep silent.

'I'm sure it will,' replied the maid, who then turned to me, determined to give me a chance to speak.

'Susannah, how long have you been working with Mistress Edgemore?'

'This is my first day, mistress.'

She looked from one to the other of us. 'I will let her ladyship know you are here. Am I to presume you will continue to make lace, for Lady FitzGerald still requires it.'

'I will, of course. I have some ready and will be coming to Watermead on Saturday.'

'That is good news; I will let her ladyship know.'

She then spoke to the milliner. 'Thank you, mistress, please send your bill as usual.' With a nod for milliner, reserving a smile for me, she left.

I watched through the window as the footman held the carriage door for her, helping her up into it and waiting until she was seated, skirts arranged, before closing the door.

'Well! You never told me you make lace for her ladyship!'

'You never asked me, mistress.'

'How much lace do you make? More importantly, how much does she pay?'

I instantly bristled. Employed here I may be, but what I did outside the shop was none of the milliner's business.

'Mistress, I beg pardon, but I believe that's between Lady FitzGerald and myself.'

She was furious.

'How dare you, girl! I'm entitled to know what you do.' Her face became red, hands clenched by her side.

'No, mistress, you're not. You're paying me for my time whilst I'm here. What I do once I leave is my business. If you are not satisfied with that, I would be happy for you to pay me for the day and I shan't return. You will, of course, understand that when I see Lady FitzGerald, I will be sure to tell her why I lost my position here.' She had no need to know that I saw Mistress Dobbs at Watermead, not Lady FitzGerald.

We stared at each other; I was determined I wasn't going to back down. 'Start as you mean to go on,' Ma had always said.

The milliner stuttered, her mouth opening and shutting, looking like a fish stranded on the shore.

Without another word, she turned and went through to the back room. I could hear her banging around in anger, but I knew there was nothing she could do. It was none of her business, plain and simple.

At five o'clock, she stood holding the shop door open.

'Susannah, you won't be free to go to Lady FitzGerald's on Saturday. Have you forgotten we are open? The hours are the same, six days a week. You will have to make other arrangements for your private affairs. I also expect you here at seven o'clock tomorrow.' She spoke for all the world as if nothing had happened between us.

'Yes, mistress,' I replied, curtsying. I picked up the dinner bag and passed through the door. At least she knew I would not be bullied. More importantly, I still had my position, though I was now even more unsure if I wanted it. I had to think about it.

I was disappointed that I would have to return to the shop on Saturday, for it restricted the time I had to go to Watermead. There would be no time to go between attending church in the morning and meeting Peter at noon. There was only one way around it, I would have to miss church, which I found very vexing. My faith had become stronger, looking forward to Sunday mornings spent in prayer and song. The church was always full, and the Rector's sermons thought provoking.

It was difficult to walk, my feet ached so badly. Every so often I had to stop to let the pain subside. I stood by the side of a house, my shoulder resting against the wall.

'Susannah, I've been waiting for you.' I started, frightened at the sight of a man who appeared from the side of the house.

'Pa, what do you want?'

'I told you before, I need support. I know you are working at the milliner's, so coin shouldn't be short. I have a new Goodwife now, a young son and daughter, too. We have nowhere to lay our heads, so I'm looking to you, Susannah.'

I had thought I had seen the last of him, but now he had come back, along with a new family. I was furious.

'No, I'll not help you, Pa. I told you before, I'll not be responsible for you, and certainly not your family. They are your problem, not mine.'

He pushed me. Hard. I fell to the ground, hitting my head with a mighty bang against the wall. I cried out. 'Stop, Pa, I'll not change my mind.' Thankfully, my shouting caught the notice of those in the house, a window opening on the upper floor.

'What's going on?' shouted the man within. 'Lass, are you hurt?'

I looked up to see a man leaning out, anxious eyes looking into my own.

'Sir, I need help!' I cried.

Pa pulled back his hand, slapping me across the face. This time he hit my eye.

'Stop, stop, Pa,' I screamed.

He hit me again, making my ears ring.

The man above shouted, 'Watch, Watch,' then disappeared, hopefully to come downstairs to my aid. I could hear the cry for the Watch being taken up by others, and I hoped he would come quickly.

My head hurt badly, and I tasted blood in my mouth.

Pa punched me hard, though this time in the stomach, shouting, 'You bitch!'

When I opened my eyes he was gone, then I heard him running off between the houses.

All the commotion had caused others to appear, along with the man from the house.

'Lass, are you all right?' asked another man as he knelt by my side.

'I think so.' I sat, wiping blood from my chin.

A woman came to my side, smoothing my hair back with a gentle hand. 'You will have a large bruise on your face come the morning. Did you see who did this to you?'

I opened my mouth to speak then quickly closed it again. I didn't know what to do. Should I name Pa? If I did, and he did have a Goodwife and children, what would happen to them, if he were arrested? They had done nothing wrong, why should they be punished for his misdeeds? I could think of no way out of my dilemma, especially with my head aching so badly.

'No, mistress, I did not.'

The man from the house spoke up. 'No need, I got a good look at him, I'll tell the Watch when he gets here. If ever he does,' he added cynically.

'No, sir, I thank you, but let it be. I've come to no real harm. I thank you all for your help, but I will be on my way.' I struggled to my feet, helped by the lady next to me.

'You're Susannah Brigginshaw, aren't you?'

'Yes, I am.' She addressed the man who had spoken to me previously, I presumed her husband.

'Go with her, John, she lodges at the Cross Keys, I don't want her to walk on her own in case the man comes back again.' She turned back to me.

'Are you sure you don't want to speak to the Watch? It's not right what's happened to you, he shouldn't get away with it.'

'Yes, mistress, I'm sure. I thank you again, but I will go back to the inn. Though I would be very grateful if you came with me, sir.'

The man took my arm as we walked together back to the inn, then accompanied me inside. I led the way to the eating room, gratefully taking a seat at the nearest table, my head throbbing with the pain.

Chapter 24 ❧

No sooner had I sat down than Master Beaker came in. He only had to look at my face to guess what had happened.

'What's this? What's happened, Susannah?' he asked, fury on my behalf clear in his voice.

'I was attacked, sir,' I replied, wiping my eyes of tears.

Hanna, hearing Master Beaker's raised voice, came through from the kitchen to sit beside me.

'Attacked? Where? Not in Honiton, surely?' he exclaimed, aghast.

'Yes, but I'm well. I'm fortunate others came to help me. They sent for the Watch, but he didn't arrive before I left. The gentlemen there,' I nodded at my guardian, 'escorted me back.'

Master Beaker spoke to the man, shook his hand.

'Well thank you for that, John.' Master Beaker had been born and raised in Honiton, and he knew all of its inhabitants. He turned back to me.

'Did you see who attacked you?' Once more I had to lie.

'No, unfortunately it happened so quickly.'

Hanna spoke up. 'I think Susannah needs to get to bed, master. I'll just get her along to her room, help clean her up.' We both stood. 'Thank you for helping Susannah, sir, we are grateful.'

'I hope you feel better soon,' the man said to me, turning to leave the inn.

Master Beaker stopped him, saying, 'Come now, John, won't you join me for some ale before you go, to thank you for your kindness?'

'That's very kind of you, Master Beaker, I will with pleasure.' The two men stayed, while Hanna and I made our way to my room.

Once there, I lay on the bed. Hanna left to get a rag and water with which to bathe my face and head.

'Now,' she said on her return, 'suppose you tell me what really happened?'

'I can't.'

'Yes, you can. If you can't, then I will tell you. It was your pa, wasn't it?'

My silence was her answer.

'I knew it. I've seen enough beatings to know when someone is standing in front of you, you had to have seen him. I'm sorry, Susannah. This must be very hard for you.'

'It's of no matter, I'm just frightened the bruises will show tomorrow when I have to go back to the milliner's.'

'Don't think on that now. I will bring you some elder tree ointment to rub on your face, it should take care of the bruises. Are you hungry? Can I bring you something to eat?'

'No thank you, Hanna, I just want to lie quietly.'

'I'll bring the ointment then, meanwhile you rest.'

❧❧❧

The next morning came far too early. My head hurt, also inside my mouth was sore where I had bitten it. Listening to the girls in the kitchen outside, I lay quietly. Eventually Hanna called to me through the door.

'Susannah, are you awake?'

I hauled myself stiffly out of bed, unlocking the door to allow her entrance.

'How are you? I can't see any bruises, it looks as though the ointment worked.' She peered intently at my face.

'I don't know which hurts more, my head or my legs.'

'What do you intend to do? Will you go to the milliner's today?'

'I have to.'

Hanna was concerned. 'What if he comes back?'

'I'm sorry, Hanna, but I don't want to talk of it. I'm sure that's the last I have seen of him.'

I desperately wanted to change the subject. 'It seems you were right, for I'm now more certain that if I had taken the room above the shop, Mistress Edgemore would have me doing work all night. I think I have made a mistake accepting the position, for she is bad tempered. I couldn't do anything right yesterday. When Lady FitzGerald's maid came to collect a new bonnet, she didn't want me to speak to her. It was only at the end of her visit that I was able to tell her I would be bringing the lace on Saturday.'

'But, Susannah, the shop would be open on Saturday,' said Hanna quickly. 'Didn't Mistress Edgemore tell you?'

'Not when I went to apply for the position, though I admit I never asked. She took great pleasure in saying as I was leaving that I was expected to be there. Now I have to go to Watermead on Sunday instead. The only way to do that and see Peter is if I miss church.'

'I wish I had never taken this position. I don't care about the extra income, Peter and I were doing well without it. Now I dread having to return.'

'Take my advice, Susannah. Don't make a hasty decision. If by tonight you feel the same way, then there's no reason why you should remain there. Go and wash up, then come to eat. You didn't have supper last night and must be hungry. We had roast lamb, I've set a good piece aside for you.'

With Hanna on her way back to the kitchen, I took a few moments to remain on the bed. I couldn't face putting my boots on again, so after locking the bedroom door behind me, I went out into the yard to wash my hands and face.

Hanna had indeed saved a good piece of roast lamb, accompanied by thick sauce with a large slab of bread. I hadn't realised how hungry I was, for I quickly devoured the platter of meat, which Hanna removed, replacing it with another, smaller one. By the time I had eaten everything my belly was aching, both from the punch yesterday and the food. I felt the need to lie down.

The eating room was busy; Hanna was rushed off her feet, so she was helped by one of the younger kitchen girls. Catching Hanna's eye, I waited for her to come to the table.

'Hanna, I need to go back to my room for my boots. I'll talk to you tonight.'

Merely nodding, too busy to talk, she continued on her way to the kitchen, carrying a large tray laden with dirty dishes.

Mistress Edgemore made no comment about the incident yesterday, and I hoped she had not heard of it. I found it very hard to do my work, thankful not to have to deal with customers, for there were hardly any. I ate my dinner as before in the garden, hardly tasting the food. When it was time for me to leave, the milliner barely acknowledged me.

I was frightened of walking back to the inn, but as I came down the steps from the shop into the lane, someone stood waiting for me.

'Master Beaker! What are you doing here?'

'I've come to make sure you get back safely.'

'Thank you, sir, that is kindly of you.' I was very relieved, and together we walked back to the Cross Keys in a companionable silence. Quickly stopping at the privy, I returned to my room. Not even taking the time to hang up my dress to release the creases, I threw it over the end of the bed. Pulling up the cover, I was instantly into a deep and dreamless sleep.

⋅⋅⋅⋅⋅

Woken early by the dawn chorus just before daybreak, I lay listening to the kitchen girls chattering among themselves, the light beginning to show through the thin linen that covered the window.

The lace pillow was always set up in my chamber, a half-finished piece lay covered by a cloth to prevent the dust settling on the delicate work. When am I going to find time to make lace now? It is dark before I get back, which means I will have to purchase extra candles from Master Beaker. The tallow ones are cheaper than beeswax, but they smoke badly, and the cost would soon add up. Would the cost of the candles make the lace worthwhile?

My legs and feet no longer ached for which I was thankful, though I had yet to put on my boots.

With my workaday dress and one good dress to my name, I decided today to wear the good one, arriving in the eating room to find it empty. Hanna must have heard me come in, as she quickly came through from the kitchen.

'Susannah, tell me the rest of the news from yesterday!'

I sat eating bread, cheese, and cold roast lamb. Between mouthfuls I told Hanna of the previous day's events.

'I'm glad you didn't take the room above the milliner's. I am sorry for your poor legs, it does take awhile to get used to standing all day, but it won't take long, I promise.' She left to serve another customer, for which I was grateful.

I sat looking out of the window. It had rained during the night, and the rooftops opposite were shining in the sun. I had stopped growing in height, my dress falling just above my boot tops, so mud from the streets was no longer such a problem. I wondered how Peter was today. His time at the joiner's was coming swiftly to its end. I knew then there would be different problems to think on.

I reminded myself I had to go to the stonemason soon to enquire about stones. I had a fair bit put by, which I kept in a chest that matched Peter's, given to me as a Christmas gift. This one differed from his own by having two secret drawers hidden in the base, which he had shown me with pride. In these I kept the larger value coins. At the time of giving he had said, 'They were difficult to do, Susannah, but it means that any contents are doubly safe, for only you, me and Master Chapman know of them.'

Hanna put the box of dinner on the table.

'I must get on, Susannah, one of the chambermaids is sick, so I have extra work to do. I hope your day is better, though, and don't forget to stand up to the old biddy! We will talk more tonight, hopefully by then you will have made a decision as to staying.'

'My thanks for the food, Hanna.' It was time to be on my way. I returned to my room to put on my boots, collected Ma's wrap and set off.

As I had thought, the streets were muddy with large puddles. I held my dress up with one hand, my dinner bag in the other as I made my way to the milliner's shop. Though early, many people were about. All bid me 'Good morning,' all friendly. I felt very fortunate to be living in Honiton where everyone was so kind.

As I walked to the milliner's, the time I was accused of stealing gloves came to mind. I realised I had never found out what happened, if the person responsible for the theft had been found, for it surely hadn't been me. I had never heard any talk of the culprit being caught. Thankfully, everyone else has forgotten about that terrible time, but I had to remember to ask when I saw the Watch, if only to help put it behind me.

Waiting outside the milliner's when the church bells rang for seven o'clock, the rain started again. With no shelter nearby, in the five long minutes it took for the door to be unlocked, I was soaking wet and as sour tempered as Mistress Edgemore.

Chapter 25 ❧

'Don't shake water all over the floor, girl! Mop it up quickly before we open the door! Don't just stand there, get on, get on.' I shook my head at the milliner's departing back.

By nature I thought of myself as a kindly soul who always thought well of others. I had originally thought that Mistress Edgemoor's bark was worse than her bite, but I had come to realise that wasn't the case. I doubted that I could ever do anything right, and resigned myself to accepting her for how she was.

When I spoke to Hanna about my concern at working with the milliner, she told me not to make a hasty decision. I had decided, after a great deal of thought, to work for one month to see how it went. That month wasn't to prove easy.

I conceded that owning a shop must have been hard for a woman alone, for I hadn't seen a husband, nor heard tell of one, and she was no longer young. Often I would see her holding her head as if it ached, her face pinched in pain, and I could sympathize with her, but that didn't excuse her hard, implacable character.

Bending over the lace pillow for hours at a time had the same effect on my back. It ached intolerably if I sat for too long at the lace, and I was considerably younger than the milliner.

Taking out the rag and bucket I wiped the floor, dusted the shelves, and then the counters. At eight o'clock by St. Michael's bells, I opened the door, turning the sign to 'Open.'

At the end of the day, instead of going back to the inn, I went to the stonemason's at the bottom of the High Street. Through the large wooden fence gate, I found myself in a large yard stacked with different coloured stone, dust thick in the air.

'Mistress, how may I help you?'

I jumped. 'Oh, sir. I've come about some markers for two graves, if you please.'

'Do you have anything in particular in mind?'

'No, but it will all depend on the cost. I have written out what I would like on each of them.' I reached inside my pocket for the paper I had prepared the night before. The mason took it from me.

'Well, this isn't much, let me see now, two markers you said?'

'Yes, sir.'

'The cost would depend on the stone, of course. If you want something to last, then it should be the granite. Would you want the markers to stand up or lie down? To have them lie down will be cheaper.'

'I hadn't thought of that. I think lie down please, and make them of the granite, if it's best.'

'Right, well, let me count the words.' He walked over to a hut that appeared to serve as both his work place and home, beckoning me to follow. Leaning on a narrow worktable, he counted, moving his fingers along to each word as he did so.

'There's thirty-seven words here. Let's say ten shillings.'

'For each one?'

'No, mistress, for the two.'

'That is very acceptable. When could they be ready? Would it be possible for you to deliver them? I would pay extra for your time. They are for my ma and baby brother who are buried in Offwell. If possible, could we take them on a Sunday afternoon? My brother is apprenticed to Master Chapman, and he only gets that afternoon off. He has an infirmity, cannot walk far, so if you could take your cart? I would willingly pay the extra required for your time and trouble.'

The mason laughed at this long reply.

'Yes, mistress, I could do that. I'll charge another shilling for hitching up my horse to the cart, but I haven't been out that way for many a year, it will make a good outing.'

'Thank you, sir'. At last! Markers. Wait until I tell Peter.

'When will they be ready?'

'Well, a week from today, which is next Tuesday. How about the Sunday after next, if your brother only has that time? You say he is infirm? If you can be here at noon, we'll go on and collect your brother, save him the walk.'

'Will you require payment in advance?'

'No, I know of you and your brother. Payment on the day of delivery will be sufficient.' I held out my hand, he taking it to seal our bargain.

'Thank you kindly. Peter will be pleased when I tell him the news.' I turned and waved to him from the gate. I was halfway to the inn when I realised I hadn't asked the stonemason his name. No doubt, Hanna or Master Beaker would surely know of it.

I was going to tell no one until I had spoken to Peter, but by the time I arrived at the Cross Keys, I couldn't hold the news any longer, and the excitement must have been plain on my face.

'Hanna, I can't believe it; I've commissioned two markers for Ma and baby William's graves! A week on Sunday afternoon the mason will take us!'

'My, that is indeed good news! I know you've wanted to do that for some time. It will help put yours and Peter's minds at rest.'

Master Beaker came into the eating room. Hanna said, 'Tell the master of your news, Susannah.'

'What news is this?' he queried, sitting down beside Hanna, he as pleased as Hanna when I told him.

٤٠٤٠٤٠

The following Sunday, I waited inside the joiner's as usual, the time until Peter was ready to leave almost unbearable. At last he was ready, and we slowly walked to what had become our usual seat overlooking the river.

'Peter, I have some wonderful news. I have commissioned a marker each for Ma and William's graves. They are to be ready one week from today.' His face lit with pleasure.

'This is indeed wonderful! Though how will you get them to the cottage?'

'I have arranged for the mason to take us. I am to be at his yard at noon; we will then come here with his cart to pick you up. From here we shall go to Offwell.'

'Us? You mean I can come, too?' I nodded. His face became red, his mouth quivering. Quickly he looked away.

Peter tried hard not to weep. Nevertheless, weep he did.

I gave him time to recover, gently touching his hand. 'It's all right, Peter, there's nothing to be ashamed of. You must be there, for I wouldn't go without you. This will be the first time you've been back, though I've been before.' To give him more time to compose himself, I told him of my visit both to the cottage then to Master Bentley, and of Mistress Bentley's death.

'Master Bentley was very kind to us both, and he promised that the next time he came to Honiton he would come and see me, but I haven't seen him since that time.' I also told him of Pa returning to Upper Hambley with a woman and child in tow, but that he didn't enquire of us. Peter sat for a while absorbing this. Deciding there was nothing to be gained from it, I made no mention of the attack on me.

'Well, we've got on all right without him, haven't we, Susannah? Thanks to you. I say she's welcome to him.'

'Yes, Peter, I would have to say she is.'

Peter, now recovered, was all excitement, his interest no longer with Pa.

'What's the cottage like? Has it fallen further? Will I recognize it? How long will it take to get there in a cart? What are the markers like? What do they say? What is the stone? How much did they cost?'

'Peter, how can I remember all those questions?' I replied, laughing. Telling him they were each made of granite, the cost, and the inscription, we spent the rest of the afternoon once more remembering our lives in Offwell, discussing how different they were now.

Towards the end of our time together, I asked Peter if he had enjoyed his apprenticeship.

'I have, though I feel badly for Master Chapman. The arthritis is very bad in his hands and knees, and he has a terrible time with the tools. I have learned so much from him. I couldn't have had a better master or mistress. I'll be forever grateful to the parish for helping me obtain the apprenticeship. I know I need to repay it one day.' He paused, looking sideways at me.

'Susannah, I've been thinking about my future, like I promised. Master Chapman cannot continue for much longer, and as you know, he has no sons. Here is a business ready-made. With my apprenticeship almost over, I am thinking of asking if I could purchase the business from him. I'm doing most of the work now, anyway, with Master Chapman spending his time talking to the customers. Perhaps we could continue in the same way, though with my name over the door, not his. It would mean that I would be able to stay in Honiton, for I've come to love it here, no wish to seek somewhere else. What would you say to that, Susannah? Would you be in agreement?'

'I would say nothing could be better! I think it would suit both you and Master Chapman. He would be able to stay involved as much as he wished, and you, as you said, with a ready-made business. But it would depend on the amount he would ask for it. I have quite a bit saved up from the lace, while you've been putting your wages aside. Between us, we should have a goodly amount. I'll count mine tonight, and you do the same. When we meet next Sunday we can talk of it further after we've been to the cottage and had the time to think it through, and make sure it is what you want.'

⋰⋱

The Friday before we were to meet, just before noon, I was assisting one of the ladies of Honiton select the right colour of ribbon for her bonnet when I heard the shop door open. Glancing up, I saw Lady FitzGerald enter. Coming from behind the counter, I curtsied.

'Your Ladyship! This is a pleasant surprise!' Hearing me, Mistress Edgemore flew through the curtain that divided the shop from the workroom behind.

'Lady FitzGerald, I am honoured you would visit my humble shop. What can I do for you?' All the time she had been talking, she had been moving in front of me, giving me no choice but to stand back, pushing up against the existing customer, who rightly objected.

'Mistress Edgemore, I came to see what new materials you have. I have need of a new bonnet; I am to attend court next month in London. I find myself in need something fresh and new.' She turned from the milliner to me. 'I also wanted to see Susannah.'

'Susannah, I heard of your employment here. How do you fare?'

'Very well, thank you, your Ladyship.' I was, in fact, worried, trying not to show it. Had Lady FitzGerald decided she didn't want the lace anymore, despite the words of the Mistress Dodd? If so, this would be a huge blow to our plans for the future. Lady FitzGerald turned once again to the milliner.

'I would like Susannah to assist me in my choice, mistress.' She untied her bonnet, placing it carefully on the table. 'Now, Susannah, what do you recommend?'

In one fell swoop she had effectively snubbed Mistress Edgemore, who looked as if she was ready to explode but daren't, fearful of losing the custom. Without a word, she swept back through the curtain to the back room. The shop was small; we all could hear things being moved about with force.

'But forgive me,' said Lady FitzGerald, 'you already have a customer. I'll wait.' She sat at the table, a small, satisfied smile on her face.

I spent another few minutes with the first customer selecting the ribbon, and when happy with her choice, she curtsied to Lady FitzGerald, and told me she would be back in a week for her own completed bonnet. I held the door open for her, bidding her 'Good morning.'

'Now, your Ladyship, do you have a colour in mind? What is the occasion?'

'I'm to go to court. My dress is green. Here, I brought a sample of the fabric with me.' She held out a large swatch.

'This makes it helpful. We do have some new fabrics in, let me show you what I think would suit both the dress and you.'

I pulled down bolts of fabric, walked along selecting various ribbons and laces, and laid all before Lady FitzGerald. Looking at them together, we discussed the advantages of each, time of no consequence to either of us.

'I think the choices you've shown me are very suitable; unfortunately, the time frame I need it in is somewhat short. I go to London in three weeks. Could you ask Mistress Edgemore to make it a priority?' However, the milliner, I knew, had been sitting in the back with ears flapping, listening to every word. Immediately she came through.

'Of course, your Ladyship, I can have it ready in two weeks, if that would suit you better?' Lady FitzGerald decided it was time to throw the milliner a small bone.

'That is quite suitable, thank you. I must say, Mistress Edgemore, Susannah has been particularly useful, you should be making more use of her skills.'

The milliner simpered. 'Oh I will, your Ladyship, thank you.'

The door opened again, all three of us looking round.

'Aunt, you're still here! How long it takes you ladies to chose a bonnet!' Lady FitzGerald stood.

'I'm finished, Thomas. I believe you've met Susannah before?' She looked between us, her eyes twinkling. The man turned to me. His smile reached his eyes, which were a beautiful dark brown. Tall and slim, he cut a very elegant figure.

'Indeed I have, Aunt.'

I frowned, trying to place him.

'Thomas Stanton at your service, mistress,' he said, bowing low. 'I believe I had the honour of purchasing a quantity of beautiful, if rather damp, lace from you years ago.'

Chapter 26 ❧

I stood still, aware I was staring, but for some reason unable to stop.

'Sir, of course I remember you, but it's been many years since we met. You have changed greatly.'

'As have you, mistress. When my aunt told me this morning she was coming to see you, I couldn't resist accompanying her. I understand you still make the lace?'

'That I do, while Lady FitzGerald,' I looked at my benefactor with a smile, 'continues to buy it from me.' I was aware that Mistress Edgemore was listening, committing to memory every word. Her face was flushed with excitement, while her hand was to her throat.

In the silence that followed, Thomas looked at me, while I looked at anything other than him. Lady FitzGerald stood up, put on her bonnet and tied the ribbons.

'Come, Thomas, we must not keep these ladies from their work. Mistress Edgemore has to start on my new bonnet, if it's to be done in time.'

Master Stanton bowed to me, then gave a very small bow to the milliner. He opened the door for his aunt, helping her into the waiting carriage.

'Well!' said Mistress Edgemore. 'Don't just stand there, girl, there's work to be done.' She gathered up the fabrics and ribbons chosen by Lady FitzGerald and hurried into the back. She was now even more full of self-importance, intent on making the bonnet that would go to court. I am almost certain that as she sat at her small worktable, her mind would have flown this way and that, imagining the custom that would now come her way. Once others found she had made a bonnet that was seen at court, it would be excellent for trade.

Within a few moments she was back in the shop to prove my thoughts correct. 'I wonder if I should put a small sign in the window. I will have to get more fabric and ribbons in, for the demand will be great,' she exclaimed, a smile on her face.

I stood at the counter gazing out of the window into the lane beyond. I knew not much more would be accomplished for the rest of this day.

Sitting in my room that evening working on a piece of lace by candlelight, I was suddenly overwhelmed with a sense of loss. What brought on these feelings, I could not say. They lay like a heavy blanket over me, threatening to push me down through the floor, never to rise again.

During the years since Ma's death, I had rarely allowed sorrow to take hold, all my energy going towards Peter and our mutual survival. For some reason, now, in the quiet of the inn as it settled for the night, Pa came to mind.

What had made him so angry? I had heard Ma tell of his young days, but his wasn't the only life beset by such hardship. How could he have been so cruel, particularly to Peter, who through no fault of his own couldn't contribute? Had Pa even given him the chance, for hadn't he done well when he started making the wood? Why hadn't he done so when our parents were alive? Or had they both assumed he was incapable? If it hadn't been for Ma, I had to wonder where we would have lived, for the cottage had belonged to her.

I was glad I hadn't told Peter of the attack on me. He could have done nothing to help, and the knowledge would only have vexed him. I could only hope no one in the town would make mention of it.

The candle spluttered, nearing its end. Thinking it would be better to sleep if I could than remain in this maudlin state, I covered the lace pillow and set it to one side. Undressed for bed, I knelt, giving thanks for the day, for those who cared for me, and for Peter. Within moments, I was asleep.

&&&&

'Susannah, wake up, for there's someone here to speak with you,' Hanna called through the door.

'For me? Who is it? It's not Pa?' I quickly put on my dress, opening the door just enough for Hanna to squeeze through.

'No, not your pa. It's a solicitor, said he had business to discuss. Quick, finish getting dressed. I told him you wouldn't be but a few minutes. Hurry now, he's waiting in the eating room.' She went back outside to disappear up the hallway.

Whatever does a solicitor want with me? I've done nothing wrong. I tied my hair back, then stopped quickly at the outside privy and hurried back into the inn.

'Mistress Brigginshaw?'

'Yes, sir, I am Susannah Brigginshaw.'

'Is there somewhere quiet we can talk, mistress?' He glanced at Master Beaker, who was hovering by the kitchen door trying not to look as if he was worried, for everyone knew that solicitors only ever brought bad news.

'Master Beaker, may we use your chancel room?' I asked.

'You may. Though I will be nearby if you need me,' he stated firmly, a warning look given to the solicitor.

Once inside, neither of us took a seat, for there was only the one. We stood facing each other.

'Mistress, I'm given to understand you are the owner of land in Offwell.'

'Me? Land? I think you must be mistaken, sir.'

'But you do have a cottage, of sorts, in Offwell?'

'My brother and I used to have a cottage in Offwell until if fell down, but that was many years ago now.'

The solicitor sighed, and persisted.

'But you did live there with your family, isn't that so?'

I was now worried, and admitted that was true.

'I understand the cottage passed to you on the death of your mother?'

'I believe so, but sir, there's nothing there now, for I was back recently, it's barely standing. I have to ask why you're asking me these questions, what business all this is of yours.'

'A fair enough question under the circumstances. However, forgive me, I should have introduced myself. My name is Jacob

Goodworthy. My practice is in Honiton. I have been asked by my client to approach you with the purpose of purchasing the land from you. Were you aware that the cottage sits on acreage?'

I felt my mouth drop open.

'No? Well, no reason why you should have known, I suppose. But it does. Four acres, to be exact. You are the entitled owner, Mistress Brigginshaw. My client, I am authorized to give her name, is Lady FitzGerald. She has instructed me to offer you two hundred guineas per acre, which would be eight hundred guineas in total.'

He hadn't taken his eyes from me all this time, watching my face turn from pink, to white and back to pink at the amount offered.

'Why would Lady FitzGerald want the land, my land, if what you say is true?'

'The towns and villages are growing by leaps and bounds; her ladyship needs the use of it, along with the access. I shan't expect an answer immediately, for I expect you'll want to discuss it with your brother. Shall we say I'll come back to see you in a few days' time, if convenient to you?'

I was speechless, my legs weak, without a word I reached for the chair, and sank onto it. Eight hundred guineas, if we were careful, would set Peter and me up for life with no more worries. We had enough of those.

'There is just one thing Lady FitzGerald should be aware of, sir. There are two graves under the oak tree by the cottage. My ma and brother William are buried there. If I decided to sell, I would need reassurance that the graves wouldn't be disturbed in any way.'

'Of course, and I thank you for mentioning it. I will speak to her ladyship about the graves. I am sure disturbing them would be the last thing she would want.'

Master Goodworthy admitted in all truth that he couldn't understand the reason for Lady FitzGerald's generosity. Land, when it did sell in Honiton, which wasn't often, went for a fraction of the price she was willing to pay. So what was behind the large amount? He couldn't work it out.

'Master Thomas Stanton mentioned he would be speaking to you, no doubt to encourage you to accept the offer.' The last barely registered; my mind was whirling round and round.

'That would indeed be convenient, Master Goodworthy, a few days' time, then.'

We spent a few more moments discussing various aspects of the arrangement, Solicitor Goodworthy eventually preparing to depart. The solicitor bade his farewell, stepping out into the hall.

True to his word, Master Beaker was outside the chancel door, arms crossed, glaring. He and the solicitor nodded at each other as the solicitor left the inn.

'Everything all right, Susannah? Not bad news, was it?'

Hanna also appeared, drying her chapped hands on a rag, also asking, 'Are you all right, Susannah? You look ever so pale. Perhaps you had best sit down.'

'I'm well, thank you both. No, it was not bad news at all. He told me that Lady FitzGerald is interested in buying the land where our cottage stands in Offwell. I always knew it belonged to me; Ma made sure I understood that, but I never realised it also had land attached. Peter and I used to think Pa was poaching when he caught the rabbits in the woods, but it seems it was ours all along. I can't believe it.'

Hanna and Master Beaker looked at each other, both wanting, but not liking to ask the amount.

They didn't have to. 'And she will pay two hundred guineas an acre.'

'How many acres are there?' Hanna asked, wide eyed.

'Four. That means eight hundred guineas for Peter and me.'

We all looked at each other.

'Eight hundred guineas?' repeated Hanna.

I nodded.

'You know what this means, don't you?' I asked, but they were both too shocked to answer. It would have been difficult, anyway, with their jaws down on their chests.

'It means Peter and me, we aren't paupers anymore.'

Chapter 27 ❧

Peter was only allowed Sunday afternoon to himself, but with news such as this, I felt a special visit was necessary.

Arriving at the joiner's just after it opened, I spoke first to Master Chapman. Explaining something of great import had occurred, I asked for time alone with my brother.

It must have been the look on my face, for he allowed the visit. We went into the back garden, taking a seat.

'Peter, I have some important news. A solicitor came to see me at the inn yesterday, a Master Goodworthy. You are aware that the cottage, along with the land on which it sits, belong to me?'

'Yes, I know it, Susannah. I didn't know about the land, though.'

'Lady FitzGerald, you know her, she buys the lace from me?' He nodded. 'She has offered to buy the land.'

Peter gasped.

'How much did she offer?'

'Two hundred guineas for each acre. All those times when we though Pa was poaching, it seems he wasn't! It was Ma's land all along! Lady FitzGerald says the towns and villages are growing, and she needs the access. What we never realised, Peter, was that the cottage sits on four acres. She requires it to widen the lane for the estate carts.' I hesitated, though Peter, I was sure, could guess what was coming, for why else would I have mentioned it?

'I have decided to accept the offer. The money can be put towards buying the joiner's business after your apprenticeship is over. You do understand why I'm selling, don't you?'

'Of course I understand, I hold no blame to you. As you rightly said, the cottage and land is yours to do with as you wish. But I want you to keep the money, Susannah, not use it for my gain. I've been fortunate enough; in truth, I have no need of it, for I've money of my own. Besides, it's important to me that I make my own way.'

I didn't stay much longer. Peter had to get on with his works, as did I. But I couldn't deny that I looked at the world through different eyes from then on.

⁂

Tuesday morning, when the bells of St. Michael's struck twelve, I called through to Mistress Edgemore, who as usual was sewing in the back room.

'I'll be gone for my dinner, mistress.' Collecting my dinner bag, I stepped outside into the fresh air. Straight away, I saw Master Stanton just turning the corner into the lane. He waved to me, and approaching, bowed low.

'Mistress, I was hoping to meet you.' He looked down at my hands, and must have noticed the small hessian-covered bag, rightly guessing it to be my dinner.

'My aunt is eager for your answer. I believe Solicitor Goodworthy told you he would return in a few days, but I am here in his stead. However, forgive me, I'll give you time to eat before I press you for it. Where do you normally go?' He looked around in puzzlement, for there was nowhere in view I could sit.

'In good weather I sit on the bench down the next lane, if that's acceptable?'

'Indeed it is.'

I was well aware of this tall, handsome man beside me, also that both of us were the subjects of intense glances from those passing by. Once settled, I opened the bag. Laying a napkin on my lap, I ate slowly, embarrassed that I should be watched.

Master Stanton, sensitive to my discomfort, quickly realised this and looked away, remarking on the various cottages along the lane, the disrepair of some, and the obvious pride of their owners in others. Farther down, two women sat outside one of the cottages with their lace pillows, and I watched them as they, in their turn, kept casting furtive glances our way.

As I folded away the napkin, returning it to the bag, I wiped my fingers.

'Master Stanton, I shan't keep you in suspense any longer. I have spoken to my brother on this matter. I have decided to accept Lady FitzGerald's offer at two hundred guineas an acre for the four acres.' I looked at him directly as I spoke. If I had learned nothing over the past few years, it was to 'start as you mean to go on.' It was best he, and his aunt, realise I would not be taken advantage of.

'I already have my aunt's instruction on this. She confirms the offer of eight hundred guineas, two hundred per acre.' He also wanted to make sure there was no misunderstanding, though Solicitor Goodworthy had made all very clear. He looked directly at me, I well aware I was blushing.

'I see.'

'That's all you have to say, mistress, 'I see?"

'Well, to be honest, sir, I thought you might be here to tell me your aunt had changed her mind.' I studied my boots. 'Are you aware my ma and brother William are buried there? I need both your and your aunt's word that nothing will disturb the graves.'

'Solicitor Gooworthy already mentioned them. You have our promise, mistress; they will both be treated with respect.'

'Then I will sell; I have already spoken to the solicitor. He has seen the deed, and will look after my interests, also.'

'Well, I expected no less from you, for you have struck me as someone who knows what they want, and more importantly, how to get it. My aunt will be well pleased.'

We sat in silence for a short while, both busy with our thoughts.

'You are going to Offwell, I believe, this Sunday?' How he knew of it I had no idea.

'Yes, the mason is taking Peter and me to place the new markers. I just hope the weather holds.' We both looked up at the sky which, for the moment, was free of clouds.

'My aunt's estate manager said his arthritis was hurting this morning, always a sign of rain, so he said. I, too, hope it stays fine for you.' He stood up. 'You'd best be getting back to the milliner's, she seems to be something of a harridan. I would not like for you to be in trouble because I have kept you talking too long.' We made our way back to the shop, neither in a hurry.

'I'll go straight back to Watermead to tell my aunt of the news. With Solicitor Goodworthy acting for both of you, the transaction should be quickly completed, maybe as soon as tomorrow.'

Still he lingered. 'Mistress, I would consider it an honour if you would allow me to accompany you and your brother on Sunday.'

'I'm sure we would both be glad of your company. Though I hope you would understand that we would like some time alone at the graves?'

All eager now, he replied, 'Take all the time you need. Perhaps the mason and I could travel farther on to Upper Hambley to check out the lane again for my aunt.'

'Until Sunday, then, we are meeting at the joiner's at noon.'

With a curtsy from me, and a bow in return from Master Stanton, we parted company at the door of the shop, Mistress Edgemore once more fit to bursting with curiosity.

I gave her a smile and went straight to work.

⁂

Sunday morning dawned, thankfully, bright and clear, though by ten o'clock clouds had rolled in, and the air was colder. I had asked Hanna to prepare enough food for four people, paying extra for the food and her trouble. When I was ready to leave the inn, I stopped by the eating room. Hanna came through, struggling to carry a large wicker basket.

'I have lots for you, a ham, veal pie, cold sausages, breads and cheeses. There's a jelly, apples, no need for anyone to complain of hunger!' She disappeared into the kitchen again, re-appearing with a large covered jug of ale.

'I've asked Samuel to come with his barrow to help you take it to the mason's.' Samuel was Hanna's friend, more than a friend really, for they hoped to be wed one day. The difference in their religion was, however, proving a barrier, Samuel's family refusing to allow him to marry a gentile. Hanna went out the front to see if he had arrived, which he had.

'Come on in to help carry the basket, if you please,' she called to him.

In he came, a dark-haired, ruddy-faced young man, with eyes only for Hanna.

'Thank you kindly, Samuel, for your help,' I said, though my mere talking to him made him uncomfortable. I couldn't help but like him. I hoped the differences could be put aside for both their sakes, for they were obviously in love.

'S'all right.' He picked up the heavy basket with ease, taking it outside, with me following, carrying the jug of ale.

'Good luck today,' shouted Hanna after us.

Samuel said not one word for the whole journey, while I took advantage of the silence by trying to decide how much to pay him for his trouble.

Once at the mason's, I knocked on the gates, which were closed, the yard not open for business on the Sabbath. Immediately they were opened, the mason waiting ready behind them with the horse and cart. Samuel loaded the basket and ale jug into the back, mumbling farewell.

'Wait, Samuel, how much do I owe you?'

'Nothing. All done.' Before I could argue, he pushed the wheelbarrow back the way we had come.

'Right, mistress. Let's go and get your brother and be on our way. I don't like the look of the weather that's coming in.'

We looked together up at the sky with its dark and lowering clouds. Hoping for the best, we arrived at the joiner's just on the stroke of twelve, Peter appearing within moments, followed quickly by Master and Mistress Chapman.

'Good luck, Peter. Good morrow, Susannah,' said Mistress Chapman as the mason helped Peter up into the back of the cart. With Peter settled, he stood in the shop doorway talking to Mistress Chapman while I took advantage of their chatter, speaking quietly to Peter.

'Another will be joining us, Master Thomas Stanton, who has helped us in the past. I hope you don't mind, Peter.'

I was worried Peter would be upset, realizing too late that I should have warned him in advance.

'Of course not, Susannah.'

Despite his words, I knew he was worried. 'Don't worry, Peter, I told him we would want to be alone at the graves.' At the sound of hooves, I looked up to see Master Stanton coming down the lane. 'Here he is now.'

All of us looked at the horse and rider, who approaching, said, 'Good morrow, mistress, Master Mason.' He looked at Peter. 'You must be Master Peter? I hope the weather stays dry for you today.'

'As do we all, sir,' replied Peter, who, I could tell by the look on his face, liked the look of this new acquaintance of mine. He also looked from Master Stanton to me, a small impish grin on his face, which I ignored.

The markers were lying flat, hidden beneath a canvas cover on the bed of the cart. Though it was tempting for us to look at them, we both, in silent agreement, decided to wait.

Once out of the town, the country sounds took over. The steady plod of the horse, Master Stanton riding behind, the grinding of the cart wheels on the hard earth. In the distance, we could hear cows and sheep, while the ever-present birds filled the world with noise, not bothered in the least by the dull weather.

Peter and me didn't speak beyond asking how each fared. My head was filled with so many memories that kept intruding one upon another; there was hardly time to finish one before another overtook it to jumble repeatedly. The time taken to reach the cottage seemed so short by cart, so long when travelled on foot. I had tried to think of a prayer to say at the graves, but now, as the time approached, I found my mind was empty.

'Here is the place, sir.' I indicated the large oak, standing tall, a goodly marker in itself. The mason pulled the horse to a stop.

'I'll get the markers down to where you want, then wait for you here.'

'I rather thought you and I could go on over to Upper Hambley, sir,' said Master Stanton. 'I have need to check the width of the lane betwixt here and there for her ladyship.'

The mason looked at me, to Peter, then up at the sky. The clouds were clearing; it was brighter, and the chance of rain diminished. He could see the cottage, or what remained of it.

He knew that if the rain did come, we would have nowhere to go for shelter.

'Why certainly, sir. We would be gone about an hour, if that's all right?' He looked at me for confirmation, as I was responsible for his hire.

'Yes, it would be. Thank you both for your understanding. The graves are round the back, sir.'

I stood waiting for Peter to be brought down from the cart and sort out his sticks.

Master Stanton slid from his horse to help the mason carry the markers round the back, both following me down the now almost lost path. Peter trailed behind as best he could, the weeds and long grass hampering the use of his sticks. I bent down, brushing aside the undergrowth. Finding first one wooden cross, then the other, I waited for Peter to join me.

'Thankfully the crosses you fashioned have made finding the graves easy, Peter.' I turned to the mason, who was behind me. 'May I see which one you have there, sir?'

He turned it around.

'That's Ma's. Here, if you please.' I pulled both the wooden crosses free surprisingly easily, laying them on the ground, then stepped aside to give him access.

He lowered the small stone marker to the ground in its place.

'The other, sir,' I looked at Master Stanton, 'here if you please.' The mason moved aside, making way. Master Stanton lowered the one he carried, adjusting it to my directions.

'Thank you kindly, sirs. Now if you wouldn't mind leaving us?' Without a word, both men walked back to the cart. Neither looked back, not wishing to intrude.

Peter looked around. 'I can't believe we used to live here; it seems so wild, so out of the way. I also can't believe how quiet it is after the noise of Honiton. Let's find somewhere to sit, Susannah.' We moved in unison towards a nearby fallen tree.

'I have spoken to Master Chapman on the matter we talked of, Susannah. He and Mistress Chapman were very relieved to hear I was interested in purchasing the business; it seems they were hoping I would want it. Without children, when something happens to him, she would be all alone. The business gave them a very good living, and while they do have some money put by, she would be out of a home. We talked long and hard, coming to an agreement late yesterday.'

'I will purchase the joinery as a turnkey business for fifty guineas which, Susannah, I have saved. Master and Mistress Chapman would continue to live above the shop, with him being as involved as he wants, only not with the making of things. Mistress Chapman would continue to keep house, and all that entails, for as long as she is able. Most important of all, the name over the shop would be changed to mine!' He looked at me, his wonderful smile spreading from one ear to the other. I didn't speak, and knew he had more to tell me.

'But that's not all, Susannah. The business is fast outgrowing the space we have now. I am looking at moving in, say, six months to a year. I already have my eye on a piece of land just outside the town for the workshop. It has the river nearby, which will make it easier to bring wood in. Everyone talks of the fires of '47 and '65 in town. The new building would be away from any danger. I plan to build a stone house on the hill there large enough for all of us.'

'None of the girls in the town seem to bother about my legs. One day I expect to marry, and anticipate many children. I would make sure there would be room enough for you, should you need it.' Here he stopped, then asked hesitantly, 'Do you have any plans in that regard?' His thoughts were obviously of Master Stanton.

'No, however, I'm young. When I do marry, I want it to be for love, to know that my husband will treat me well. I will not live a life like Ma's.'

This comment turned our thoughts back to the reason for our time here. We both looked over at the markers.

'I said one day there would be markers here, Peter. I am thankful I was able to keep my promise.'

'That you have, though I never doubted you would. Ma would hardly recognize us now, you so beautiful, and me soon to be a joiner with my own shop! Tell me, do you still have the doll I made for you?'

I laughed. 'Yes, Emma. She is still with me; she stays on my bed where I can see her every day. I talk to her, too. Remember when I said one day we would live in a house like Watermead, how silly I must have sounded.'

We sat in the shadow of the oak, the sunlight dappling through the branches, content just to be together.

'When I build my house, I will call it Watermead, if you want!'

'No, I thank you, Peter, besides, there can't be two houses in the town with the same name! No, this must be my house, paid for with my own funds.' I gazed off across the woods. 'Who knows, it might already have been named.'

'I so wanted to say a prayer, Peter, but now I'm here, I find I can't, the words won't come. I am so afraid of forgetting Ma and William.'

'That's all right, Susannah, there's no need. I'm sure we've both prayed enough over the years. Ma would understand. Neither of us will forget her nor William, never fear that.' He looked over at the graves. 'Having the markers is very important to us. I like the words you had the mason scribe on them. Let them be our prayer.'

We sat on the log, holding hands as we listened to the birds, to all the memories, while we waited for Master Stanton and the mason to return, so we could eat.

All four of us sat on the log behind the cottage, the food spread before us on a cloth Hanna had thoughtfully placed in the basket.

Eagerly munching our way through the feast, there had been little time for talk, each enjoying the sounds around us, each relishing the moment in time, if for different reasons.

Chapter 28 ❧

On the journey home, we stopped at the joiner's, the mason helping Peter down from the cart.

'Thank you for your many kindnesses, sir,' Peter said, 'Susannah and I are most grateful.'

'No need for thanks. It was a pleasant day, especially as the rain held off.'

I was standing beside the cart, waiting to hug my brother. 'I'll see you next Sunday, Peter, we'll have more plans to make by then.' I waited until he had gone into the shop, and turned wearily back to the cart.

'I'll take you back to the inn if you wish, mistress, for you won't be able to carry the basket and jug alone,' said the mason.

'I am grateful, sir. I find I am tired, and I have yet to pay you.' I pulled the coins from my pocket, handing them to him.

The mason put them into his own pocket, not checking the amount. He helped me into the cart, though this time to sit next to him, all the time watched by Master Stanton. In silence, the three of us made our way to the inn. Hanna came out to take the basket and jug. The mason bid his farewells, turning his weary horse towards the yard and its well-earned rest.

Master Stanton and I stood facing each other. 'Thank you, sir, for accompanying us. Also for giving us time to be alone.'

'Think nothing of it, it was my honour. But I must thank you, in turn, for the food, which was very thoughtful of you.' He paused. 'I understand the solicitor now has possession of the deed to the land?' asked Master Stanton.

'Yes, he collected it this morning on his way from church. With the proceeds of the sale, I shall require more advice, though I am unsure where to obtain it.'

'What kind of advice?'

'It will be a vast amount of money. Although I have a chest of Peter's making in my room here,' I indicated the inn, 'more will be too much to keep safe. I need to find somewhere safer.'

'Yes, I can see that. Would you leave that worry to me? I'm sure I can think of something.'

'Yes, sir, I would. Thank you again.'

With a final curtsy from me, and a bow from him, we parted company.

I went straight to my room, lying on the bed, holding Emma to my breast. I spoke aloud to the doll. 'Well, no one can ever say Ma and William lay in unmarked graves.' Before I realised it, I was asleep, the emotion of the day finally taking its toll.

I slept through supper, even though Hanna told me she knocked twice on my door. Unable to enter, for I always kept the door locked whether in or out, she had no choice but to leave me sleeping. Talking to her the next day, she had thought of trying to look through the window to make sure I was well. However, she thought that now the worry of the markers for the graves was over, I would be bone weary. How right she was.

꽃꽃꽃

The following week passed much as usual, the shop busy with autumn laying a heavy hand on the land. Ladies wanted new bonnets 'that are in fashion in London.' Both Mistress Edgemore and I were kept running.

The milliner, whether she admitted it or not, was rapidly coming to realise that I had a very good eye for colour and detail. With each passing day she left the customers more and more to my attention, whilst she was busy sewing frantically in the back room to keep up with the demand.

One evening, after a particularly tiring day as I was on my way back to the inn, I bumped, literally, into the Watch. Turning the corner into the High Street, my mind elsewhere, I hadn't heard the approaching footsteps. Apparently, neither had he, for we met with a bump.

'Oh! I'm sorry, mistress, forgive me. I wasn't watching where I was going.'

He stopped, peering at me.

'You are Susannah Brigginshaw, am I right?'

'Yes, sir.'

He shuffled his feet, looking down. 'Right, I've often seen you about town. I wanted to speak with you, but there has always been others around. I needed a private word, if you know what I mean.'

'No, sir, I don't.'

'No. Right. Well, I wanted to apologize, mistress. I know it's been a good few years that I should have spoken before, but, well, I hope you'll understand. It's about the gloves, you see, the ones you were thought to have stolen.'

'That I hadn't!'

'No. Right. Exactly. That you hadn't.' He drew himself up. 'What I wanted to say was, I'm sorry I had to take you into custody.'

Try as I may, I couldn't stay angry at this poor embarrassed man standing before me. My voice gentling, I replied 'I know that, sir, and I do thank you for the apology. Tell me, did you ever find the true culprit?'

Now he obviously regretted he had brought up the matter in the first place.

'Well, yes, but it's all in the past.'

'Not for me it isn't. Who was it, sir? I believe I'm entitled to know.' I looked right into his eyes, daring him to refuse.

'Yes, well, no doubt you are.' He looked around, making sure he wasn't overheard. 'It were one of the ladies in the shop that day, mistress, it was her what took them.'

'I see. I remember two ladies. Which one?'

'Um, right.'

'Come now, sir, you have just admitted I have the right to know. After all this time, I believe I deserve an explanation as to why my name was blackened.'

'Aye, well, it wasn't for long, you were out of gaol before you were hardly in it, as I recall.'

'That's not how I remember it. Her name, sir.'

'Um. Well, on the understanding it's not repeated?'

I gave no such understanding, just continued to look at him.

'Well, all right. It turned out it was the Widow Ribble.' He hurried on. 'But she's been dead these two years or more, so nothing to be done about it now.'

'Apparently not, but what was done about it before she died?'

'Um, well, nothing. You see, she returned the gloves, stating it was all a misunderstanding. With you coming into the shop all dirty, the glove-maker shouting at you like she did. She said she became frightened, put them in her bag by mistake in her rush to escape, and no one to argue with that.'

I stared at him, silent.

'Well, I must be off, for I've a lot to do before I can return home.'

Quickly he walked on before I could say anything else, though he plainly hadn't wanted to give Widow Ribble's name.

Well I never, the Widow Ribble! The Watch was right, who was to argue with her? She was one of the wealthiest people in Honiton. He would have been brave indeed to confront her. He was right; it was all in the past. In some ways, I regretted I had insisted on knowing the name of the culprit.

❧❧❧

The following Sunday, I was late arriving to meet Peter. I had suffered a sore stomach during the night and felt out-of-sorts on wakening. Foregoing breakfast, I stayed in bed all morning, visited once or twice by Hanna knocking on the door, asking if I needed anything, each time declining.

When the bells struck eleven, I dressed ready to leave, only to return to sit on my bed until nearer noon. Slow of foot, it wasn't until nearly a quarter past the hour when I arrived to find Peter, very agitated, standing outside.

'Susannah, what's the matter, why are you late? You are never late.'

'It's nothing, Peter. I felt a little unwell when I awoke; it's taking me a time to recover. But enough of me, what news do you have?'

He led me by the hand to the lane, a look of concern on his face.

When we were seated he said, 'I wondered if you could introduce me to the fellow who is helping you with the sale of the land. What was his name?'

'Solicitor Goodworthy.'

'That's it.' His face cleared, a smile appearing. 'I have such plans, Susannah; I can see them all in my head. I have a whole book of drawings. The most expensive part will be obtaining the wood I want to use, some of it will be very exotic and rare, but I know without doubt my plan will work.'

I was very quiet, not my normal voluble self.

'Are you sure you are well? Should you not see a physician?'

'No, Peter, do stop worrying. I am fine, I'm sure. I feel better just for seeing you. I think it's just, well, now the markers are on the graves, and you buying the joiner's business, it's all made me think. Am I going to be content to work with the milliner for long? I'm not interested in getting involved in trade. I only took the position to allow me to meet more people, and I have.'

I turned to face him squarely.

'As you know well, making lace is a very solitary occupation. I know the women of the town meet sometimes with their pillows to talk and exchange ideas, but I'm not one of them. I'm repeatedly making the same patterns, and to be honest, I'm tiring of it. I want more for my life, Peter.'

'I can understand that. I'm sorry if you are not fulfilled, but I'm at a loss to know how I can help. I would offer you a position in the shop, but with Mistress Chapman there, I cannot. You're right, you do need something more. You must have given it some thought?'

'Yes, but my mind goes round and round in circles, never coming to an end. With the money from the sale of the land I feel I should be using some of it for good, but what that is, I just don't know. I can't help all the families in town, but how can I even help one without the others?' I beat my fists on my lap. 'Peter, this is very irritating to me. I have to think of something!'

He laughed. 'You will, Susannah, you will.'

'I feel uncomfortable staying at the inn. Word will soon get around of my good fortune, then Master Beaker may feel I am taking advantage of his good will.'

'Then speak to him first. Ask him if he wishes to make changes to the arrangement. Even if he increases the rate for the room, you can afford it, Susannah.'

'Yes, I can. That's what I'll do, but why couldn't I work that out for myself? I do thank you, Peter. I knew once I spoke to you I'd feel better!'

The rest of the afternoon was spent in chatter, the final day of Peter's apprenticeship almost upon him.

As we parted, he said, 'If I think of anything of interest to you, I'll be sure to let you know. In return, if you would speak to solicitor Goodworthy on my behalf, I would be grateful.'

'That I will. I expect to see him very soon, for the sale of the land must be complete. I'll see you next Sunday, on time!' Waving goodbye, I walked back to the inn in the gathering dusk, the evenings already beginning to close in.

I stopped to speak briefly to Hanna, to be soon joined by Master Beaker. In thought of Peter's advice, I asked if I could speak with him privately. He was already aware of the offer I had received, though not that I had accepted it. When I told him the sale was almost complete, he was, as I expected, very pleased for me.

'That's wonderful news, no one deserves it more than you.'

'But, sir, because of it, I find myself in an awkward position. You have been very kind to me these past years, allowing me to stay here for such a peppercorn rent, but I have to ask if you wish to re-think my tariff, knowing as you do, of my good fortune.'

'I see, I hadn't thought of it.' He settled himself in his chair, steepeling his fingers as he looked out of the window. 'Well, let's say another shilling a week, how would that do?'

'If you're sure, sir, that would do well.'

'Right then, lass, we have an agreement.' He held out his hand, which I took gladly.

❧❧❧❧

Solicitor Goodworthy came the following day while I was at work. Telling him I could only speak to him during my dinner, and it was now nearly a quarter to twelve, he returned outside to wait, and paced up and down in front of the store.

When I emerged at noon with my dinner, he didn't wait for me to speak, plainly in a hurry to be on his way.

'Mistress, the sale of the land is complete, the deed now given to Lady FitzGerald. The funds, in gold coin, are in my possession. What would you have me do with them?'

'Could you hold them for another two days, sir? I have asked another for advice. I expect him to speak to me any time. Then, I will come to your room with my instructions.'

'That will be fine, mistress. If I am not there, speak to my clerk, he's always in, and he is aware of the transaction.' With a hasty bow, he hurried down the lane, intent on his next task.

I had eight hundred guineas. Me. Little Susannah Brigginshaw from Offwell. What should I do with such a fortune?

The afternoon trickled by, with just a few customers coming. Mistress Edgemore was sour tempered with me. It had proven true, my statement to Hanna, I could do nothing right. For no reason she would shout, waving her arms about like a windmill while she ranted and raved over the most trivial things. I had to wonder, yet again, why I continued to stay.

When five o'clock sounded on the bells, I was more grateful than usual to head back to the inn.

I quickly washed, and sat at a table near the window, well away from the fire. The wind had got up, causing it to smoke again. It gathered under the ceiling, movement below causing it to swirl about as if dancing with itself.

Hanna set a platter before me while I poured ale into a beaker when we both heard the front door of the inn flung open, and heavy footsteps pounding down the passageway. We looked towards the door as Solicitor Goodworthy ran into the room. He looked dishevelled, his eyes wide with fear. Obviously, he had been running, for he was out of breath.

'Mistress Brigginshaw, thank God you are here.'

'Sir, whatever is the matter? You looked scared to death,' said Hanna.

He ignored her.

'Mistress, I have terrible news.' Without asking permission, he sat at my table as he ran his fingers through his long, greying hair. 'I have terrible news, terrible news.'

'Sir, what is the matter?' I asked, now starting to worry.

'I hardly know how to tell you. It's my clerk, you see, mistress.'

'What about your clerk?'

'He's gone.'

'I'm sorry to hear that, but what has it to do with me?' I was relieved, for I cared nothing for his clerk.

'That's just it, mistress. He's taken your funds with him. I wasn't out of my room for long, just long enough to speak to you at the milliner's. Then I had two more errands to complete. Master Warren, he's dying, you know, he needed to make a new will before he meets his Maker. Then to Master Winston Greene who has business in London, though why he doesn't use a solicitor there, I'll never understand.'

I sat looking at him, my food untouched, glancing from time to time at Hanna, who looked as bemused as I felt.

'When at last I returned, the door to my room was open, the strongbox broken into. He's taken your money, mistress, every last gold coin.'

I could hardly believe it. My money was gone? On the same day I received it?

Hanna, seeing I didn't understand, took over.

'Have you called the Watch?'

He looked at her, aghast. 'No, I never thought of it, needing to tell Mistress Brigginshaw first.'

Hanna replied angrily. 'You should have called the Watch first. Every moment without the Hue and Cry means the clerk is getting farther and farther away.' She ran out, yelling for Master Beaker who was in the kitchen.

I sat, stunned.

'I'm sorry, mistress. He has been with me for five years, and never shown any tendency for thieving before, or I assure you, I would not have kept him in my employ.' He continually wrung his hands, as if hoping that would help his case. I was vaguely aware of Master Beaker coming and Hanna returning.

Within minutes the Watch appeared, only to drag Solicitor Goodworthy out of the room to be spoken to in private.

My only thought was, what would I tell Peter?

Chapter 29 ❧

The whole town was in an uproar. The Watch called for a large search party, all able-bodied men and boys assembling outside the inn. Most carried flaming torches, for night was rapidly approaching. While he waited for the men to gather, he asked the solicitor, amongst other things, if the clerk had kin nearby.

'Over to Alphington way, he does,' replied the solicitor, worry clear in his voice. 'His parents have a farm there. I dread to think what they will say when they hear what he's done.' He put his head in his hands, all apparently too much for him to bear.

'Are they still alive?' the Watch demanded roughly.

'He came to me a few years ago; perhaps they are, perhaps they aren't. I don't know.'

'If we had been told earlier, we could have caught him in daylight. Now it's going to be much harder.'

He glared at Solicitor Goodworthy who, with his face buried in his hands, didn't see. He seemed to have aged some ten years in the last few minutes.

The clerk had always been known as 'Solicitor Goodworthy's clerk,' his given name never used. Master Goodworthy roused himself enough to volunteer information.

'His name is Nicholas. Nicholas Skerrett.'

With a last annoyed look at the solicitor, and based on this information, the Watch and his group headed out of town, northwest to Alphington in search of the thief. Other men, settling into groups of eight or ten, went in different directions. All shouted the 'Hue and Cry.'

Master Beaker joined one of the groups, while Hanna and I sat on my bed waiting for news. I had no hope of sleep. Unfortunately, when it came, the news wasn't good.

The Watch, along with his group, returned just after dawn looking tired and drawn. He came, he told me, straight to my chamber.

'We found the farm he comes from; his parents were heartbroken when I told them. They thought their son had escaped their own life of hardship, and now they find he is a thief. Even I felt sorry for them. We searched in all the barns and outbuildings, but there was no sign of him. All the men will be making their way back by now, hopefully one of them have better news. Don't despair, mistress, we will find him sooner or later.' He left shortly after to well-earned sleep.

Master Beaker returned. With a shake of his head he told us they, too, had no success, leaving immediately for his own bed.

I was exhausted, Hanna also, though she headed to the kitchens just before dawn to prepare breakfast. Most of the men of the town had joined the Hue and Cry, but there were others who would need feeding, like the elderly and infirm.

As much as I wanted to stay awake in case of good news, or otherwise, my eyes closed of their own accord.

I didn't go to the milliner's, deciding instead she might as well be upset about this as for any other reason. I spent the day sitting in the eating room, though unable to eat.

≀▲≀▲≀▲

At ten o'clock the next morning, the Watch and his men set off again. Stopping to speak briefly to me, he said, 'I have an idea, mistress. Don't despair; I feel all will turn out well.'

I could only thank him for trying.

News came just before supper. Cheers could be heard, growing louder as they approached the inn. Hanna and I looked at each other, hardly daring to hope. The Watch came in first, followed by the men who had been out on the hunt with him, all smiling, all hot and thirsty.

'We got him! He was at his parents' farm, as I thought.' They all sat down at different tables, while Hanna rushed out to get ale and food for everyone.

'We searched the farm yesterday, as I told you, but then I thought, where else could he go? So I decided to go back to the farm again today. And I was right! He was hiding in the barn under the straw.'

I gave a huge sigh of relief. 'Thank you, sir, I am grateful. What of my money, sir, did he have it?'

'He did. I don't know how he got it all that way, for it was very heavy, being all gold coin. I've not heard a report that a horse and cart has been stolen, so he must have carried it, which is hard to believe. No doubt I'll get the truth of that out of him; I would hate to think he had an accomplice. It took all of us to bring it back, for it's a long walk and it is so heavy. We took it to Master Goodworthy's room, and left him counting it. It will be locked up safe and sound this time. I left two men standing guard over it, and over the solicitor.'

'Nicholas Skerrett is locked up in the gaol. He won't escape from there. The fool hadn't had time to spend any of it, he was too busy running away like the thief he is. Now he'll be transported, his parents out his support just when they need it most. What a fool.' He shook his head at the poor man's folly.

It took a long time to thank everybody, more and more men arriving at the inn as each of the search parties returned. It is a day I will never forget. No matter my feelings towards the Watch before, I had now been forced to rethink. It was only due to him that I had my funds returned to me.

In spite of all he had done, I did feel sorry for the clerk. He had to have been desperate to steal; now he would have to pay a harsh penalty, indeed. I didn't envy him or his parents.

Solicitor Goodworthy didn't appear, still feeling shame that his clerk had done such a terrible thing. I hoped he would come to see me, for I didn't hold blame to him. He had hired the clerk in good faith, and had no way of telling he would commit such a crime. I just hoped the Watch was wrong about an accomplice.

⁂

The following Sunday I spent as usual with Peter, then returned to the inn after six o'clock. I was no sooner through the door than Hanna caught me, tugging at my sleeve, pulling me into the eating room.

'Susannah, have you heard the news?'

'What news? I've been with Peter and heard nothing.'

'You'll never believe it!'

'Probably not until you tell me,' I laughed.

Hanna flapped her hands. 'It's all over the town; I thought you would have seen the crowds. Mistress Edgemore has had some kind of fit! Her niece came from Exeter on the coach for a visit, only to find her on the floor of the shop. I hear her mouth was spewing froth; her eyes were every which way, with hands and feet jerking around! Well, she called for help, the niece, not Mistress Edgemore, and people went running both for the Watch and the physician. By the time they arrived, she'd died, God rest her soul.' Hanna crossed herself. Though she wasn't Catholic, she liked to make sure she was fully covered by God's grace.

I stared at her, my mind trying to grasp the implications.

'What of the shop? The bonnets and caps? What of Lady FitzGerald's bonnet? She needs to go to court. Who's going to make them now?'

'I don't know, all I do know is it won't be the milliner! The niece is all of a twitter, apparently, hardly taking the time to bid her aunt a proper farewell. She didn't shed any tears, even false ones, that people could see. She just rushed upstairs to see what was there, according to the Watch. You mark my words; anything of value will already have been claimed. I expect she was looking for a will or some such. The talk is she's the milliner's only relative, so everything will go to her now. Can you imagine!'

I could. More importantly, what of my own position? And Lady FitzGerald's bonnet?

Chapter 30 ≈≥

I reached for the table nearby to steady myself, feeling with my hands for the bench, so I could sit down. I told myself to stop and think. With the loss of the position, for I was sure it was lost, what difference would that make to me? Was this really such bad news? With the sale of the land, I knew I would not be poor, the lack of wage not desperate for me. Try as I might, though, I couldn't feel grief-stricken. I had, after all, only known the woman a short while, and to be honest, had never actually liked her.

However, that didn't mean I couldn't feel sorry for her. I did. I also had to think of myself, of Peter. I knew he would do well, with such a promising future ahead of him. I had the lace, and Lady FitzGerald was still buying it.

Lady FitzGerald's bonnet! Someone had to tell her that now it wouldn't be finished for her journey to London. I jumped up.

'I have to go to Watermead right away. Lady FitzGerald was relying on the milliner for a new bonnet, for she is to go to court. She should know of this immediately.'

'But you can't! It's almost full dark, you can't go now.' Hanna was openly panicking.

I knew she was right, that I shouldn't go, for there was no telling what terrible things could befall me alone and in the dark.

'Well, I'll hire a cart to take me.' I stood up, turning first one way then the other, unsure what to do first. Hanna pulled at my sleeve.

'Susannah, sit down!' she insisted. 'You can't go now. You won't be going to the milliner's tomorrow, or do you have a key to the door?'

I shook my head.

'Then you can go to Watermead tomorrow, in the daylight. If you left at dawn, you would be there early, with no danger to you. Think, Susannah, this makes more sense.'

Hanna was right; I knew I had to wait until the morning. 'Yes, that does make more sense.' I laid my hand on Hanna's arm. 'Thank you, for I wasn't thinking clearly; after all, it's just a bonnet!' But a very important bonnet.

I spoke to Master Beaker and told him I had to leave early tomorrow morning, for I must go to Watermead to tell Lady FitzGerald of Mistress Edgemore's death.

'She has need of a very important bonnet, which remains unfinished,' I explained.

'Aye, I heard the news. Tragic, very tragic. She'd been a widow for many a long year, her husband dying of the fever quite young. She also lost two children, both stillborn. A sad life for sure. An even sadder ending, dying all alone like she did.'

'I never knew of her losses, for she never spoke of them.' Though I felt sorry for the milliner and the way of her passing, I was determined not to dwell on it. My thoughts were for the living.

'I bid you good evening, sir. I must have my supper and get to bed. I have a long day ahead of me tomorrow, and I'm no longer used to walking such distances.'

After supper, I locked myself in my room, lying once more on my bed. Cradling Emma, my thoughts ran to how insecure my life had become. When I had left the shop last, Mistress Edgemore had been well, and for her, relatively happy. I knew I had to make the most of my life, every single moment of it, for none could tell what the future would bring.

It was strange the next morning, walking up the drive to Watermead with no lace in my hands. I knocked on the back door, then stepped back as I waited for someone to answer.

The frightened face of a maid appeared round the barely opened door.

'Oh it's you, Susannah, I was afeared it was a wanderer. There have been sightings lately, and they have done some dreadful things! But come away in.' She stood aside while I entered, then peeked furtively outside, making sure no one else was about. Closing and locking the door, she said, 'You are here early, have you brought some lace for her ladyship?'

'No, I need to speak to Mistress Dobbs, if you please.'

'Wait here. Would you like a drink? Or something to eat? There's some nice fresh bread just out of the oven.'

'No, I'll just take a seat, if I may, for my feet are very sore.' The maid disappeared, returning shortly with Mistress Dobbs.

'Hello, Susannah, you are here early.' She looked at my face, knowing instinctively something was wrong. She took a seat beside me at the long kitchen table.

'Whatever's wrong?'

'It's about the new bonnet her ladyship ordered. I'm afraid it won't be ready.'

She was instantly alert. 'What do you mean, it won't be ready? Her ladyship told the milliner it was to be made a priority!'

'I know that, but the milliner died of a fit yesterday.'

'Died? Of a fit? The milliner?'

I sat silently while she absorbed this.

'How could this be?' She looked at me. 'Can't you finish it?'

'Me?' I squeaked. 'No, I can't. I have no idea how to make a bonnet, let alone one for someone as important as her ladyship. No, I'm afraid that's out of the question.'

'I see. Wait here while I speak to her ladyship,' and she almost ran out of the kitchen.

'Are you sure you wouldn't like something to drink?' asked the maid who had let me in.

'No, but thank you.'

Within very short order, the lady's maid returned. 'Follow me,' she said, slightly out of breath.

I had never been past the kitchens before, and I trailed behind her, trying to look in all directions at once. Through doors, along corridors, up and down stairs, until we came to a stop before two large wooden doors.

'Wait here.' She knocked on the door, and then entered without waiting for a reply, at least, none that I could hear.

I looked around. We were on the second floor of the house, and I could look over the banisters to the floor below. The black and white floor showed beautifully from on high. All those years ago I had promised myself I would have a fine house like Watermead one day. What a silly girl I had been.

'Come in, if you please,' said the maid.

I turned to see her holding open the doors.

The room I entered was beautiful, full of light even though it was early in the day. Large red rugs covered the floor, with hardly space between to see the wood, and mirrors on every wall, which reflected the light even more. At first glance, the whole room seemed to be a sitting area. The chairs, of which there were many, were large and comfortable looking. Tables holding branches of candles stood against the walls.

A fire burned in each of two grates, one at either end of the huge room. All the tables had candles, either singly or in candelabra, burning on them. What a waste of candles, there is light enough without them.

Mistress Dobbs gestured. When I looked to my right, I saw Lady FitzGerald sitting, waiting for me.

She was dressed in a beautiful blue silk over-robe, and matching slippers peeked out below. Her hair had already been arranged, blue ribbons that matched her robe woven intricately between the curls.

'Come here, Susannah, what's this I hear about my bonnet?'

I walked over, stopping to curtsy as I drew closer. Only then did I notice another, who stood at my arrival.

'Mistress, this is a pleasant surprise!'

'Master Stanton, good morning. I've come about her ladyship's bonnet.' I turned to Lady FitzGerald. 'I'm sorry to bring such sad news, but Mistress Edgemore died yesterday. I wanted to come last night to tell you, but couldn't make the journey in the dark. I came as soon as I could. Your Ladyship, I am unable to finish the bonnet. I have had another thought, though. There's a milliner in Exeter who has a good reputation for work of the very highest standard. You have chosen all the ribbons, lace and fabric, and I know that Mistress Edgemore had already formed the base. May I have your permission to take it to Exeter and explain the situation to the milliner there? I would be willing to stay there until the bonnet is finished, then bring it straightaway to you. I could be back by Wednesday, Thursday at the very latest.'

Lady FitzGerald sat back, her hands relaxed on the arms of the chair.

'Sit down, Susannah. I would need the bonnet by Friday morning, you are aware of it?'

'I am, your Ladyship,' I replied, taking a seat on the edge of a chair.

'Where would you lodge?'

'That I cannot say, for I've never been to Exeter, but I am well able to take care of myself, never fear.'

'I know you are,' she said drily. 'How do you propose to get to Exeter?'

'There's a coach that leaves Honiton this afternoon. If I hurry back, I could hire passage on it.'

Lady FitzGerald sat watching me, while I thought how she had aged since we had met in Offwell.

'Tell me, are you interested in learning the milliner's trade?'

'No, your Ladyship. I was only interested in keeping busy, meeting new people, new experiences. But becoming a milliner? No, that's not for me.'

'I am relieved to hear it; you are far too intelligent for that. I believe you read now?'

'I do, and write well, too.'

'Who taught you?'

'My brother, Peter. He had to learn for his apprenticeship, and in turn he taught me. I knew my figures before, I learned those with Ma. She would hardly believe I can now read.'

Lady FitzGerald stood up, me following. 'Very well, take the bonnet to Exeter. But if you are to get the coach in time, you must hurry. I'll get my estate manager take you back to Honiton in a cart. Do you have money for lodgings?'

'I have the coin you paid for the land in Offwell, though that is kept locked up, and I don't have ready access to it.'

She called her maid who was standing away from us by the door. 'On the way out, give Susannah ten guineas to pay for expenses.'

The maid bobbed up and down in acknowledgment.

'Keep close account now, Susannah. No doubt the milliner will require extra for the rush.'

Her ladyship addressed Mistress Dobbs, 'Leave us alone.' Without a word, she left the room, closing the door quietly behind her.

'I am glad you are here, Susannah. You are sure you are content with the sale of the land?'

'Yes, your Ladyship, for I had no use for it. My only concern was of the graves, but Master Stanton has put my mind at ease.' I looked at him with a small smile. 'Peter and I recently put gravestones there. Master Stanton was kind enough to accompany us. I feel at ease to know they will come to no harm.'

'Rest assured nothing shall be allowed to disturb them. Be on your way, and come back to Watermead as soon as you can. Godspeed, Susannah.'

I curtsied to Master Stanton, who had opened the door for me. I followed the maid back to the kitchen. If I had been left to find my own way, I would have been hopelessly lost. She handed me the ten guineas, sending the estate manager to arrange a cart and driver, but before he could be called, Master Stanton appeared, addressing the maid, 'No need, I'll take Mistress Brigginshaw back to Honiton.'

The women in the kitchen stood still, gaping. I knew what they were thinking. Master Stanton himself driving this girl back? Whatever was it coming to?

'Oh no, sir, I will be grateful for the estate manager to take me.'

'I have to go to Honiton as it happens; I'm joining friends for dinner. We'll take the carriage, if that's all right with you?'

Before I knew it, I was on my way, riding in style. Sheltered from the wind, I sat opposite Master Stanton.

'This is very good of you, mistress, to care so much for my aunt's bonnet.'

'Her ladyship mentioned it was needed for court. I wouldn't see her disappointed.'

'Still, it's a long way to Exeter. Have you been before? Indeed, have you ever ridden in a coach?'

'No, sir, never to Exeter. Though I've been in a coach once before, her ladyship took me to Watermead to show me where to bring my lace.'

He laughed. 'Well, you are in for an experience,' though he didn't elaborate further. I tried not to keep looking at him, looking instead at the countryside as it sped by. Whenever I gave him a quick glance, his eyes were on me, a small smile on his face. I looked at his hands, noticed they were large and strong, the nails well cut and clean. He sat, relaxed, leaning against the side of the carriage, completely at ease, while I sat in the middle of the opposite seat, upright and stiff.

'It seems such a long time since I met you by the stream. How you've grown,' he commented.

'Well, sir, that was many years ago. I notice changes in you, too.'

'You do? So you remember me?' He leaned forward, his arms resting on his knees, eager to hear more.

'How could I forget the man who bought my lace the day I turned my ankle?'

He waved his hand in dismissal.

'It was nothing, and the lace was very fine. You still make it, I believe you said.'

'I do, her ladyship's kind enough to buy it from me. Though what she does with it all, I just can't fathom!'

'I believe she sells it to someone who truly appreciates it.'

'I would hope so, for it is very time-consuming work.'

'Is that what you want to do for the rest of your life?' I was taken aback, for this was a question far too familiar for such a rare acquaintance. I looked at him, eyebrows raised.

He saw he had offended. 'Forgive me, I don't mean to pry. There's nothing wrong with making lace, I just wondered if you had other dreams, as yet unfulfilled?'

'All I know, sir, is I want something more for my life.' I indicated that was all I would say by looking out of the window.

The carriage stopped outside the milliner's, the footman helping me down.

'Thank you for the ride, sir; it has saved me a good deal of time.'

'Good luck in Exeter, mistress. If you need assistance, send word to me.'

Before I could answer, the carriage started on its way, leaving me standing in the street, wondering what assistance I could need, or that he could provide.

Chapter 31 &

There were three women waiting outside the milliner's shop to speak to the niece, who wisely kept the door locked. Two of them, it turned out, had already paid in full, and were now demanding their goods, finished or not. The niece, only speaking to them from the upstairs window, well out of harm's way, was in turn demanding more money for the bonnet's release.

When I arrived by coach, then awaited entry after stating I was there on Lady FitzGerald's business, I explained to the women I was to go to Exeter on behalf of her ladyship with a bonnet. It added fuel to the fire when the niece came downstairs, only allowing entry to me.

She had been obstreperous, refusing to hand it over until she had been paid. Thankfully I had the ten guineas I had received from Mistress Dobbs, and used some of it to claim the bonnet. I also asked for a hatbox in which to keep it safe. When I came out, the women were still there.

'Why should Lady FitzGerald's bonnet be more important than our own?' One of them asked, but I had no ready answer. When I looked back into the shop, the niece had already retreated upstairs.

There were, it seemed, only two items of talk in the town. The first was of the milliner's funeral, which had been arranged for the following day. The second, seemingly more important to the ladies of the town, was what would become of the shop's contents. It appeared that most of the bonnets had been left half finished, causing me to wonder what Mistress Edgemore had been doing in her workroom the last little while. All knew I had been employed there, so I couldn't help but feel it a good thing

I would be in Exeter for the next few days. The furor would soon die down, some other piece of news taking its place.

From there, I had gone straight to the inn to pack some clean linen along with my best dress.

Hanna prepared some bread and cheese wrapped in a cloth for the journey, handing it to me as I made for the door. I had asked Master Beaker if he had a bag I could borrow, and Hanna brought it to my chamber.

The coach stood waiting in its usual spot for its passengers at the bottom of the High Street. Black with gold paintwork round the wheel arches and doors, it looked large and impressive. There were stains on the paintwork on the outside of the doors and the windows, which I couldn't recognize, though I didn't think too much on it, so much else catching my attention.

The four horses, unmatched in colour, stood with their feedbags on, contentedly munching as they rested in the sunshine. It wasn't until I was standing at the side of the coach that I realised how big it was. I had seen it before, of course, but never this close. The coachman stood beside it shouting loudly, 'Departing. Departing in five minutes.'

'Please, sir, may I buy one seat to Exeter?'

He turned to me. 'You have the fare? It's sixpence.'

I held out a shilling, waited for the change.

'Hand me your bags, I'll put them up top.' He saw my look of concern. 'Don't worry, it shan't rain.' He made as if to take the hatbox from me.

'I'll take it inside with me, sir. The other bag can go up top, and thank you.'

'Suit yourself.' The second coachman stood on top of the roof. My bag was flung up to him, and he secured it with rope.

I climbed up the steps and took a seat next to the window, the hatbox held safely on my lap.

I thought it very dark and small inside the coach, full of odd smells that bothered me. The seat was hard, and with space for a further five passengers, it would be very cramped should all the seats be occupied. There was space for another passenger outside, between the coachman and his companion, the man who blew the horn.

One other lady paid her fare, climbing up to sit opposite to me. She was older and smiled as she settled.

'Good morning,' I said, to be answered with, 'Good morning to you, Mistress Brigginshaw.'

'You know of me?'

'Of course, I know most of Honiton's inhabitants. I was sorry to hear of the death of Mistress Edgemore, especially that your position there had come to an end.'

'Yes, thank you, but forgive me, for though I recognize you, I do not know your name.'

'I am Mistress Troak. I do not, or perhaps under the circumstances I should say, I didn't, use the milliner in Honiton. I prefer to buy my bonnets and caps in London. I travel there regularly to meet with my brother.'

'I've never been to London. This will be the first time I've visited Exeter, I hear that's very large. Is London larger?'

Mistress Troak laughed. 'Yes, many times larger than Exeter. What's the purpose of your journey there, if I might ask?'

'I'm on an errand for Lady FitzGerald. Mistress Edgemore was making a bonnet her ladyship requires quickly. I have to take it to a milliner to get it finished before Friday.'

'It must be a very important bonnet to require you to take it all that way for finishing.'

'Yes, it is. May I ask in return, why you are travelling?'

'I usually visit once every couple of months, just to make a change of scene. Also, it gives my maids a chance to air out the house. I'm a widow and find my life here grows tedious after a while. Where do you intend to stay, mistress?'

'That I don't know until I arrive. My first thought is to find a milliner prepared to help at such short notice, and only then will I look for lodging.'

'I know of a milliner, I'll show you the way to her shop, if you wish. I could also help you with lodging. I stay with my nephew who has a very large house with many empty rooms. You can stay there with me.'

'That would be very kind, on both counts, mistress. But are you sure your nephew wouldn't object to having a stranger in his house?'

'I can vouch for your good standing, so don't worry about that. His house is always open. Tell me, what do you mean to do with yourself now your employment with the milliner has ended?'

'It's been such a whirlwind, I haven't really given it thought.' However pleasant she seemed, I did not intend to discuss my recent good fortune with a stranger.

It was apparent there were to be no more passengers this day, for we felt the coach sway wildly as the driver climbed up to his seat.

With one hand I clung on to the window frame, and with the other I put the hatbox on the empty seat beside me. I found myself excited at the mere thought of my journey.

'Departing, departing!' cried the coachman again, the loud horn blowing a warning for everyone to be out of the way of the speeding horses, their feed bags now removed.

After only a few moments of the bumping and swaying, I felt sick. This didn't bode well, for we were still in Honiton.

'Are you not feeling well, Susannah?' Mistress Troak looked at me with concern.

'No, I feel very sick.' My face felt hot, beads of perspiration quickly gathering on my brow and upper lip.

'Quickly, take this.' She reached under the seat, pulling out a dirty tin bowl. Handing it over just in time, I retched, then brought up my breakfast.

'Don't be embarrassed, it used to happen to me all the time before I got used to the motion of the coach. When we slow down we can empty the bowl out the window.'

I realised, with horror, what the strange marks were on the sides of the coach. I thought I would never feel well again. Clutching the bowl, my stomach heaving, I just wanted this nightmare to be over. The very thought I would have to return the same way was too much to bear.

Several hours later, all best forgotten, Mistress Troak spoke. 'Look, this is the beginning of Exeter.'

In my misery, I didn't look outside; the countryside rushing past was making me feel worse. I sat as still as the swaying coach would allow, my head back, eyes closed. Travelling at unbelievable speed, we hadn't slowed sufficiently to empty the bowl, the stench now almost overpowering, which Mistress Troak kindly pretended not to notice.

When we eventually stopped moving I cautiously opened my eyes as the coachman came to the door, pulling it open.

'Give me the bowl.'

In one movement, he tipped the contents into the street.

My stomach heaved again.

'Don't look,' my companion advised. 'Take up the hatbox and let's look for that milliner.'

I felt far too ill to walk, indeed I didn't think my legs would carry me; all I wanted to do was to lie down.

Emerging with caution from the coach, I saw my, or rather Master Beaker's, bag brought down from the roof and dumped on the street.

'Come, Susannah, you will feel better soon.'

With no choice but to follow Mistress Troak, I picked up the bag.

The comparatively fresh air of Exeter did, in fact, clear away some of my wobbles, but not enough to make me feel like my old self. Certainly not enough to look where we were heading, so I merely followed the skirts of Mistress Troak in front of me.

'Here it is. You go in first.'

I looked up; a double-fronted shop stood before me. The doors and windows were painted a bright blue colour, while each window was full of the most beautiful bonnets and caps. Ribbons hung in a cascade of hues to the side.

Inside there was not one, but three tables with mirrors for customers, and easy chairs available for those waiting.

'Yes, how may I help?' A rather large lady stood behind the counter. On her head was an exquisite lace cap with flounces and ruffles abounding, steel grey hair peeking from beneath. She wore a dark red dress, over which a large Honiton lace stole covered her shoulders. It was, quite simply, breathtaking.

Mistress Troak stood aside, letting me speak.

'Please, mistress, the milliner in Honiton died yesterday. She hadn't finished a bonnet for Lady FitzGerald, who requires it for a visit to court this Friday. It is almost done, but her ladyship has asked me to bring it here for you, hopefully to finish.'

'You said it was for Lady FitzGerald? Well, open the box, let me look.'

I put the box on a table, taking off the lid.

The milliner took out the base of the bonnet, holding it up while twisting it this way and that, inspecting the inside as well as the outside.'It is nearly finished. Did you bring the rest of the fabric?'

'Yes, mistress, it's in the box.' The milliner delved in once more, bringing out handfuls of lace and ribbon.

'When must it be finished by?'

'Wednesday morning, for I have to get it back to Watermead by Thursday morning.'

'It will be expensive,' she warned. 'I'm very busy with my own work, as you can see.'

Indeed, I could. In the short time we had been in the store, several ladies had entered, approached immediately by one of the milliner's assistants. When I looked around, all three tables were occupied with customers.

'Yes. Her ladyship is aware it will be.'

'Very well, return Wednesday morning. The cost will be three guineas. In advance.'

I handed over the coins. 'Thank you, mistress.'

With a small nod, the milliner quickly disappeared behind a door, presumably to a workroom beyond, leaving her assistants to earn their wages.

Mistress Troak had been looking at the displayed, finished items, holding up bonnets to her face, looking in the wall mirrors.

'Thank you, mistress, for bringing me. It's a relief to know all is in hand. More importantly, that it will be ready in time.'

'It was not an effort; it is on the way to my nephew's. If you're finished here, we will go straight to his house. I could do with a wash and something to eat. No doubt you could, too, after losing your breakfast.'

My bag grew heavier with each step, the street seemingly endless; I hoped we didn't have to walk the length of it. With traders crying their wares at every shop front and people shoving to get through the crowds, the racket was indescribable.

Just when I couldn't go any farther, we turned off the main street, walking along for another few minutes. We came upon a waist-high gate set in a dry stone wall on our right hand. It was only when Mistress Troak stopped to open it that I looked up to see a church, and realised we were about to enter a churchyard. I found myself, gratefully, in an oasis of calm.

Mistress Troak's nephew was the Rector. No wonder she said he had many spare bedrooms, for the manse, set to the left of the church, was huge. I counted ten windows across the top, four on each side of the front door. A large porch protected the front door from the worst of the weather. On either side were wooden benches, handy for sitting and removing wet or muddy boots.

Mistress Troak used a metal pull to the right of the door, but no sound could be heard either inside or out. I stood nervously, wondering what I would do if her nephew considered it an imposition, his aunt bringing a stranger to his home.

The subject of my concern opened the door himself. A small, almost stunted man stood before us, a smile of welcome on his face.

'Aunt, as usual, a delight to see you,' he came forward to kiss her. 'Who is this with you?' He looked inquisitively at me.

'Richard, please allow me to introduce Mistress Susannah Brigginshaw.'

I curtsied.

'I know of her from Honiton,' she said. 'As we were travelling together in the coach, and she had no plans where to lodge, I knew you wouldn't mind if it were here.'

'No indeed, Aunt. In God's house, all are welcome.' He stood back, bowing us inside then leading us into a sitting room. We both removed our wraps, for the room quickly proved to be very hot, a huge fire burning in the grate.

'We would welcome something to eat and drink, Nephew. Susannah was dreadfully sick on that awful coach, I'm sure her stomach must be empty,' she smiled at me in sympathy.

The Rector immediately rang the bell beside the fireplace.

While waiting for it to be answered he said, 'I expect you would like to refresh yourselves first.'

'I'll get a maid to show you where you will sleep, mistress.'

'Thank you, sir, I would be most grateful.'

The door opened, the young maid standing there silently.'Ah, Daisy, my aunt has brought a guest. Would you show her to one of the bedrooms? While they are refreshing themselves, please bring in some food and drink for us all.'

'Yes, sir. Follow me, if you please.'

I presumed she was talking to me, though she didn't glance in my direction, appearing shy. The girl picked up my bag while I carried the empty hatbox. At the top of the stairs, we turned to our right down a long, dark corridor.

'This room if you please, mistress. Shall I unpack your bag for you?'

I was taken aback. 'No, but I thank you. I just have a few things. Perhaps I could wash. I was rather unwell in the coach.'

'I'll bring hot water straight up. Nasty things, those coaches.' She disappeared back down the hall while I walked into the bedroom, standing with my mouth open.

A huge four-poster bed draped with embroidered curtains took pride of place between two long windows. There was a fireplace to the left, laid ready, but not alight. At an angle in front of the fireplace stood two comfortable-looking chairs. A wooden cabinet was behind the door, and when I looked inside, I saw it was a place for storing clothes and linens. With such a fine house and contents, this, surely, was no ordinary rector.

The maid returned with a jug of steaming water carried carefully in both hands, a white linen cloth over her arm.

Pouring the water into a bowl on a table by the cabinet, she said, 'If there's anything else I can do, just call down. I'll come back to light the fire a bit later, it gets real chilly at night.' With a quick curtsy, she disappeared once more.

I sat on the bed, which was so high a small ladder was necessary to climb up. I felt utterly exhausted, wanting only to lie down, though I knew I couldn't stay upstairs; I had to go down, be polite.

Rousing myself with an effort, I quickly washed, returning downstairs to the sitting room to rejoin Mistress Troak and the Rector.

Chapter 32 ❧

I tapped on the door of the sitting room, waiting to be beckoned in.

Pulling it sharply open, the Rector said, 'Come in, come in, no need of knocking, mistress. Think of this as your home. Do you feel better? Good, good. Do sit down; we have tea and cake ready. We will be dining at seven-thirty, after Evensong.' He guided me to the settle, indicating for me to sit beside his aunt.

'Thank you, sir, Mistress Troak, for your kindness. I do feel better. It's the first time I've ridden in a coach. It was the movement that, well,' I paused, remembering the journey with a shiver.

'I understand, no need to go further,' said the Rector, interrupting me with a smile before I could go into detail. 'My aunt tells me you have brought a bonnet to town to be finished. You will be with us until Wednesday morning?'

'That is right, sir, but if you feel it an imposition, I can find lodging elsewhere.' I accepted tea and a plate of cake from Mistress Troak, placing them on a small round table beside my chair.

'Not at all, it will be good to have someone young in the house, won't it, Aunt?' Though he addressed her, his smile was for me.

'Indeed it will, Richard.'

I looked around the elegant room. I hadn't realised that Rectors were so well paid. Surely, he had to have a private income to supplement his clerical wage. There was a large oblong table in the corner, set against the wall. It held various magazines, stacked one on top of another. I longed to look at them, so leaving the Rector and his aunt to talk of familial matters, I wandered over to it.

'Please, sir, would you mind if I look at these?'

'Not at all, mistress, read whatever you want.'

He turned to speak to his aunt, but she waved her hand, indicating he should be silent.

'You read, Susannah?'

'Indeed I do, mistress.'

'Well, I never. Where did you learn that skill?'

'Ma taught me numbering and my brother taught me to read. He's apprenticed to Master Chapman, that's where he learned.'

'Can you write, also?'

Proudly, knowing I was one of the few girls of my standing with this ability, I replied, 'Yes, I can. I love the feel of the parchment beneath the quill, watching the ink form the words.' Aware I had distracted their conversation. 'Forgive me, I never meant to intrude.'

'You're not intruding. What do you like to read?'

I put down the magazine, turning to my host, 'Whatever I can find. Master Beaker has a few books. I've already read each one three times. Reading opens so many doors, allows you to see things you've never dreamed of, wouldn't you agree, sir?'

'Indeed, I would!' replied the Rector eagerly. 'Do feel free to look in the library. It holds a vast amount of reading material, a lot of it ecclesiastical, of course, but there are other subjects. I am sure you will find something of interest to you. My aunt can show you where it is later.'

'If you wish to borrow a book, you may take it back with you to Honiton. My aunt can then return it upon her next visit.' He glanced at the large grandfather clock in the corner.

'Perhaps tomorrow?' I asked Mistress Troak, who nodded.

'Forgive me, Aunt, mistress, I must prepare for Evensong. I shall leave you ladies.' Bowing, he made his way through the door.

'I need to rest, Susannah, I'll also need to change. I keep clothes here; I come so often it became pointless bringing a bag with me every time. Will you join me for Evensong?'

'Thank you, yes. I would enjoy that.'

'Good, I'll be back in an hour. As Richard said, feel free to read the magazines there.' She indicated the table. 'I bring them back from London each time I go; it gives my nephew a different perspective for his sermons. I consider it an act of charity, for it also saves his parishioners from complete boredom. My brother works at the magazine, you know.'

'I didn't. That must be an interesting occupation.' I was going to ask more questions about her brother, but Mistress Troak yawned, obviously tired. Questions could wait until tomorrow.

She went upstairs to rest before the service, leaving me alone to sit quietly in the sitting room reading the magazines, the name printed in large black letters at the top. Instantly I was enthralled.

The articles all seem to have been written by men. Why was that? Why don't women write? Or do they write, but the broadsheets won't print their work? There's so much to say. I can't be the only woman who thinks so, surely? I looked through the window and out to the tranquil rectory garden, watching the sparrows and thrushes fighting for drinking space from the large round blue dish set on a stand.

Thoughts whirled in my head. I have so much to say, but how do I say it? Would anyone want to read it? I have only known Mistress Troak for a short while, could I ask her or would she think it an imposition? Would I be taking advantage of her kindness? If her brother works at the magazine, would he be able to assist me? Dare I ask?

Chapter 33 ❧

While I had been vacillating at the rectory, Peter had been sitting in his chamber with Solicitor Goodworthy looking over the papers for the purchase of the joinery.

'This all looks in order, sir. Is Master Chapman using a solicitor in this regard?' He held the papers in his hands, hardly able to believe his name, Peter Brigginshaw, was writ on such a document.

'I am acting for both of you, a little irregular, but with my being the only solicitor in town, well, there's no other way. He and I have been in discussion already. From a purely personal position, I believe you are extremely fortunate to be able to purchase the business. Master Chapman enjoys a very good reputation, not only in Honiton, but all over Devon and Cornwall.'

'I know that for a fact, for there are frequent commissions coming from the surrounding area. I intend for that reputation to not only continue, but to grow.'

Solicitor Goodworthy stood up.

'Master Brigginshaw, this will be final on Monday when your apprenticeship is over, all that's required is the payment be kept in readiness.'

'When do you require that, sir?' Peter was reluctant to go to the chest where he kept his hard-earned money. He had no quandary about the solicitor himself, but more from whom the solicitor should speak to. It would be easy to inadvertently divulge its location and contents, however innocently. It would also take a long time for the solicitor to regain the town's trust where money matters were concerned.

'I will need it by Friday morning, at the latest, in order for the sale to go through.'

'Very well, you shall have it then. I'll bring it myself.'

'Are you sure?' He looked down at Peter's legs, thinking of the painful climb up the stairs, unable to stop himself looking at them. 'I can return, if you would prefer.'

'No, sir, I thank you, but I will bring it during my dinner hour, I'm sure Master Chapman won't object to my leaving for such a reason.'

The solicitor laughed in agreement. 'I'm sure not, under the circumstances.'

'I understand Susannah's money has been returned?'

'Yes, though now it is being held by a reliable agent. I feel very badly about my clerk, feel I am to blame.'

'I have spoken to my sister, she holds no blame to you. These things happen, it's how it's handled that is the important thing.'

'Yes, I agree. Though, I feel that my reputation has suffered. I hope that people will remember all I have done right, and forgive me in time. Well, I can't sit here talking, lots to do, lots to do.' He bid farewell to Peter, calling farewell to Master and Mistress Chapman on his way out.

Chapter 34 ❧

Mistress Troak came back downstairs. 'I'm ready, Susannah, do you need your wrap? The church can get quite chilly.'

'I have it ready, thank you.'

Together we set off along the path to the church, following others across the grass for this, the final church service of the day.

Taking a seat in one of the back pews, leaving the front for the regular churchgoers of Exeter, we knelt together in prayer, but I found my mind couldn't settle where it should.

As a family, when Ma and Pa had been alive, we had very rarely attended church, certainly never Evensong, so I knew I would be unfamiliar with the responses. After moving to Honiton, and after a deal of soul-searching, I found what little faith I had once possessed had almost gone.

For how could a loving God have taken William when he was just four days old? Why hadn't He stopped Pa from drinking after all the prayers Ma had sent skyward? How could He have allowed Pa to take off when Ma died, leaving Peter and me alone to die, defenseless and scared?

I had attended church in Honiton, along with Master Beaker, Hanna and the townspeople. But each time the Rector called us to prayer, I knew I should be saying a small prayer asking for forgiveness for Ma and William for whatever sins they had committed. But what sin could a four-day-old possibly have been guilty of?

My thoughts kept straying to the magazines I had read in the rectory. I wondered again if I dare ask Mistress Troak for assistance. What would I say?

I told Peter I wanted more for my life, and here was an opportunity, seemingly ready-made; I had to grasp it with both hands. Ma's words kept coming back to me, urging me onward. 'Don't look back, Susannah, only look forward.'

The service began. The Evensong prayers and responses flowed in its age-old rhythm, and the hymns at last soothed me. When the final blessings had been given, I knew exactly what I was going to do.

As Mistress Troak, the Rector, and I sat down for our evening meal, I felt an extraordinary peace, at last a decision made, just the action to be done. After the blessing, the little maid served the food, then withdrew to the kitchen. Alone, the three of us ate in silence for a while, all hungry.

'Tell me, Susannah,' said the Rector, 'did you enjoy the magazines? Did you find my library?'

'The magazines are very interesting, sir. I have also found two books that I would like to borrow. May I show them to you later, to see if you agree?' I turned to Mistress Troak, glad to have been given the opportunity to speak of it. 'I believe you said your brother worked in London, mistress?'

'Yes, he has done so for the past six years.'

'And what is his position there, if I may ask?'

'He is the editor. I don't know whether you noticed or not, but the sheet leans more towards men's interests.' She gave a sniff of disapproval.

'I did, and find it fascinating. I noticed that all the articles were written by men, also.'

'That is so.'

'Is that usual? Do women never write?'

'Yes, they write, but I've not seen anything in those sheets. I know women write whole books, though usually poetry and such, for I've even read some of them. Why do you ask?'

'I just found it fascinating there were no women writers.' I looked from my new friend to the Rector, putting down my implements.

'I have already spoken of my interest in books, my love of writing.' I paused. Now that it was time to speak of my longing out loud, I was reluctant, afraid of them thinking me, a young single woman, of takings airs above my station. My hands were gripped below the table, and I forced myself to go forward.

'I make the lace, as you know. Lady FitzGerald has been kind enough to purchase it, for which I shall always be grateful. My brother, Peter, is apprenticed to the joiner. With that coming to an end, he will be purchasing the business within the week.'

Mistress Troak and the Rector glanced at each other, each with raised eyebrows.

'Now I find myself to be unsatisfied, wanting more in life. I have been working for the milliner, but with her death, I no longer have employment. The magazines have opened my eyes to a different world, a world I wish to become part of.' I was now very excited, my words coming faster, easier. Neither had shown surprise that I should have voiced this, giving me courage to continue.

'Mistress Troak, how would I find out how to have an article published in the magazine?'

'That's easy, Susannah. All I need do is write to my brother, Richard's father, and ask.'

'Would you be willing to assist me?'

Mistress Troak, finished with her meal, sat back comfortably in her chair. She looked at the Rector as if silently asking his opinion, he returning it with a small nod of his head.

Turning back to me, she said, 'I would, Susannah. I would, however, suggest you take the time while you are waiting for the bonnet to complete a piece of writing. Let me read it before I contact my brother.'

My heart was beating so loudly I felt sure the others could hear it.

'Thank you, mistress. I shall.'

Looking at the Rector, I asked, 'May I use some parchment and a quill, sir?'

'Of course, I will have the maid bring some to your chamber; it would probably be quieter to sit there.'

'May I use the sitting room?'

'Certainly, if that's what you would prefer. Now, ladies, if you would please excuse me, I have to go to my study. I need to pen a long overdue letter to the bishop.'

Leaving us together, the room settled into quiet. 'Are you sure of this, Susannah?'

'I've never been so sure of anything in my life, mistress.'

'Then this is what you should do. Now, if you will forgive me, I'll also retire, for some reason I'm more tired than usual after the journey. It must be my age.'

I stood and curtsied, bidding her a good night. She paused at the door, turning to look back at me.

'I feel we are to become great friends, Susannah. You must call me Eva.' Before I could give my thanks, she disappeared.

Leaving the dining room, I gravitated once more to the sitting room. Candles had been lit on the mantle over the fireplace, and another on the round table, the magazines moved out of harm's way. The flickering remains of the fire, which had been lit while we attended Evensong, cast shadows on the walls.

The room felt warm and comforting, and I was reluctant to go upstairs to my chamber. Sitting by the fire, I wondered how Peter was faring, how excited he would be for me when I told him of my yearning, for I had never mentioned it before.

Tomorrow, I would begin writing. Though writing what? Should I write of the plight of widows and orphans left to fend for themselves like Hanna and her mother? Perhaps I could write of the lacemakers who work long hours in bad light for very little reward? Alternatively, should I write of something I've never given thought to before?

I climbed the stairs carrying the candlestick the maid left on the table in the hallway. All my thoughts filled with the coming morning.

Chapter 35 🐦

After breakfast, I left the rectory immediately, heading for the milliner's. Thanking the Rector profusely for his hospitality, and Mistress Troak for her support and advice, I felt very emotional as I prepared to leave.

'Thank you both for everything you've done for me, your kindness shan't be forgotten. I thank you, Eva, for taking my poor writing, and for sending it to your brother. Should he need to contact me, I can be reached at the Cross Keys.'

'I know, Susannah, now do stop fretting. All will be well, mark my words.'

From the rectory library, I had borrowed two books, both by the same female author, Aphra Behn. The first was entitled, *Love Letters between a Nobleman and his Sister*, the second *Poems on Several Occasions*. I had chosen them because most of the other books were written in another language, which, from the little I knew of church services, I supposed to be Latin or maybe Greek.

Carrying the bag now heavier for the two books, along with the hatbox, I set off. It was a fine day and the walk pleasing. The bonnet was ready and waiting for me, and with time to spare before the coach departed for Honiton.

While I was waiting for Lady FitzGerald's bonnet to be brought from the workroom, I noticed one other customer in particular. Dressed in a fashion a little different from what I was used to seeing, she also spoke with a different accent.

It appeared she was purchasing a new bonnet, but giving her current one in part exchange. I tried not to overhear her conversation with the milliner's assistant.

The assistant had spoken in a quiet voice to the milliner, asking how much to allow for the exchange. The milliner hadn't been pleased, but custom was custom, and a price was given and accepted by the customer.

When the lady left the store carrying the new bonnet in a hatbox, the other was left on the counter. Made of straw, it had a large, multi-layered bow on the front with straw flowers around the back with ribbons trailing behind. I thought it beautiful.

I spoke to the milliner. 'How much would you accept for the bonnet, mistress?'

She looked at me. 'Five shillings, and no less.'

'I'll take it,' I replied. The assistant brought it over to me, and I looked in the mirror as I tried it on. It fit me very well, and I was thrilled with my impetuous purchase.

I handed over the coin, and thanked her profusely. The assistant offered a shabby hatbox for its transport, provided for no extra charge, but I preferred to wear my beautiful new purchase.

I made my way to the coach stop. Paying another sixpence, I climbed aboard, though this time with horror I found the coach full, and prayed I wouldn't be sick. With no room inside, my hatbox had to go outside on the roof.

It may have been the many other thoughts filling my head that gave my stomach more to think of so that I reached my destination without having to use the tin bowl.

Three other passengers, though, were not so lucky. We were all grateful for the wind that whipped through the coach to blow away the sour odours.

The journey was speedy, and we arrived in Honiton with plenty of daylight left. There was enough time to go to Watermead tonight, and hopefully I would be able to ask someone to bring me back in the cart as before.

Leaving the bag, along with my own new bonnet in my chamber, I told Hanna I would tell her everything on my return.

Eager to stretch my legs, I set off at a good pace, breathing deeply of the sweet air. Making good time, I knocked on the back door of Watermead.

'Susannah, we were told not to expect you until the morrow. Come in,' said the young kitchen maid.

'I didn't expect to be here until then, but the coach from Exeter made good time. I thought it would help her ladyship to know the bonnet was safely back.'

'Indeed it would, I'll go and tell Mistress Dobbs. Wait here, I want to hear of your journey.' She was quickly back, followed by the maid.

'Susannah, her ladyship will be pleased. She is just preparing to go out, but leave the bonnet with me.' I handed over the hatbox. 'Do you need a ride back in the cart?'

'If it's not too much trouble, for I'm a little tired.'

'No trouble, I will get someone to tell the carter to take you straight away.' She disappeared through the door, eager to show the bonnet to her mistress.

That evening after supper and her work over for the day, Hanna and I sat on my bed. Tales of the journey, including the tin bowl in the coach, made Hanna roll around with laughter until tears streamed down her face.

She in turn told me of a visit by Master Bentley, passing on his good wishes. What with one thing and another, it was late before we had finished talking, and Hanna left for her own bed. I gratefully climbed between the sheets, asleep before my head lay on the pillow.

The next morning I woke early, listening to the familiar and comforting sound of the girls preparing the food for the day, thinking.

Why hadn't I mentioned the writing to Hanna? How was Peter? Are the papers for the purchase of the joiner's in hand? With my mind going round and round, it was pointless to continue to lie abed. I might as well get up, eat early, then get on with lace making. It was two more days before I would meet Peter again. There was so much to talk about, so many plans to make. I couldn't wait to tell him of the writing. Perhaps I should have spoken with him first, listened to his opinion, but it had not been possible.

I returned to my chamber, settling down at my lace pillow, the bobbins making their comforting clacking noise as I moved them around, the pattern forming slowly before me. But my mind wouldn't stop working.

With the gold coin safely kept, I realised with a start that I didn't have to make lace any more. I had made it all my life, couldn't think of not making it. What would I do with my hands? I couldn't think of the writing until I heard from Master Jenkins, Mistress Troak's brother. What will he say? What if he declines? What if he wants me to write more?

I must to go to Mistress Troak, Eva, and let her know of his decision, for good or bad. I had asked my new friend where she lived. I couldn't believe that it was so close to the inn and was surprised that we hadn't met before. It would be easy to visit her and, hopefully, she in turn would visit me.

⋆⋆⋆⋆⋆

On Sunday, Peter and I met. I told him of my unexpected trip to Exeter, Mistress Eva Troak and the Rector befriending me, and more importantly, of my writing.

'Susannah, this is indeed good news! You enjoyed it, the writing, I mean?'

'I did, but Peter, I know I should have asked for your opinion first, but I couldn't. I pray you understand. It was very short, barely anything of note. Indeed, I will be very surprised if I ever hear any more of it.'

He sat quietly, gazing at me.

'I've no doubt you made the right decision, for I've never known you to make a wrong one. You did bring us to Honiton and put me apprenticed with Master Chapman.' He stopped, gazing down at his feet. 'What would we have done had we stayed in Offwell? Slowly starved to death, I've no doubt. But here you are, almost a writer! And look at me, instructing a solicitor! Now I am buying the business from Master Chapman, with money worked for honestly. No, Susannah, never apologize to me, for I wouldn't be where I am if not for you. I will forever be grateful to you.'

We both sat quietly on the bench, soaking up the soft Devon air, grateful for each other's company.

'By tomorrow night, the sign with my name on it will be over the shop, with me responsible for it all from here on in. One day,

Susannah, my name will be known the length and breadth of this country.'

'I'm sure of it, Peter. Perhaps my name will also be known, if for a different reason.'

Two long weeks later a letter came on the coach for me, the coachman handing it to the ostler at the stables when he changed the horses for fresh ones, he in turn delivering it to the inn. Hanna brought it to me.

Closing the door to my room, I sat looking at it, at my name written on the front.

'Susannah Brigginshaw, care of the Cross Keys, Honiton.'

Carefully picking open the seal on the back, I unfolded the sheet.

Mistress Brigginshaw,

My sister, Mistress Troak, has inquired whether our magazine has interest in your writing for publication. The short article she forwarded on your behalf, 'A Lacemaker's Life in Devon,' we find very acceptable and would like to publish it next month (December 1777).

The usual payment for such writing is two guineas, which I anticipate in advance will be acceptable to you. Should you wish to decline, please advise the writer forthwith.

If you wish to send other writings, we would be pleased to accept them, as we find your article thought provoking, of interest to not only ladies, but gentlemen, also.

Truly,
Jeremiah Jenkins, Editor

I sat, trying to absorb this news. They have accepted my poor piece! I had to tell Peter. Now I didn't have to wait until Sunday to see him, he is nearly the owner of the business, with no limits on our time together after seven long years.

I sat, sobbing, my heart so full it felt as if it would break. 'Oh, Ma,' I cried, 'how I wish you were here.'

Gathering Hanna from the kitchen to take along with me, I went to Master Beaker's chamber.

'I have received some wonderful news. While in Exeter I wrote an article for a broadsheet and Mistress Troak sent it to her brother, who is the editor in London. I have just heard that it has been accepted!' I waved the letter in the air.

They both looked at me, unable to grasp the full impact.

'Well, that's grand,' said the innkeeper.

I was disappointed they didn't seem very excited. 'It means that so many people will read it, it is wonderful news.'

'What did you write of?' asked Hanna.

'It's called 'A Lacemaker's Life in Devon.' It's very short, barely any length at all. It tells of the lacemakers and their hardships. I never thought it would be accepted; now I can't wait to tell Peter!'

'Well, if you're pleased, that's all that matters,' said Master Beaker, returning to his ledgers, not really understanding why I was so excited.

Then I realised, who was able to read around here? Certainly not the subjects of my writing. I had to think of a way to get the news out to the lacemakers; perhaps I would gather them all together and read the piece aloud when it was published.

⁂

I went along to the joiner's, calling to Peter as soon as I entered. He was talking to customers, and having to wait to speak to him was torture.

He was thrilled for me when I told him. 'You have achieved what you wanted, well done. I am so proud of you.'

Mistress and Master Chapman came through, curious about the commotion, then delighted to hear the news.

'We'll tell all we know of your success,' Master Chapman said.

I laughed. 'It's just one small article, sir.'

Peter and I sat together in the shop, the smell of sawdust and glue in the air.

'What a way we have come, Peter.'

'All thanks to you.'

'No, thanks to us both, Peter. The land sale has gone through, and I am now wealthy. Master Stanton came to see me yesterday, and has arranged for me to meet with the agent who cares for his aunt's funds tomorrow.'

'That is good news. You care for him, Susannah?'

'How could I? He's well above my station, Peter, as you well know.' I looked away. 'But if things were different, then yes, I could care for him.'

'Maybe once upon a time I would agree, but not now. Our family is coming up in the world, Susannah, there's none can deny that. There's no holding us back now, you'll see. You are an independent woman who earns her own living, though maybe it's time you looked for somewhere else to lodge.'

I looked at Peter as he spoke, and saw a handsome young man with a face full of confidence and promise.

As I walked back to the inn, I reflected on the talk with Peter. Yes, if things were different, I would care greatly.

Chapter 36 &

Lady FitzGerald had been accepting a glass of ale from her nephew in the drawing room at Watermead. News of my success with the writing had raced through the town, spread mostly by Mistress Troak, who had also received a letter from her brother advising of his decision. It was brought to Watermead seemingly by the wind, relayed by the kitchen staff to her ladyship's maid, who told Lady FitzGerald, who in turn told Master Stanton.

'What are your intentions to the girl?'

'She wouldn't have me, Aunt, though I've loved her since that day I bought the lace, but she hardly notices me.'

'Nonsense, Thomas. What of your own estates, titles? Is she aware of them?'

'That I don't know; surely she must have heard from those in the town, but I would give them up in a moment for her hand.'

'My, but you do have it bad, Nephew. But I have to ask, what of that trouble in London? Is it all settled?'

'No, not yet. That's part of the problem. The family of the girl is threatening to take me to court over the trouble. Until it is all settled, I can't ask for Susannah's hand.'

'Is it your intention to tell her of it?'

'I suppose I have to.' It sounded like a question.

'I would say so! I know it's almost acceptable these days to get a girl in trouble, but the way you handled it made you look very bad, Thomas. Society in London will take a long time to forget about it, if they ever do. You just have to accept that fact.'

'I know, Aunt, that's why I haven't been back for a while. I'm better in the country until it all dies down.'

'A wise decision. The only advice I can give, if in fact it's advice you are seeking, is that you are honest with the girl, if you are to have any kind of lasting relationship with her. If you're that serious, Thomas, you have to speak to her brother.'

'You would put no objections in the way? She is of lowly birth, what would the family in London say?'

'Why should I object? What do you know of my own beginnings? Nothing. My father was a furrier, while my mother took in washing to survive. I'm the very last person to put obstacles in the way of true love. Moreover, do you care what those in London say? Life is too short, Thomas, not to live it in love. If you've found it, grab hold, and the family be damned! Yes, she had lowly beginnings but has survived, indeed has prospered. No, I have no objection. She is a delightful girl, will grow even lovelier. Follow your heart, Thomas.'

Sitting in the drawing room, surrounded by so many beautiful objects, Thomas knew that upon the death of his aunt – though, please, God, that wouldn't be for many years – all this would be his. His older brother should have inherited the title and estates, but as he died ten years previously, Thomas, was now the heir.

He was only too well aware his past behavior hadn't been that of a gentleman. He had just hoped that memories over the other business would grow dim sooner rather than later. If his aunt and Susannah could forgive him, that was all that concerned him.

He would have given it all up if necessary, he added, for without me by his side, what good were mere possessions? He couldn't sit with them of a winter evening before a roaring fire discussing the events of the day, nor could he walk with them beside a fast-running river watching a kingfisher break the surface, a writhing fish in its beak. One could grow old with possessions, but what a lonely aging.

Master Stanton smiled at his aunt. She knew he had decided to follow his heart.

Peter had been surprised to see Thomas Stanton in the shop, indeed hardly before he had opened the door.

'Peter, I'll not beat around the bush. I ask you for Susannah's hand in marriage. I don't expect you know much of me, besides being Lady FitzGerald's nephew, but truth to tell, I am wealthy in my own right. I have four estates, two in Norfolk, one in Dorset, another in Wiltshire. I inherited the title of Lord Stanford on my brother's death; I have more than enough money to ensure that Susannah will be well cared for all of her life. And I love her with all my heart.'

'I must, however, tell you that I was in some trouble in London two years ago. It concerned a girl, the usual problem.' He looked down at his boots, embarrassed. 'My solicitors are working on resolving the matter, indeed it should be finished by the end of this month. You have my word, Peter, that all that is behind me. May I have your permission to ask Susannah to marry me?'

Peter had been delighted, a broad grin on his face. Stepping forward, he shook Thomas' hand.

'With pleasure, sir, do I grant it, though do I understand you've yet to ask Susannah?'

'Yes, I can only hope she will have me.'

'She will have you, never fear, whether you have estates and a title or no, she'll have you.'

Thomas left, making his way directly to the inn. He asked Hanna to tell me that he was waiting to speak to me, spending the time pacing up and down the eating room.

'Master Stanton. You wish to speak to me?'

Now the moment had come, Thomas was tongue tied.

'Susannah, I've come straight from your brother. I have asked his permission for your hand, which he granted. Surely you must know that I love you, and have no wish to live without you?' He had gone on to tell me of the trouble he had been through, assuring me profusely all was behind him. 'I know we don't know each other well, and I don't expect you to answer me now, but please tell me you will think on it.'

'Sir, I have no reason to wait to give you an answer. I accept, and willingly.'

Thomas had stood, hardly daring to believe what he'd heard. 'You will?'

I laughed. 'Of course I will. How could you doubt it?'

He took me in his arms and held me close, unheeding of the faces peeking round the door of the kitchen.

'But you do realise I intend to keep writing, don't you, Thomas? Would you have an objection?'

'I would expect nothing less.'

Master Beaker appeared and we told him. He bowed to Thomas and called for ale to toast us. Hanna and the kitchen scullions were all there, giving congratulations to me, eyeing Thomas as if weighing up his suitability. Hanna, who had been able to hold back the tears in front of Thomas, predictably cried with joy. Once everyone had stopped congratulating us, the kitchen girls spinning it out as long as possible to avoid returning to work, I asked Thomas if Lady FitzGerald was aware of his proposal.

'Indeed she is, and has already given her blessing. She asked me to bring you to Watermead to meet with her. Can you come now?'

Thomas had ridden in his aunt's carriage from Watermead to Peter's shop, then to the inn. Firstly, we went to Peter to tell him of my acceptance.

As he embraced me, Peter said, 'This is indeed a wonderful day, Susannah. I'm happy for you and wish you both much happiness.'

Master and Mistress Chapman were summoned to be told, though they had already heard of it from their neighbour, who had herself heard the news on the way back from the church, it being her turn to arrange the flowers.

⸎⸎⸎

For the first time, I entered through the front doors of Watermead, standing on the black and white chequered floor.

I was greeted by Lady FitzGerald with warmth. The three of us sat discussing arrangements for the wedding, which we decided would take place in two months' time, none thinking of a reason to wait longer. Banns were to be read at St. Michael's over three Sundays, which would give all time to plan. I sent a written message to Master Bentley advising of the arrangements, asking him to join us in the celebration.

Watermead had its own chapel in the grounds, and Lady FitzGerald offered its use for the service, but my wish was to be married at the church doors of St. Michael's in Honiton, with as many people of the town present as possible, for they had all been my family in one way or another since we moved there.

Chapter 37 ❧

Arrangements were made for my wedding dress to be started immediately. Lady FitzGerald's dressmaker was summoned to the inn, bringing with her swatches of fabric. I quickly decided on a light blue silk, the neckline made especially to fit the piece of lace I had cut from Ma's woolen dress so many years ago. I had kept it safe in the box Peter had made me, unable to sell it, the last thing I had of Ma's.

❧❧❧

I met Mistress Parnell in the town the following day, and stopped briefly to talk. With so much to be done, just as I was thinking I should be on my way, she asked me if the lacemakers could make something in lace for my wedding day, in memory of Ma. I was very touched, gladly accepting. We returned to the inn, sitting in my chamber discussing what it would be, how it would look.

She told me how all the lacemakers were overjoyed at my good fortune, how she had already spoken to them, all wanting to be a part of it. She asked was there anything special I wanted included, to which I replied I would leave all decisions to the makers. She hurried off to gather all the women together to discuss who would work each piece. With time short, it would take a mighty effort to finish the piece in time.

I was aware that the women would be out the buyer's funds for their work, with efforts now concentrated on myself. I gladly arranged with Solicitor Goodworthy to generously compensate each and every one, not wanting to be responsible for their lack.

Mistress Parnell knew she would need to chivvy the women, for time was short for the large amount of work required, though I had no doubt Mistress Parnell would make sure the lace was perfect.

Hanna was an important part of the wedding. My best friend, she had encouraged and supported me through the years. Now she would stand with me at the church door while Thomas and I gave our vows to each other.

This would be the biggest wedding seen in Honiton for many a long while, and all the workers on her ladyship's estates were given the day off in celebration. Amid all the hurly-burly, I had just one task I was reluctant to complete, saying goodbye to Master Beaker and Hanna.

They had become my good friends, more of a family. With time fast approaching when I would leave the inn, I felt greatly saddened, promising to stay in close touch.

Thomas and I had discussed at length where we would live. I preferred Dorset for its close proximity to Devon and Peter, but recognized that we would probably be travelling to each of Thomas' estates in turn. I remembered when I had thought Exeter was a long way away.

The Banns had been read in church for the first time, two more to go. How I wished Ma was here, even Pa to give me away. Conversely, I just hoped he didn't return to spoil what I knew would be the happiest day of my life. Giving me to Thomas would be Peter's duty now, done with joy.

જાજાજા

At Watermead, the staff there all delighted with my good fortune. They walked around with smiles, the cleaning and polishing done with enthusiasm in readiness for the wedding day. The gardens, always immaculate, were made even more so. The cooks spent hours deciding on the menu for the wedding breakfast, decisions made then sent to Lady FitzGerald for approval. Orders for meats, game and fish were given to the estate manager. Orders for vegetables and fruits, along with flowers for the church, were given to the head gardener. The pastry cook made samples, all tasted with gusto; choices discussed, then discussed again.

I still lodged at the inn, reluctant to move to Watermead until I was wed. On market day, I wandered down the High Street, standing at the top of the hill to look down at the businesses.

The farmers from the surrounding area had brought all their animals in from the countryside for sale or barter, makeshift pens were set up to contain them. Stalls had been set up along the street with fresh vegetables and other goods on display.

Suddenly, without warning, a mighty shout went up, easily heard above the general noise, everybody turning to look. Farther down, I saw one of the bulls was trying to break free from its restraint, the poor farmer hanging on to the rope grimly with both hands while people nearby raced out of the way. The mighty head was down, foam dripping from its mouth onto the cobbles.

I watched, frozen in horror as the rope snapped, the farmer fell back in shock at the short piece left in his hands, the longer end still attached to the ring through the bull's nose. It stood, pawing the ground while it decided which way to go.

The screaming was terrible as mothers scooped up children, running for cover, stalls overturned in the rush to escape.

One man approached the beast, perhaps with the thought of holding on to the broken rope, though what good that would have done, I couldn't imagine. A woman came from between two broken stalls to tug frantically at his arm, obviously terrified for him as she tried to get him away and out of danger. He shrugged her off and she fell. He looked quickly at her as she lay on the ground in horrified tears.

The beast shook its head, while the man slowly began edging towards a gap between the houses that led into the empty fields beyond. He must have thought if he could distract it, he could save the woman on the ground as well as others. It would also give a better chance of capturing it or destroying it.

The bull started running, attracted no doubt by his movement, heading straight for him. In a moment too brief to note, the man had no chance to hide behind the house wall before the bull was on him. I watched helplessly as he was tossed into the air, landing on the cobbles with a thud I could only imagine, but couldn't hear above the panicked voices. The bull stood still, legs splayed wide next to the poor man who lay motionless, his lifeblood already starting to flow onto the road.

From nowhere, thankfully, the Watch appeared, pushing his way through the running crowd. Standing calmly in the face of such terrible danger, he fired his pistol, the shot hitting the bull right through the eye. A great burst of blood spewed forth. In an instant, the animal dropped to its knees then slumped over. The Watch approached cautiously, pushing the beast with his foot to see if it still lived. But it was quite dead.

The whole thing had taken no time at all, but at the end of it, a man lay badly injured.

Once certain the bull was beyond doing any more damage, people rushed to help, but it was too late. The horns had caught the man's throat, his life surely ending instantly. The farmer stood close by, wringing his hands in anguish while being consoled by those around him.

I drew closer, wanting to catch a glimpse of a man who would knowingly put his own life in danger to protect others. I was jostled by those who, like me, wanted a better view. Instantly I felt a cold chill run down my back, a throbbing in my chest.

It was my pa. Pa had tried, in vain, to stop the bull. Pa had, in the last moments of his life, been so foolish, and so brave.

I was suddenly aware that Peter stood beside me. He had been on his way to a customer with an invoice and been drawn by the screams. The look on his face was something terrible.

'Come, Susannah, there is nothing we can do here.' He ushered me away back to the inn, taking me directly to my chamber. He fetched Hanna to stay with me, and then went to speak to the landlord.

Hanna brought ale, sitting with me, soothing me.

Peter returned, asking Hanna to leave us alone for a few moments.

'I'm sorry you had to see that, Susannah. I have heard from others that Pa was very brave trying to stop the bull. I have to say it though. I'm glad he's dead. You won't be bothered by him any more, no more attacks on you.'

'You know of it?'

'Yes, nothing is secret here. I knew the day after it happened. At least Pa did one good thing; let's remember him for that, not all the other.'

I nodded, trying to take it in. Pa was dead.

'Why did you never speak of it to me?'

'I know you, Susannah. You wouldn't have wanted to trouble me. I knew, that was all that mattered.'

'Is someone taking care of him?'

'They are. I'll arrange with the Rector for him to be buried in the churchyard, which is more than he did for Ma. I'm sorry, but perhaps it's all for the best.'

I nodded, but couldn't believe how cold his voice was.

He left shortly after, and Thomas arrived before supper. He had been told of the terrible tragedy, though he didn't know it had been our pa. When I told him, he didn't know what to say.

❧❧❧

Peter and I were alone with the Rector when Pa was buried in the churchyard. We didn't want anyone else there, all in town respecting our wishes. We never heard mention of his other family, and his wife did not turn up at the service.

I had given brief thought to burying him next to Ma and William in Offwell, only to decide against it.

The mason was commissioned once more to complete a simple headstone. I knew I would never be able to forgive Pa; it was best he didn't lie under the oak.

❧❧❧

The one thing we all had in common was praying for good weather on our wedding day. Thankfully, it dawned dry and clear, if unseasonably cold. Those who possessed them were wrapped in fur and wool, all except me, for I refused to cover the lacemakers' work they had toiled long and hard over. Today of all days I knew I wouldn't feel the chill.

Mistress Parnell had directed the lacemakers to make a magnificent lace stole. It was as if she knew I had seen the milliner in Exeter wearing one.

The women had reproduced it nearly exact. Sprigs of flowers, bees and birds, bells and blossoms covered the handmade net. It was the most beautiful piece I had ever seen.

At ten o'clock in the morning we exchanged our vows amid a great crowd, everyone cheering, then went back by carriage to Watermead for the breakfast, with all welcome. Most of the town was there; some came from curiosity at seeing Watermead, only heard of before. I like to think all came from joy.

Peter closed the shop for the day, and Master Beaker closed the inn, as all the staff attended both events. Hanna spent most of the day crying, beyond happiness for me. Samuel came with her, wide-eyed when he saw Hanna dressed in her finery.

Eva Troak was there, raising her glass often, telling everyone she was responsible for my literary success. Richard, the Rector, also journeyed from Exeter.

At the end of the day, I had but one request of Thomas. 'May I take my bridal flowers to Ma and William's grave? Would someone take me?'

'Susannah, you must realise that now you command, even at Watermead.' He laughed at me, kissing my cheek. 'I will call for the carriage, we'll go directly.'

Leaving the guests to continue the celebrations, with Peter alone joining us, we rode to Offwell, my wedding flowers clutched tightly.

Behind the cottage, hard to find now, Thomas cleared the undergrowth and last year's dead leaves, the markers thankfully still clear of moss. The words showed well in the dying light.

Here lies
Emma Brigginshaw
Much loved ma of Susannah and Peter Brigginshaw
Died in the year of our Lord, 1770

❧❧❧

Here lies
William Brigginshaw
Much loved son and brother.
Died in the year of our Lord, 1767

Laying the bouquet on Ma's grave, I bowed my head in a quiet prayer, one hand holding the hand of my new husband, the other of my dear brother.

Full circle. With life ahead of us all.

❧❧❧

Author's Note ❧

Honiton lace is one of the finest laces and I have nothing but admiration for the women, men, and children who sat in dark, cramped houses by candlelight making beautiful pieces of lace for a pittance. *The Lacemaker's Daughter* is dedicated to each and every one of them.

I would like to express my thanks to Allhallows Museum, www.allhallowsmuseum.co.uk, in Honiton, Devon, for their unfailing commitment to keeping the beautiful craft of lace alive. I visited the museum in 2009 and was truly inspired by the exquisite work done by lacemakers, not only in the past, but also in the present. I strongly recommend, if you have a love of lace, that you visit. Margaret was of special help to me, and I thank the trustees and volunteers for their dedication.

The Lace Guild, www.laceguild.co.uk, is another excellent source of information about different kinds of lace.

I owe a debt of gratitude to so many people: Wilda Schutz for her unfaltering faith in me; Susan Armstrong for listening to my readings on the high seas; Pamela for finding Susannah for me; Joyce Himes, for my web design; my test readers, Carolyn Sheppard, Pam Glew and Keri Kahle; and to my husband, Cam, for his infinite patience while I wrote *The Lacemaker's Daughter*. To all who helped bring Susannah into the light, thank you.

Susannah Brigginshaw was a member of my family. As I said at the beginning, all I wanted to do was give her the life she never had. I hope she would have been happy with it.

All the characters, besides Susannah, are straight from my imagination and have no relation to any person, living or dead.

Any mistakes, however, are mine.

In the 17th and 18th centuries, it was known for authors to give thanks, 'For reading my poor book.'

Therefore, I, too, hope you have enjoyed my poor book.

Diane Keziah Robertson
Canada 2012
❧